# AFT CURTAIN FALLS

BY

# AINSLEY SHAY

Quixotic
Publishing

After The Curtain Falls
Copyright © 2014 by Ainsley Shay
All rights reserved.

*After The Curtain Falls* is a work of fiction. The characters, incidents, and dialogues are products of the author's imagination and are not to be construed as real. Any resemblance to actual events or persons, living or dead, is entirely coincidental.

Quixotic Publishing LLC
P.O. Box 1311
Boynton Beach, FL 33474-1311
www.quixoticpublishing.com

Edited by: Todd Barselow
Cover by: Najla Qamber

After The Curtain Falls / Ainsley Shay. —First Edition

ISBN 978-1-939588-02-9 (print edition)
ISBN 978-1-939588-03-6 (eBook)

*For Kevin*

# CHAPTER 1

Three minutes.

I roll my sleeves up to my elbows and take one last look in the small mirror hanging to my right. Beneath dark strands of hair, black-lined eyes flash with uncontained eagerness. Their engorged pupils mostly hide gold-flecked blue irises. They always look like this just before the curtain goes up.

Two minutes.

Just beyond the wall of fabric dividing me from my audience, fragments of conversations fuse together and flitter to my ears. To any other person the sounds and syllables of each broken sentence would create a chain of meaningless nonsense. But to me, they are strung together in such a perfect way they cause my nerves to whine with excitement. "Magician," "illusionist," "a fake," "an act," "how much longer?" Ah, what bliss to savor the anticipation; they are starving for me, and I drink in every drop of their expectations and accusations alike.

One minute.

I shake out my arms and roll my neck to loosen and warm my muscles, preparing for the surge of blood about to storm through my veins, and the brilliant energy that will race alongside them. In moments, raging heat will consume me, and with pleasure, I will lose myself in it, inviting it to ignite every cell in my body. The

1

curtain cannot open soon enough.

The lights dim, and the hum of a long single note resonates within the walls of the red tent, suspending half spoken words in mid air. I bring the inside of my wrist to my lips and kiss the inked dragonfly.

It's time.

The music ripens into a haunting rhythm drowning out the roar of the roller coaster and the screams that follow as it falls back to the ground. As the curtain opens one hundred pairs of eyes return my stare. Their expressions are the usual collection of amusement, suspicion, disbelief, and even a fair amount of hope as they search my face for the truth.

I reveal nothing.

The black satin cloth slips between my fingers as I grasp the corner of it. Expecting to possess each one of their morbid curiosities, I open my arms and pull away the smooth cloth. The spectators' gazes fall to the three small tables between us. Murmurs and whispers escape their open mouths. I steal my attention away from the audience and focus on the dead things surrounding me.

Some of my guests fidget in their seats; others are motionless, but all appear impatient to see the phenomenon they've paid their five bucks to witness. In the second row, a teenage girl with red hair looks up from the tables to me. Her eyes are wide. She inhales sharply, puffing up her already too large chest. I glare at her, feeding on her apprehension as she reaches for the hand of the blonde girl sitting next to her. Redhead's eyes dart from me to the stage. I tilt my head, focus in on her, intent on nurturing her anxiety, she is after all a witness to a freak show. She cowers, tucking herself deeper into her seat, and looks down at her lap.

The blonde looks at me and leans into the redhead and I hear her say, "Don't be such a wuss. Besides, he's hot." And then she winks lasciviously at me.

These are the moments I feel like a rock star, and there's no other place than on this stage I'd rather be. It's that shot of adrenaline that triggers the unnatural energy inside of me. The feverish excitement rides along my veins as I pick up the butterfly by one of its delicate blue wings.

A fat woman in the front row eyes me with skepticism. Her dress has risen and settled on her thighs, presenting me with the mortifying view of thick calves stuffed into flesh colored socks reminiscent of horrid sausages straining to burst forth from their restrictive casings. To her left, a boy about eight or nine sits as still as a cactus in the desert. His eyes are nearly glazed over and his mouth hangs open as if I've already performed my trick. The woman holds one of his hands in both of hers on her lap. She kneads her fingers over his, the movements animating the purple and yellow flowers on her dress.

"Young man, would you like to assist me?" My tone is deep and insinuating.

His mouth closes, and he points to his chest. Wide-eyed he whispers, "Me?"

"Yes. You, in the red shirt."

He looks down at his red t-shirt and then up to the fat woman. His head bounces up and down. A plea spreads over his freckled face, as if his dream to be a freak's assistant has finally come true, and she's the only one standing in his way.

Hesitantly, she releases his hand. He tears out of her grip and climbs onto the stage, not bothering to use the stairs, and hurries to my side.

"What is your name?" I inquire. He smells of rotten fruit and dirt, the pungent odors of a boy who hasn't yet found the marvelous invention of deodorant.

"Riley," he says. His lips are outlined with a caked-on white substance. His fingers twist around and through each other like a ball of knotted, writhing snakes.

"Please welcome Riley." The audience claps for the pudgy

3

boy.

"May I put this dead butterfly in your hand?"

"Yeah! Yeah!" His smile divides his face in two, and he opens his hand. White speckles dot his fingertips. No doubt, the same as the once powdery sugar that's around his mouth.

I place the insect on his palm. "Do you believe the butterfly is dead?"

He studies the motionless insect and shakes his hand, as if the jarring might wake it from a deep sleep. After poking at its bulbous head, Riley nods in short bursts and says, "It's dead."

"Thank you," I say.

I wait a few more beats and for effect only, circle my hand over the butterfly's lifeless body. The boy's nerves get the better of him and he shifts from one foot to the other. I place my free hand under his to keep it steady. "Riley, please stay still," I whisper.

"Sorry." He bites his lip nervously.

The music heightens and intensifies. Each blow to the invisible drum matches my pounding heart. The energy begins to writhe inside me. Everything under the tent fades as I focus on the unexplained vigorous force taking over my body. My eyes dance in rapid jerky movements behind my lids, and the fierce flood of heat courses through me. Scorched streams of energy furiously wake each cell in my now slightly vibrating body.

I open my eyes and touch the butterfly. A single drop of sweat rolls down the side of my face as the intensity of the energy leaves my body. Waves of dizziness immediately take its place. The creature mere moments ago, void of life, once again comes alive. It flexes its wings as if emerging from the cocoon for the first time, and then lifts each leg until all six have exercised the movement.

Gasps echo throughout the tent. Riley's eyes are huge as he stares at the butterfly moving on his palm. I raise the boy's hand so the audience can see the creature is alive, and the movement sends the butterfly into flight. As if rehearsed, it flies over a spot light,

4

magnifying it a thousand times against the backdrop of the tent. The audience "oohs" and "ahs" as they watch the butterfly flutter over them. Arms reach up, eager to touch it, but it flies to the tallest part of the tent and disappears into the darkness.

From the corner of my eye I see a streak of pink—CeCe, my little sister, dressed in a tutu. The curtain veils her from the audience. I imagine the smile on her face, and her brown ringlets bouncing with excitement. She is, by far, my number one fan. Her happiness is infectious and it pulls a smile from me.

Whistles from the audience resonate around me; they clap and yell for more. Their excitement stirs the simmering warmth inside my bones, and I'm impatient to continue.

I thank Riley and guide him to the stairs. He turns and looks up at me, his mouth once again gaped open. "You were the best assistant I've had the pleasure of working with. In fact, you were so good, you yourself might have a future as a Freak." His face beams with undeniable happiness. The audience chuckles, all except the fat woman. She's glaring at me with pure hatred as she grasps the boy's hand and returns it to her lap. I flash her a wicked smile and wink.

When I glance up, Zane, my best friend, gives me the corona gesture and mouths, "You rock." Half of him is tucked in the shadows behind the audience. The unhidden half flickers in the light. He lifts the corner of his mouth and the metal spikes and rings piercing his entire face glint from the light hanging to his left. I stifle the grin that threatens my lips, and lower my eyes to the corpse on the second table.

The dead frog feels like a flattened rubber ball in my hand. Wart-like bumps are scattered over its dark green body. The energy continues to weave itself through my body like a slinking reptile, begging to be released. And this time, without an assistant, I repeat the process. When I pull away my hand, lightheadedness creeps into the crevices of the relinquished energy. Fatigue, a recently found acquaintance, greets me early this evening. I spread my arms to the

5

audience, more to steady myself than to imply they are witnessing greatness.

After the third resurrected corpse scurries off the stage, I thank the audience for attending and give a final bow as the black velvet curtain falls and pools in front of my feet. My head falls to my chest, and my shoulders slump surrendering to the exhaustion.

"Erik, you were fantastic," my dad says as he slaps me on the shoulder.

I offer him a tired smile. "Thanks."

"Hey, you okay?"

I should have tried to hide the weakness I feel, but that would have taken more energy than I had to give right now. "Yeah, I'm fine." I plaster a smile on my face that I hope looks convincing.

His eyes gleam in the spotlights; they portray skepticism tempered with pride. He nods and forces a smile of his own. "Watching you night after night makes me want to start performing again." A proud father that, up until four years ago, was a great illusionist in his own right. Then one night he put his thirteen-year-old son on the stage and laid a dead dragonfly at my feet, and I did what only comes natural to me. The theatrics of it were never planned or practiced, and without any uncertainty, word of my performance spread and gathered many and they wanted more.

I pull back the curtain and see the last of the crowd have left.

"Your mom and CeCe should be back soon. I bet they'll sell out tonight." At the end of my performances, CeCe and my mom sell autographed pictures of me at the exit. Most of the audience buys them; they're still on the high from the show and want whatever memorabilia they can get.

"You look tired. Why don't you head in and we'll be over after we finish here?" He lifts the bottom of the tent and nudges the frog through the small hole. It hops away.

As I leave through the back of the tent, I sense someone watching me. About twenty feet away, a man leans against the

6

supporting rope of a tent. His arms are crossed over his chest, and he's staring in my direction.

"Hey, Mister."

With my attention on the man, I didn't notice the little girl standing next to me. Blonde pigtails frame her doll-like face. A pink purse hangs on her shoulder, and she's holding a bag of cotton candy. "Yes?"

"I just saw you bring those dead things back to life." Her voice is shaky like she's been crying. The light is sparse in the alley behind the tents, but there's just enough of a glow to catch the streaks of wetness forging trails from her eyes.

I glance up and the man hasn't moved. His expression is barely readable, but his guarded stance suggests I proceed with caution. Unnerved, I rub the back of my neck.

"Was it real?" the little girl asks.

A request. One I've been asked a thousand times before. Now all of this makes sense. She wants me to bring Fluffy or Rover back from the dead. People come to the carnival to be entertained. The only thing that needs to be real, and I want to be real, is the illusion I bring back the dead. Nothing else. But, out of all the people that come to my show, the children are the most difficult to fool. They believe what their eyes see. Adults are easy to deceive; they're immune to magic, enchantment, and fairy-tales alike. Sad really, but it's a belief I thrive upon. I'd rather be in a freak show than a science lab.

Avoiding her question, I ask, "What's your name?"

"Sophie."

"It's nice to meet you, Sophie." I put my hand out for her to shake, but she ignores the gesture and pushes her small purse farther up onto her shoulder.

"It looked pretty real to me."

"I'm glad. It sounds like you enjoyed the show."

As if I'd never spoken, she asks, "Can you bring back my

7

mama?"

Her mother. Why couldn't she want me to resurrect her dead goldfish or hamster? Not that I would have, but that request would have been a hell of a lot easier to dismiss. I close my eyes and try to shut out the sight of this motherless child. The lights from the Ferris wheel blaze behind my lids. Nubby balls of fabric rub against my fingertips as I dig my hands into the pockets of my jeans. I've never wanted to have the talent of Houdini, the man I was named after, but I would give anything to be able to escape this moment.

When I open my eyes, Sophie is looking at me, waiting for an answer. She reminds me of CeCe, not in looks, but age, and most of all, her bravery. My fatigue multiplies as I watch this little girl suffer for want of her dead mother. Her pain, her plea, her desperate hope is etched on her face and I have to look away.

The mass of air I suck in tastes sour. I kneel down so we are eye level, giving her the respect she deserves. "Sophie, I wish I could, but that's not something I can do." As the words leave me, I've never felt so helpless.

She says nothing else as the hope slides down her cheeks. Her arms slack at her sides and her pigtails flop forward with the fall of her head.

"I'm sorry." The need to comfort her is overwhelming. But, I stand and do nothing except fight the urge to fold in on myself.

Without another word, she turns away from me and walks toward the man propped against the rope. Her purse falls off her shoulder, and the bag of cotton candy drags on the ground. He gives me a slight wave. I return a nod that I hope conveys the regret and remorse I feel. He holds out his hand, the little girl puts her small one into it and they walk into the blinking lights of the carnival. I collapse to my knees with unbearable exhaustion and the bitter taste of regret in my mouth.

# CHAPTER 2

"Erik, don't you dare press that snooze button again!"

I hit the obnoxious invention silencing the relentless beeping. The rain pelting against the RV's canopy takes its place. "Wake me up at nine," I yell back to my mom, and pull the pillow over my head.

"Come on, your physics book is beckoning for you." Pots and pans clunk and clang around her words.

"I don't think that's physically possible."

"You're hilarious. But that's not going to help you on your test tomorrow." Aside from being my mom, she's also my teacher. "If you went to public school—"

"I'd be sleeping in, it's Saturday." Days of the week mean nothing to my mom. Our studies come first, I know this, and it's always been this way, but it's still fun to argue with her.

"Let's go. Breakfast is almost done."

The covers fall from my chest as I sit up. Cool air rushes my warm skin and goose bumps coat my arms and upper body. The nightmare crashes into me, and I fall back on my bed. A hysterical little girl clung to my leg while she screamed for her mother. I was bound in chains, useless. Her doll-like face was filthy from tears mixed with the dirt that I kicked up as I dragged her through the

9

carnival.

I try to shake it off and get up before Mom calls me again, but the feeling lingers as I walk down the thin hallway towards the common area. I think my mom's done a good job making our home on wheels as close to a stationary home as possible. When bacon isn't wafting through the air, it smells like vanilla and lavender from candles and oils; we have a surplus as my grandmother owns a whole shop of the stuff.

I slide into the booth seat at the table and turn on the TV.

"Thanks for joining me," Mom says as she grabs the remote and clicks the "off" button.

I'm too tired to protest. "You're welcome. But, it was the bacon's siren call that I could not resist." I rub my tired eyes.

"What? I can't hear you through the mumbling." She sets a plate of eggs, bacon, and toast in front of me.

She's blurred when I look at her. "I said, 'it was the bacon that got me out of bed, not your nagging.'" A dishrag hits the back of my head. "Hey. I'm just kidding."

"Yeah, right. Eat. You'll need all your energy to get through today's lesson." She nods toward the open book.

At her mention of energy, a slice of uneasiness and torment glides down my throat with the eggs I just swallowed.

"You were sleeping when we got in last night. Are you coming down with something?" She rests her hand on my forehead. "No temperature."

I'm not sure how much longer I'll be able to hide my post-show exhaustion from her and my dad, but there's no other option. I have to. As soon as they find out, they'll cancel all of my upcoming shows.

"I'm fine." I pull away from her hand and it drops to her side. Alarms buzz in my head like a million insects fighting to be freed from a jar. I don't dare look up at her, and instead shove another bite into my mouth. Eager for a change of subject, I ask, "Where are Dad

10

and CeCe?"

The buzzing weakens into a hum when she answers. "They went to get donuts. Your sister saw a Krispy Kreme as we came into town, and she's been hounding your father ever since." Her arm brushes against mine as she sits down next to me. The air condition kicks on and her perfume floats along the cool stream that blows by me. It's light and always reminds me of honey.

"I hope they bring some back," I say around a mouthful of food.

She rakes her fingers through her short spiky hair. "And they're still hot."

"Stop pushing me!" The door to the RV swings open.

"I'm not pushing you. It's called nudging," Dad says. "Come on, let's get inside where it's dry."

"Leave those wet jackets by the door," Mom says.

"The wind is so strong, it's blowing the rain sideways, and everything under the canopy is soaked." Dad shakes his arms and drops of water collect on the floor at his feet.

CeCe sets the box of donuts on the table and wiggles out of her purple raincoat. "Don't touch them until I get back." She hurries down the hall and closes the bathroom door behind her.

"Hey, son. Thought you would've slept in today." Dad sits down across from me. Mom tosses him the dishtowel and he rubs it over his head.

"That would've been nice." I toss Mom a look of blame which she ignores and takes another sip of her coffee.

"Ready for another perfect show tonight?" he asks.

"Sure thing." I reach for the box of donuts. "But right now—"

"Don't even think about it." CeCe rushes towards me and slaps my hand. "If it weren't for me, they wouldn't even be here, so I get the first one."

"Fair enough," I say and shove a forkful of eggs in my

11

mouth.

"You're a pig."

"Yeah, and how many of those donuts are you planning on eating?" Not that it matters. The girl looks like a stick you could snap in half.

"How about I let you know when I'm done." She lifts the lid and the smell of sugary glaze wafts up.

Mom eases the lid back down. "Hold on, little girl. Before you eat any of those, you're eating eggs and bacon."

CeCe stands, picks up the box of donuts, and stomps off toward the back of the RV.

"Nobody look," she hollers over her shoulder.

"She's freakin' hiding those donuts. The girl definitely has issues," I say.

"I heard that!" Twenty seconds later she sits back down at the table, empty-handed. "The only issue I have is you." She sticks her tongue out at me.

I pleasantly return the gesture. Egg particles cover my tongue like confetti, adding to the insult.

"You're gross." Mom puts a plate of food in front of her.

"Yeah, but you love me anyway."

CeCe picks up her fork. "Not enough to give you a donut."

I flip through the pages of the physics book. Only a few more months of studying and schoolwork then I'll be free to just be a freak; although Mom's mentioned college several times, none too surreptitiously, either.

"Mom, you gonna help me on this exam or what?"

She pastes the "poor baby" look on her face, tilts her head. "Sure, honey, right after I read that chapter for you." She pats my cheek. "My job is to teach you psychics—not how to cheat."

The equations on the page start to blur together. I glance at my watch; no wonder, it's almost noon. "Taking a break. I'm going to set up for tonight's show," I call out to whoever's listening.

12

No one responds as the door shuts behind me. The pounding rain has ebbed into a faint curtain of falling mist. The ground is soft from the rain and my boots sink into the mud. I hope the rain is done for the day, giving the puddles and mud pies enough time to dry up before we open. The last show has to be a sell-out, just like the rest in this town. A hundred puddles splotch the slick ground. I jump to try to dodge one. My boot rolls along loose pebbles, arms flailing like a mad man to get my balance. I regain control exactly in time to step into a pothole when I hear my name.

Cold water seeps through the laces soaking my sock.

"That bloody sucks." Zane and Lars serpentine puddles as they walk toward me.

"Thanks to you," I say, stepping out of the puddle and shaking my boot towards Zane.

"Eh, watch it!" Zane jumps back before my wet boot connects with his leg. "Don't blame me." He holds up his hands in defense. "I wasn't anywhere near your ass." The lit cigarette perched on his lips bobs as he pleads his innocence.

"Distraction, dude. So definitely your fault." Lars points an accusing finger at Zane.

"Man, you were brilliant last night." Zane takes a drag off his cigarette before continuing, "I mean the way you hold the audience in the palm of your hand." He holds his hand out in front of him, his fingers curved into a fisted cage. "Fucking brilliant."

"Yeah, well, sorry I missed it." Lars stares at Zane. "I, alone, was setting up for our show." Zane, oblivious to Lars's penetrating beady glare, watches his smoke rings drift away and disappear.

"One day you're gonna have to tell me your secret to how the bloody hell you do that shit," Zane says.

"Yeah, one day." A slow grin eases over my lips.

"You're never going tell me shit, are you? You know it's not right to keep secrets from your best friend?" he fires back, although his not-quite black eyes have understanding in them. He looks away

13

and stares somewhere past the Ferris wheel. "Yeah, well, guess we all have our secrets."

Lars takes hold of my wrist and turns it over. "Hey, how about we add to that? Tonight? You can be our volunteer for tonight's show."

"I've already been your volunteer, hence the dragonfly you're staring at." I was sixteen when they tattooed me.

"Isn't it perfect?" Lars asks no one in particular. He twists and turns my wrist studying the dragonfly's blue and green wings and tapered body. He would volunteer at his own show if he had any un-inked skin left. Tattoos cover every inch of his body, from his bald head to the soles of his feet.

"Of course it's bloody perfect, I did it," Zane says. He happens to be an amazing artist who, ironically, hates tattoos. His stage name is InZane, and his choice of body art is piercings. And like Lars, would be his own volunteer if it weren't for the shortage of exposed flesh. Metal rings, spikes, and bars decorate his entire body except his hands. And they probably would be too if he wasn't the tattooist at their shows.

"He wants more holes not ink." Zane flicks the rings in my earlobes, and points to my eyebrow. "That's real beauty there. Let's put a bar through your tongue tonight, no one will even see it." He takes the cigarette from his mouth and throws it to the ground. "It'll be our little secret." His smile is framed with metal hoops. It looks like the gesture would hurt, but I've never asked.

"Don't even bloody think about damaging his canvas more than you already have." Lars shakes his head in disgust.

"Thanks for the offers, but I'm gonna pass on both."

"No worries. We'll find another sucker to prick or ink; ha— or both." Zane wriggles his eyebrows. "You know how easy I am on the eyes."

"If I know you like I do, you'll choose some hot naïve chick and talk her into piercing her belly button or tongue," Lars says.

14

"Ah, brother, you know me all too well."

"I gotta set up for tonight. I'll stop by after my show to check out your victim." I bump my fist against each of theirs.

I'm thinking about past shows and the request of that sad little girl when something catches my eye at the edge of one of the tents. The small brown body is wet, the fur matted as it lies dead in a puddle. The field mouse swings, its body stiff when I pick it up by its tail, a perfect specimen for tonight's show.

A dry red silken cloth lay by the entrance to my tent. My heart aches for the person who has left it for me. Serpentina, the freak-show's snake charmer will come later for her scarf. She won't infer how her pet is, and she won't ask for it back, but I believe somehow she'll know it's alive and well.

The thick fabric of the tent folds onto the floor when I untie the cords. The inside is just large enough for ten rows with ten chairs each, a stage, and a small area behind the stage for our equipment.

The dead mouse looks even more pathetic on the table. After lifting out the wilted snake, I toss the silk cloth, a ribbon of red flies through the air before it lands in the corner. Irony is sometimes sick, I think, as I lay the snake on the table next to the mouse. Hunter and prey lay side by side, embraced by the same cold death.

~~~

From behind the stage curtain, I watch my audience settle into their seats. Another sell-out. Perfect. The music starts and the energy begins to quiver under my skin, but the heat that accompanies it is only faintly warm. If I can get through tonight's performance, I'll have the next few days to rest before we arrive in New Orleans for my next set of shows.

The skin is soft against my mouth as I kiss the dragonfly on the inside of my wrist. My blood begins to simmer with the thought of resurrection, and my mouth turns up, the cocky half-grin eases its way across my face and into my eyes. This is what I do.

A faint rush of air skims my cheeks when the curtain opens.

15

The sweet pungent scents of the carnival drift into my nose as I inhale deeply. With my head lowered, I lift my eyes and penetrate the audience with my glare. The fascination on the faces and the expectations in their eyes causes the ends of my nerves to blaze with the hunger to bring back the dead, and with it, relief. I'm ready.

With its fur now dry, the field mouse feels soft on my palm. The dramatics of tonight's show progress swiftly as I speed through the setting up of the resurrection. The life force inside of me comes fully alive. Heat surfaces at a furious speed, and the energy is manic as I touch the small body. The energy is coming too fast and I take a deep breath and ease my hand away to slow the rip current flooding my veins. The rodent's tail whips back and forth first, and then his head lifts off my palm. It shakes its head when it gets to his feet. When I lower my hand to the ground it runs back stage, claws tapping the canvas floor of the tent.

While the energy is still strong, I quickly pick up the dragonfly from the second table. As soon as it darts away, my energy is mostly dissolved and I'm exhausted. But, as with the rest of my shows, the finale requires the most energy. I pick up the wilted snake and ask a big guy with a buzz cut to validate the creature is indeed lifeless yet real. He walks up to the stage and picks it up by the tail and wiggles it in the air. Serpentina would have her rattlesnake strike him down if she'd witnessed that. He then takes the snakes head in his hand and looks at it, eye to eye. "You can't get any deader than that," he says.

I thank him and he returns to his seat. As I lay the snake across my palm, I close my eyes and will all of the energy inside me to bend to my mercy. The familiar current courses through me, weak, but it's there. The snake rolls and I curl my fingers to keep it from rolling off my hand. The heat rises and what's left of the little energy I have moves fast through my body. Controlling the flow, I guide it into my fingertips and touch the dead reptile.

As the energy drains from me, I watch the snake's muscles

16

fill with life. The limp line of its body begins to coil around my hand. It raises its head and looks at the audience, its tongue slithering out and in.

The outline of a standing crowd wavers before me, and I barely hear the applause as everything starts to fade. I manage a bow.

The curtain falls—and so do I.

# Chapter 3

**I**'m still on the stage floor when I wake up; my parents are standing over me. I try to focus but the highest point of the tent looks like it goes on forever.

"Oh, thank God." My mom's voice is frantic.

"I told you he'd be fine. He just fainted." The shakiness in my dad's voice doesn't back the confidence of his words.

Mom ignores him. "Honey, can you hear me? Are you alright?"

"Yes. And yes," I manage to croak out. I try to sit up and a world of dizziness greets me. I lie back down and shut my eyes.

"We should take him to the hospital," she says.

"Just give him a few minutes, he'll be fine."

CeCe leaps onto my chest, knocking the wind out of me and wraps her arms around me. "You're alive!"

"Honey, give him a few minutes," Mom says.

"It's okay." I hug her against my chest.

"Never do that again, okay?" CeCe wraps her arms around my neck.

"Okay, I'll take it out of the act." No one laughs at my joke. "How long was I out?"

"Ten minutes," Dad says.

Only ten minutes, yet it felt like I'd lost hours. I'm tired and weak, but I feel different—like something's missing. I try to ignore it and ease into a sitting position, only slightly lightheaded now. "See, I'm fine." I smear a smile over my mouth.

"Don't you give me that grin." Mom crosses her arms over her chest and gives me the evil eye.

Damn it, didn't work.

Even the illusionist doesn't buy it this time, I know he wants to, but he doesn't.

Creases I never noticed before etch their way over my parents' faces. "What? I'm fine." CeCe sits in my lap. She takes the small brown field mouse I brought back during my show out of her pocket. "He looks fine, too."

"He is. I'm going to keep him. His name is Scooter. Cute, huh?"

"Perfect."

My parents are staring at me like they're waiting for me to understand something. Something obvious. "This may not be perfect timing," my dad says, "but you haven't had a break in a long time and we think," he places his hand over my mom's, "it's time to—"

"You're right," I say. "I'm not going to argue. I'll cancel the next couple of shows, rest, get my strength back up—"

"No." Mom shakes her head. "This is serious. Your father and I have both noticed you're strength has—is…" She glances at my dad and expressions pass between them that I don't like. What are they getting at? My stomach tightens when I register their wordless exchange, and resentment sits on the edge of every one of my nerves.

My dad realizes that I've finally caught on. "Your mother and I think it's for the best. Your body…your energy isn't recovering quickly enough to perform night after night."

"No!" I yell, and mimic my mom's shaking head. CeCe puts Scooter back in her pocket and gets up from my lap. Finding my calm, I say, "I just need to eat more, and…um…get a few more

19

hours of sleep each night." I hate that I'm stammering. Even I'm unsure of my own words, barely believing them myself as they spew out of my mouth. How can I possibly convince them that I'll be ready in a couple weeks?

This isn't happening. I'm not ready for my life to end. Not in death, but the only way I know how to live it, as a freak. "So what? We're just going to follow the other freaks around, town after town, watching their shows, until you guys feel like I'm ready to perform again?"

"What you do, your gift, it's not…ordinary."

"Oh really, Dad? Thanks for explaining that. I've been wondering why we travel in a freak show!" My head falls in my hands and I grasp chunks of hair in my balled fists.

Dad's hand is heavy on my shoulder. "I'm sorry, Erik, but it's time for you to rest." His tone is soft but unarguably firm.

In a voice that sounds unrecognizable to me, I say, "This is all I know." Tears are threatening as my new reality slams into me, and before they come, I need to get out of here. Blood rushes to my head as I get to my feet. Steadying myself, refusing to sway, I pretend to look stronger than I feel. I walk toward the curtain and push it to the side. One hundred chairs are side-by-side, empty, and I already long for the moment when the curtain opens and every one of them is filled.

I'm not sure why I turn around, but as soon as I do, I wish I hadn't. CeCe is huddled next to my mom; she's crying. My dad's head is lowered and his arms are crossed over his chest as though he's trying to hold in a thousand emotions. Mom is watching me, and her face looks ready to break apart any second. She steps closer to me and reaches out, but I back away before she can touch me. The oncoming tears are so close to shattering my resolve; I turn away from them.

I close my eyes and take a deep breath. "I need some space right now." And like Sophie and her dad the night before, I escape

20

into the blinking lights of the carnival, letting the curtain fall behind me.

I run toward the RV, to where my motorcycle is parked. The air is heavy and damp and it's hard to fill my lungs with oxygen as I try to catch my breath. Weaving through the crowd of people, their gleeful shrieks pierce my ears as I pass roller coasters, fun houses, and carousels. A quick turn around the ticket booth brings me face to face with a giant stuffed bulldog, a plastic spiked collar around its neck. The owner displays the proud look of a winner with the useless mutt barely tucked under his bulky arm. I don't smile back. Cutting around him, I bump his shoulder.

"Hey! What the—"

Ignoring him, I pick up my pace.

"Jerk!" Bulldog owner bellows over the noise of the carnival.

When I turn the corner into the area designated for us carnies, I see my motorcycle and the hysteria in my chest starts to thaw. I'm grateful no one is around to hear the sick choked-off noise that comes out of me. The thought that I'm running away from something I love so much scares the hell out of me.

I jump on my motorcycle and start the engine. It roars, and in a wake of dust, I skid out onto the main road and twist the throttle. The bike responds and I hold on tight. Tiny drops of rain strike me, stinging my face and arms. The wind beats against me as if punishing me for giving up or giving in, I don't know which.

Only a pinprick of brightness remains in my side mirror. Ignoring it, I focus on the long, dark stretch of highway ahead of me. A lazy moon drifts alongside me, its glow muted as it floats through clouds as thin as floss. I have no idea where I'm going as I follow the single headlight illuminating the broken white lines of what seems like an endless road.

At least an hour later, a flickering light comes up out of the darkness. The closer I get, it morphs into a half-lit sign: 'Diner.' A few semis idle in the parking lot. A rusted blue truck occupies the

21

one pump at the gas station, a huge rebel flag hanging out the back of the bed. The owner looks at me, nods. I nod back.

As I climb off my bike, I glimpse the dragonfly that rests permanently on the inside of my wrist. It reminds me of the first time I ever brought back the dead. I didn't even realize what I'd done. It was a moment I will never forget and it was in those seconds that I was transformed into something else, no longer just a regular boy. I was a freak. A lifeless dragonfly had changed my life forever.

A bell on the door jingles as I pull it open. "Have a seat anywhere you'd like," a girl with bleached hair says from behind the counter. She waves her arm around the empty restaurant.

I slide into a booth by the window. A menu lands in front of me. "Coffee?" When I look up, a face with colorless eyes, a thin nose, and a glossed smile framing slightly crooked teeth is waiting for an answer. Her nametag reads "Madison." She pushes the braid from her shoulder to her back and taps the pen on the small notepad.

"A Coke," I answer.

She jots it on the pad. "Special of the day is pot roast with mashers and peas." She turns and heads toward the kitchen. A tattoo rests on the thin exposed area on her lower back; a fish or maybe a mermaid.

A loud grumble draws my attention outside. The rebel truck pulls out of the parking lot. I stare past the gas station and lights into the murky void beyond. My emotions are a quilt of confusion, anger, frustration, weakness, and hopelessness. There's also a sliver of relief, only a sliver, but it's there, and that confuses me the most.

Madison sets the Coke on the table with a wrapped straw. "What can I get ya?"

I didn't hear her approach. Without looking at the menu, I order a grilled cheese and fries.

"You got it," she says. She yells over the music blaring from the kitchen, "Wally, I need a grilled cheese and fries."

I already miss the warm tingling feeling just below my skin.

The energy that coursed through me just a short time ago and ached to be freed is conspicuously absent. Will I ever feel it again? A crash in the kitchen rips me from my thoughts.

A few minutes later Madison sets a plate of food in front of me with a bottle of ketchup. "So, what's your story?"

"Excuse me?" I ask, caught off guard by her forwardness.

"You look like someone just strangled your puppy." Tearing off my check, she tucks it under the saltshaker. She crosses her arms and cocks her hip.

"That's morbid," I say, delaying my answer and trying to use the few moments to concoct a lie that sounds halfway believable so I can eat in peace.

"Yeah, well, it's true. You're the best looking, and saddest guy I've ever seen come in this place and I've worked here—" she looks up to ceiling and then back to me, "goin' on three years," she shrugs, "off and on."

Embarrassed by her comment, I pick up the ketchup and tilt the bottle on its end, waiting for the red goo to plop onto my plate. "Just a little mid-life crisis."

"A mid-life crisis—at what—eighteen? Yeah right."

"Seventeen," I correct her.

"Oh, then that makes perfect sense."

A quirky grin along with a puff of air releases some of the tension inside of me.

She sits down across from me. "Do you mind?"

The last thing I want is company, but I wave my hand holding the grilled cheese, and say, "Nope."

She props her hand under her chin. "Where you from?"

"All over." I take a bite of the sandwich.

She must see my reaction because she smiles and she asks, "Best one you ever had—right?"

"Yeah, it's really good," I say with my mouth full.

"I know it. It's because Wally—" she thumbs in the direction

23

of the kitchen, "puts the butter on both sides of the bread. Who would've thought it'd make a difference?" She holds up her hands and shrugs.

I glance in the direction of the kitchen; through the pass-thru window, a guy strums an air guitar to an unidentifiable song blasting from the radio.

"You a runaway?" she asks.

"I guess you could say that. But probably just until morning." I pick up the Coke and sit back to look at her. "Do you ask all of your customers this many questions?"

"Nah, just the ones with a story on their face and a thousand pounds of shit on their shoulders." Pointing to me with a bitten down nail she adds, "There's something different about you, or something familiar...I can't figure out which."

Please don't let it be either, I think. I pick up a fry and on the way to my mouth I stop. "You know when things are going to be different from now on, different than everything you've ever known, but you're not sure different how?" Where did that come from? And why am I talking to this stranger? But, after I say the words, I realize they're true. I'm scared of what's to come...the unknown. As far as Madison is concerned, maybe I opened up to her because I know I'll never see her again. I don't know, maybe I'm desperate to hear everything will be okay, or I just need to get if off my chest. Who knows? And, instead of a thousand pounds of shit on my shoulders, now it feels like it might be closer to a hundred.

"Life is what you make it. No matter where you are, what you're doing, what it was before, doesn't matter. It's all about the now." She takes one of my fries and eats it. I would normally consider that the rudest thing ever, but somehow the act fits perfectly in this surreal moment. She continues. "What's important is the present and how you choose to live it from here on out."

I take her words as if they came straight from the bible of life. They make sense.

"So?"

"So…what?" she asks.

"It's your turn."

She takes another fry and points it at me. "I see how this works. An eye for an eye, huh?"

"Something like that." I pick up a fry from the pile, dip it in ketchup, and pop it in my mouth.

"My dad's sick." She purses her lips and looks out the window. I don't think she's going to continue, but then she says, "So, I moved back here from New York City to take care of him. I was going to school for art, had a scholarship and everything." She sounds sad, but on the fringes of her words, there's pride and gratification. "But, things happen, and he's the best man I've ever known. He raised me all on his own. Always supported me with all my artsy stuff and let me be my own self. So, I got my job back here," she waves her arms around, "at this grand-ole place." She laughs. "But, I would do anything for him, just like he did for me." Cocking her head, she smiles. "I don't know what my future is. It's different than the one I had planned, that's for sure. But, I live for today, and I can't afford to have second thoughts about coming back to this dead-beat town." She shrugs. "So come Monday morning, I'll get up and go to class at the local college, where they think art is a joke, but I'll go and make the best of it until something changes." She takes another fry.

"Would you like me to order you some?" I ask.

We laugh, and then ease into a comfortable silence. The truth in her words and the honesty and pride in her nature weighs heavy on me. Madison is a person without judgment. In just these last few moments, I feel less scared of my future.

She stands and looks at me. Her smile comes easy when she says, "Whatever it is, you'll figure it out. It's all just part of life's little process." She picks up the check, and tears it in half. "It's on me," she says and walks away.

A mermaid tattoo.

# CHAPTER 4

$\mathcal{T}$ he sun begins to peel itself away from the horizon as I pull into the carnival. I get off my motorcycle and walk around the nocturnal playground. It rests, so it can offer the people in this town one last night of fun. Remnants of sugar and grease drift by on the slight shifts of warm damp air.

When I round the corner, my parents are sitting in the lounge chairs under the canopy of our RV. Each of their faces share the same concern. My mom gets up first, and as with a small child, takes me by the hand and leads me up the steps into the RV. Dad follows and puts his hand on my shoulder.

"Want something to drink?" Mom asks.

"Sure, thanks."

Here goes nothing…"You're right. I need to rest."

Their simultaneous heavy exhales are proof of their relief. But, their exchanged glances don't look as if they're buying my argument-free-confession.

"We're only doing this—"

"Don't." I say, cutting off my mom as I hold up my hand to ward off more explanations. "Even though I've accepted this decision, it doesn't mean that I have to like it."

She hands me a mug of hot chocolate, and the warmth feels

27

good in my hands, a much needed comfort right now. "Just tell me what happens now."

They look at each other again; this time it's not shock on their faces, but uneasiness. My mom lowers her head, and the gesture makes me nervous. Dad twists his hands around each other like he's washing them. They're both quiet. They're both delaying. Mom looks up and nods to my dad.

"Your mother and I think it's best if you stay with Oli for a little—"

"What?" I bolt up and my leg hits the table, splashing hot chocolate out of the mug. "Damn it!"

"Watch your mouth," Mom warns.

"I…I'm not sure what I was expecting you guys to say, but it sure as he—heck wasn't that." My grandmother, Oli, is great, but I'm meant to be on the road.

"CeCe is going with you," Dad adds.

"And what about you guys?"

"We're going to stay on the road. Your dad is going to start performing again."

"This will give you a chance to rest and try to have somewhat of a normal life. Go to school—"

"School?" I sink into the chair and squeeze my eyes shut. This is not happening—can't be happening.

"Erik, look at me…please." I open my eyes and my mom is kneeling in front of me. She takes my face in her hands. "You've worked so hard and you're so close to graduating."

I want to look away from her pleading eyes as she throws me to the wolves, but I can't.

"Erik, it's going to be fine. I promise. You'll make friends—"

An edgy laugh escapes me. "Fine? You really think so? How is it going to be fine when I'm a freak? Are you listening? A freak!" I feel the anger and pain digging trenches into my face as I glare at her.

28

"No one knows that, but you." Her tone never changes, the softness and evenness of it grates on my nerves instead of soothing them. "You've made friends with Lars and Zane."

"Maybe you didn't notice, Mom, but they're freaks like me. You want me to make nice with jocks and geeks?"

I can feel my energy heating inside me, wanting to escape. I push it down. I've never hated who or what I am, or what I can do, but right now, I despise being different. Most of all I hate that it's failing me. Weakening me into something I'm not—normal. I take a deep breath. I get up and walk to the kitchen sink, turn on the faucet, and splash water on my face.

"This carnival-freak show life that your mom and I have brought you and CeCe up in, it's not..." Dad shakes his head. I hear the guilt in his words.

"You always told me and CeCe it's not where we are or what we're doing, but that we're together...as a family. I don't know about you, but those words meant something to me."

I watch tears pool in his eyes and he pulls me to him and crushes me in a hug. "I know, son. I know. This arrangement won't be forever," he whispers, sadness straddling every word.

Breaking free from his embrace, I ask, "Did you tell CeCe yet?"

"Tell CeCe what?" my sister asks as she comes into the room wiping the sleep from her eyes.

"No, but I guess now's as good a time as any," Dad says.

"I'll let Mom and Dad tell you what's going on." My parents give each other the look, again. This time my stomach doesn't do flips, but it hasn't fully recovered from the first blow either.

She stops and her face pales. "Whoa! You guys all look so serious. What? Tell me. You're scaring me. Is Erik going to die?" she asks frantically and embraces my waist. It's no wonder she thinks that after last night's episode of me passing out.

"Erik!" CeCe screams as she squeezes me tighter.

29

"CeCe, I'm not dying." I hug her back. Her small frame seems so fragile against me.

Mom comes to the rescue. "Honey, let go of your brother." She guides CeCe to the table and beckons her to sit, patting the seat next to her. My dad sits and so do I. "CeCe, you and Erik are going to stay with Oli for a while." CeCe's mouth opens to protest, but my dad holds up his hand for her to wait. Mom continues, "Erik needs to rest and we think it's best if you guys settle down."

"For how long?" CeCe asks as she wraps one of her curls into a tight spiral around her finger, the tip of it turning a deep shade of purple.

"Probably until June," answers Dad.

CeCe lowers her head and cries into her hands. "That's a long time away."

"It is, but you won't even notice we're not around. You'll be busy with school and—"

CeCe's head pops up. "School? An actual school—really?" Her excitement replaces the shock. "I'm really going to get to go to school? Make friends?" She claps and bounces in her seat.

And just like that, with CeCe's newfound happiness, the tension and stress in the room starts to dissolve. In one of the most difficult times in my life, it's again that that little girl makes me smile.

~~~

And like we've done a thousand times before, we prepare to move on. Only this time it won't be to perform another show, in another town. Not for me anyway. And this time when I say my goodbyes to my friends, it seems absolute.

"Until then, my friend," Zane says and he grips my hand and leans in.

Lars slaps me on the back and says, "Take care of yourself, man."

"Don't worry about me. I'll see you guys soon."

After I start to walk away, Lars calls out to me, "Maybe you'll be ready for more ink by then."

I turn around in time to see Zane hit Lars in the arm and say, "He's gonna want bloody holes."

Laughing, I think of how much they have been part of my family. I'm going to miss them.

Then it's time to say goodbye to Serpentina. I pull back the cloth of her tent. "Serpentina," I call.

"Back here."

I walk toward the voice and look behind the curtain. She's sitting on the floor leaning against the huge pillows with a snake draped around her neck. The space is decorated like a gypsy's home; a large rug is in the center surrounded by a pile of large colorful pillows in the corner, and a dressing table.

"I'm heading out and I wanted to say goodbye."

"You're not staying for tonight's show?"

"No. It's time for me to take a break."

Nodding in understanding, she stands and positions the snake on a wooden perch. It slithers and coils around the knotted branches until it rests on a limb near the top.

Serpentina wraps her arms around me and whispers in my ear, "Who's going to bring all of my beloved creatures back to life?"

I don't give her an answer; I know she's not expecting one. Her question only makes me smile as I hug her back.

Standing in the shadows, I watch the Ferris wheel, the enormous ring starting and stopping, the cars rocking and swaying a hundred feet off the ground.

"Erik."

I knew it wouldn't be long before they'd be calling me.

It's time to start over. This is for the best. Right? Maybe, if I keep telling myself that, I'll start to believe it.

We pull onto the highway and exhaustion overwhelms me. I just want to sleep. Need to sleep. As I close my eyes, I swear to myself I won't dream of my past or have nightmares about my future. And, I pray that my mind doesn't betray me.

# CHAPTER 5

I sit alone in the RV. The scents of lavender and vanilla surround me. Mom always told us the lavender is relaxing and the vanilla is homey. Until this moment, I never thought about it one way or another, but she's right, they are the scents of my home. The home I'm leaving for a new one.

I grasp the handle; pulling it up and opening the door seems like the hardest thing I've ever had to do. I inhale as deeply as I can, holding the scents I'm leaving behind in my chest. I pull the handle and push the door outward. I grab the strap of my backpack and step out onto the sidewalk, the hole in my jeans tearing more at my knee.

Florida's heat immediately surrounds me. The humidity I always seem to conveniently forget about coats my skin. The next breath I take is heavy, thick, and scented with recent rain. Low dark clouds still hover above me, concealing the blue. More rain is still to come.

I stare at my grandmother's house, my house. It looks the same as it always does, and this brings me a small measure of comfort. At the edge of the sidewalk is a gate that opens up into her yard. A stone path weaves through a perfectly manicured lawn, past statues of garden gnomes, flowerbeds and overflowing birdbaths, ending at the foot of the wide white wooden steps of the porch.

I'm not dreading the walk up to the quaint white house with the red door, but rather the walk I won't be making back to the RV later today, tomorrow, or even in a week. This will be my home for the next year, or at least until I graduate.

Dragonflies dart back and forth through a swarm of gnats, snatching and eating their prey in mid-air. The sight of them makes my chest ache. I push away the reasons of why I'm here instead of on my way to New Orleans for my next show.

I walk along the white wooden fence that surrounds Oli's property, running my hand over the top of each piece of wood. The prickle of the dry slats threatens to bless the tips of my fingers with splinters. They are the smallest fragments, minuscule really, that stab through your tender flesh and shoot raw pain through your entire body.

Today, I welcome the pain.

A huge ficus tree with its knotted trunk umbrellas the house, dwarfing it under its outstretched limbs. From one of its thick branches hangs the swing I would endlessly push CeCe on when she was little. She'd yell, "Higher! Higher!" then giggle as I sent her flying into the air. Things were so simple once.

"Let's go, son." Dad lifts the latch on the gate and we walk through. The sound of it clicking back into place, that small *clink* sounds so final.

CeCe is already standing on the porch, the handle of her purple suitcase in one hand and Scooter's cage in her other. "Would you guys hurry up!" Her face is beaming as we walk up the stone path. She looks over her shoulder at me. "Erik, I'm so excited, I can't stand it." A high squeal follows her statement.

Nervousness ricochets behind her words, but I don't acknowledge it. For her sake, I act excited too, and tug on one of her curls. "It's going to be great," I lie.

The ache in my gut sends me doubling over as I climb the few steps up to the front porch. A crushing feeling of emptiness

34

overwhelms me, like I'm forgetting something, something almost as important as breathing. With my hands on my knees, I close my eyes.

"What's the matter?" Dad asks.

"Nothing. Just…a little nauseous from the trip." He knows I'm lying, but he doesn't call me on it.

I ease into an upright position just as the door opens. Oli, short for Olivine, who thinks she looks too young to be called Grams or Grandma—which she does—stands in the doorway with her arms wide as she welcomes us into her home and her life, for keeps this time.

~~~

My room is at the end of the hall. I toss my backpack in the corner and sit on the bed. The headache that's been brewing for the past hour has finally surfaced.

"Erik, any particular place you want this?" my dad asks holding my duffle bag.

"No, just drop it anywhere."

He sets the bag on the floor by the closet and sits down next to me. Scents of the RV waft off him, vanilla and lavender, slightly tinged with sweat. My stomach aches with feelings of homesickness already.

Detachment surrounds me like a cyclone. Everything that's transpired in the past twenty-four hours has happened to someone else and I'm just a bystander wearing 3D glasses. It seems like days—no, months—since I've performed and it's only been a day.

As if he knows what I'm thinking, my dad rests his hand on my leg. "This is a good thing. You know that, right?"

Answering him would be giving in to this moment and these feelings. Instead, I ask, "What if someone recognizes me?"

"No one's going to recognize you. Don't worry about that. Listen, after graduation—"

I look at him then. "I'll be back to performing as the freak

35

that I am."

"That's my boy. I couldn't have said it better myself." I hear the smile in his words. "I'll be counting down the days."

"I've already started." I look down at my watch. The wide black leather band wraps around my wrist, the silver face stares back at me. The second hand ticks toward the day I get my life back.

"Come on, let's eat," he says and gets up.

"I'll be there in a minute."

He closes the door behind him.

I get up and walk to my duffle bag. Crouching next to it, I unzip the side pocket, take out the framed picture, and set it on the dresser. It's a picture of me the first time I ever performed, a dragonfly resting on my palm.

Only 253 days.

~~~

We say our goodbyes. I fight the tears that threaten to sting my eyes as the RV, my home, my parents, drive away. I watch until it turns the corner and is out of sight. When I look up, only a sliver of the moon is visible, like it's flashing a lopsided grin, mocking me and my newfound circumstances.

I climb the few steps to the porch and sit on the swing, not ready to go in yet. Exhaustion once again consumes me and I give in to it, closing my eyes.

A whistle jars me and I look at my watch. Only fifteen minutes have passed. Gus, Oli's tiger-striped cat has crept up and fallen asleep against my thigh. He purrs as I pet the soft gray fur around his neck. The front door opens and Oli holds out a mug to me. " I thought you might like some cocoa." I take it and she sits next to me with her own.

"Thanks." We sway on the swing like we used to when I was small and my feet couldn't reach the floor.

"It's been a long day, but I'm thinking tomorrow will be even longer," she says.

36

"I think you're right. Unfortunately." I've tried to avoid thinking about what the first day of school will have in store for me. The warmth in my hand brings me back to the moment. The tiny marshmallows have almost disappeared. I take a sip from the mug. "This hot chocolate is amazing."

Oli chuckles. "Just like your grandfather, he wasn't a tea drinker like me, or even a coffee drinker for that matter, hot cocoa was his thing. Every morning I prepared a thermos for him." She looks out across the yard. "You both have the same blue eyes, clear and bottomless. You remind me so much of him."

"I miss him."

She smiles. "Me, too."

I don't say anything as I watch her, and she looks lost in her memories.

She tilts her head a little, and the expression on her face looks sad, but in a weird way, content. "Your grandfather was a great man; brave, intelligent, kind, and it didn't hurt that he was extremely good looking." She blushes. "He was everything that I could have ever wanted in a husband." She takes of sip of her tea and lowers the mug back to her lap. "And, with all of his redeeming qualities, he also came with something extra."

"What?"

She looks directly at me. Her voice loses its lightness and takes on a sobering edge. "Like you, he too could bring back the dead."

# CHAPTER 6

Heat creeps up my throat, and the porch shrinks around me. Impossible. I had to have heard her wrong, or the woman's gone crazy. No. It has to be true. I want it to be true. I'm paralyzed as I wait for her to continue.

"Erik, you were born with a gift," is all she says before she picks up her tea and takes another sip, leaving me in agony.

A thousand questions crash about in my head. What am I? Why me? Like the bumper cars at the carnival, they collide into one another, jerking and fighting to be freed. I want to shake the answers from her, but afraid of disrupting the moment, I stay silent and motionless.

"Maybe we should continue this tomorrow, after school. It's been a long day, and it wasn't fair of me to bring it up now."

Oh no! A tease this enormous is cruel at best. "Come on, Oli, you can't stop now," I say as calmly as I can. She smiles, and I hope this means she's going to continue.

Gus climbs onto her lap, lies down on his side, and curls his tail around his body.

"How come Mom never told me?"

"She couldn't. She never knew." She strokes the cat's fur.

The shock must be evident on my face because Oli explains, "We decided not to tell her. We couldn't risk her telling her friends;

that was the main reason. But, we had no answers to her no doubt endless questions. And, it didn't seem fair to ask her to understand something that went against everything we'd taught her about life and death."

I understood. I remember trying to explain it to CeCe, and Oli was right. I had shrugged off all of her questions, because I had no answers, except one. And thinking of it now makes me smile. I had just finished my performance and we were on our way back to the RV. "Erik," she said in her six-year-old voice.

"Yeah?"

"Are you an angel?"

"No." That was the only answer I had to any of her questions. And, even that one wasn't good enough.

She said, "I know you don't have wings because I've seen you with no shirt on. But, maybe they forgot to grow, or maybe when you're daddy's age you'll get them."

"Maybe." I conceded to her angel theory only to make her happy, and because I had no other explanation.

Oli continues, "Another reason—and I'll plead the fifth if you even speak of this, but your mom had this horrid cat—" A quirky hiccup laugh escapes and she covers her mouth. "Not like Gus here. That cat was— well, your grandfather and I hated the thing. She found it on her way home from school when she was seven and insisted it already loved her. I don't think that mangy orange mess could love anyone. But, we let her keep it and she took care of him for almost ten years before it died. And we knew if we ever told her the secret, then for certain she'd want that cat brought back from the dead." She holds up her hand. "Mean I know, but ten years was long enough to be stared at by those beady pink eyes."

I laugh.

"Didn't she ever tell you about Bones? Short for Lazy Bones, he slept all day. But by night, he was the hunter. Brought all kinds of presents home, you know the ones, the kind that aren't too pleasant to get."

"Oh, I know all about Bones. But, I've never heard that version of him. The Bones I heard about was a fluffy, purring tabby. According to Mom, he was the best pet in the world."

Oli hiccups again. "Either way, that whiskerless cat made her happy."

We gently sway back and forth on the swing like a pendulum, and I can't tell if the time is passing slow or fast. "Why me?" I ask.

Whispering, she says, "I don't know." She shakes her head and looks off into the distance. "Do you remember that night in the hospital?"

The instant the words leave her lips I'm taken back to a moment that I have tried to forget every day for the last seven years. I slowly nod. "Yes."

"You were only ten years old when you tried to bring your grandfather back."

I lower my head and rest it in the palms of my hands. "I was weak then."

"You're weak now."

Her words sting, but they are true. I feel her hand on my back and she circles it around and around trying to ease the pain of failing.

"The second he released his last breath, you were next to him. Your body was convulsing with so much energy—" She takes her hand away from my back and I turn my head in my hands to look at her. "The heat...I've never felt anything like it. When I touched you to pull you away from him, your skin was scorching." She huffs. "Then you fainted, I thought you were..." She doesn't finish.

I hear her sniffle and it's my turn to comfort her. I put my arm around her shoulder.

"If it weren't for your father pulling you away from him, you would have died—you know that, don't you?"

I do, but I don't answer her. "Oli, it's okay."

40

She pulls away from me. "No." She shakes her head. "No, it's not okay, because, even as I watched you suffer, I wanted nothing more than for you to succeed." Guilt accents her every word.

I don't blame her. How can I? I'd wanted him to come back, too. "If it makes you feel any better, I wasn't suffering."

She pats my hand and gets up. "I'm going to refill my tea. Would you like more hot chocolate? Or would you like to go to bed?"

I hand her my mug. "No, I'm good, thanks. I'll be here when you get back."

She smiles and walks into the house.

Quiet blankets the night. I think about the night my grandfather died, and every second in that hospital room is still crystal clear. I knew he was going to die that night, my parents told me as much. When we walked into the room, Oli was holding onto his hand. She looked up at us and her face was wet, her eyes red, but she was smiling. That part I didn't understand until years later.

I watched his chest sink as he exhaled for the last time. Oli reached up and closed his eyes. I didn't even think as I ran to him. My body was already prepared to give back life, the heat, the energy, and the love for him; I thought it would be enough. But after touching him for only a few seconds I started to see nothing, only blackness, and my skin began to cool, then nothing. When I woke up, I was lying in the bed next to my grandfather's; his bed was empty.

Oli sits down on the swing, steam rising from her mug. "Are you alright?"

"Yeah. Fine." I rub my eyes trying to erase that night like I've tried to do a thousand times before. "What now?"

"Well, tomorrow you'll start to live a normal—well, average seventeen-year-old life."

Temporary. My temporary normal life, I think. "You act like it'll happen automatically."

41

She laughs. "I wish I could say it would." She puts her arm around me and without acknowledging it aloud, she senses that I'm scared. And she's right.

"Look at this move like a new beginning. Try to accept the boy inside, not the gift living inside the boy. You're not destined only to be a performer. After you graduate, you can be whoever and whatever you want. Who knows, maybe you'll go to college and learn to be an architect."

Not a performer? That's exactly what I am.

"I see you don't believe me."

"I do," I say as the lie breathes through my lips.

She frowns at my untruth. "Erik, I'm going to share something with you." Staring into her mug, she continues. "This gift will break you, if you let it. And I promise, it'll take you—and everything you live for—down with it." She looks at her wedding ring and spins the diamond around her finger.

My stomach clenches at her words. I close my eyes and exhale.

"Your body is not an endless well of energy, and right now it's weak; you need to give it time to heal."

"How long?"

"I'm not sure to be honest. For the next few months try to not focus on your gift. I know it may not feel right here." She places her hand over my heart. "But, I promise it will. It will take time, but it will."

I almost believe her. But, bringing back the dead is part of who I am. And performing, it's what I do. It's what I'm great at. It's what I love. It's all I know.

"Are you okay?" she asks.

"Yeah, I'm fine."

"I still see the disbelief in your eyes—"

"No, Oli, it's not...I...it's just..."

"Erik, it's alright." The corner of her mouth lifts and she

42

touches my cheek. It's warm from holding the steaming mug.

Again, I'm lost for things to say.

"I watched your grandfather live most of his life trying to understand why a simple man like himself possessed such an ability. He never found any answers. I don't want you to spend your life looking for answers that aren't there. Some things don't have an explanation, they just are. You have your whole life ahead of you."

Laughing, she covers her mouth with the back of her hand to hide her amusement.

"What's so funny?"

Shaking her head, she says, "Not funny, unimaginable…your grandfather never told or showed anyone on this earth what he could do, except for me. And to imagine what he would do if he knew that his grandson did it every night in a show as a hoax."

"Would he be mad?" I feel a sudden tremble in my stomach.

"I don't think so. Honestly, I think he'd get a kick out of it."

Relief floods through me and I nod, feeling better that I have his approval.

"Why don't you get some rest? I've kept you up late enough." She kisses my cheek and gets up, walking toward the door.

"Oli?"

She turns around.

"Thanks."

She smiles and turns away disappearing into the house.

After a few minutes alone on the swing, I get up and go to bed.

I close my eyes and lay back against the headboard. Sleep isn't going to come easy tonight. I miss the moans of the semi engines and the whooshing sounds of passing cars. Tonight, there will be no highway melody to lull me to dreamland. Tonight, the silence offers only the swishing of the paddle fan, and the deafening memories of a life I've only recently departed from, but that I so desperately miss already.

# CHAPTER 7

"You forgot to put on your makeup," CeCe says and giggles.

"It's too early for your comments, little one." I pour some juice in a glass. "And besides, eyeliner isn't makeup."

"Yes it is."

"No it's—"

"Good morning. How are we doing?" Oli walks into the kitchen in workout clothes.

"Hey, Oli," CeCe and I say together.

"There's nothing like a morning walk to keep me young." She takes a plate from the microwave and puts it on the table in front of me; pancakes. "Don't get used to it, I'm a huge fan of cereal."

"Thanks," I say, smiling.

"You guys ready for today?"

CeCe and I look at each other and exchange I-guess-so smiles.

~~~

The rumble of my motorcycle draws attention as I pull into the parking lot. I park in a spot close to the school's entrance and take off my helmet and rake my fingers through my hair, messing it even more.

"You can't park there."

44

I turn around to see a girl with short blonde hair wearing very tight jeans. "And why not?" I ask, leaning against the motorcycle and crossing my arms over my chest.

"Because that's Aiden's spot." A deep-throated engine rears up behind me. "I tried to tell you."

A Mustang pulls into the spot next to me. The engine cuts off and the door opens. "Hey, babe," the driver says to the girl standing next to me.

In less than a second, blonde girl's face changes from bitch to angelic. "Hi." Her voice is almost melodic.

He pulls her to him and kisses her. When he comes up for air, he looks at me and says, "It's obvious you're new here," he slaps me hard on the shoulder, and nods toward my bike, "so, I'll let it slide today."

"Aw, thanks man," I say, showing him the same curiosity by slapping him on the shoulder and adding a tight squeeze. "You're too kind."

The smirk falls off his face. "Let's go," he says to blonde girl. He throws his arm around her and they walk away. She glances over her shoulder, her eyes warning me.

Strike one against the new kid.

The first thing I notice when I pull the door open to Student Services is her long wavy brown hair. Her back is to me, and within seconds, I concoct an image of her face. I hope I'm not disappointed.

"May I help you?"

Startled, I jerk my head toward the voice. An office lady stands at the counter in front of me. Hair dyed the color of dead leaves surrounds her fat, wrinkle-less face while new growth of white continues to creep out of her scalp. Before I can answer, she says, "Ah, you must be the new student." It's not a question. "I'm Ms. Perks."

Behind her, the girl with the long hair looks in my direction. She's beautiful. Without taking my eyes away from the beautiful

45

girl, I ask, "Is it that obvious?"

Beautiful girl looks away.

She laughs. "No. Well…yeah, and only because I know everyone here, not because you look the part. And when I came in this morning, everything to get you started was on the fax." She opens a drawer and pulls out a file. "Here it is, Erik." She hands me my schedule. "Your locker number and the combination to the lock are on the back." She opens another drawer, takes out a piece of paper, and hands it to me. "And here's a diagram of the school. Should help you find your way around."

"Thank you."

"Starting a new school is hard enough, especially in your senior year. But, never having gone to a school before is, well—it must be a very difficult transition." She's shaking her head and I can only begin to guess at what's going through it. "So, if there's anything I can do, don't hesitate to ask."

Refraining from reaching across the counter to pinch her lips shut, I say, "Thanks."

Behind Ms. Perks, beautiful girl turns her head slightly. Listening? She affords me her profile as she tucks hair behind her ear, still studying the paper in her hand.

"Addison."

"Yeah?" says beautiful girl.

Addison. She looks more like an Autumn or Summer, but I can get used to Addison. Her hair falls over her nearly bare shoulder; only the thin line of a white strap on her tanned skin.

"Don't you have Mr. Tauras first period?"

"Yes."

"Great. So does Mr. Davenport." Addison looks up then, right at me. Her eyes are pale green. "Would you be kind enough to show him where it is?"

"Sure." She sets the paper back in the pile and picks up her bag. Walking past me without saying a word, she shoulder opens the

46

door and pushes out into the hall.

"She's a nice girl, just has her own way, that's all," Ms. Perks says.

I thank her, and catch up to Addison. The halls are crowded and it's difficult to stay at her side, so I walk close behind her and try not to imagine what's under her almost sheer, flowing white skirt. "I'm Erik."

She says nothing and continues to charge through the hall.

"I said, I'm Erik."

"I heard you the first time," she says over her shoulder.

When we get to class, she walks down the aisle and sits at a desk, never looks or says anything to me. I stare at her, baffled as to what I did wrong.

"You lost, son?"

I realize I'm standing in the front of the class looking exactly that. Everyone who is already in their seats is staring at me, smirks smeared across their faces. Hoping I can be heard over the class snickering, I say, "No. This is room 128, right?" I hand my schedule to, who I assume is Mr. Tauras. His comb-over, stained the color of brown shoe polish, falls over his forehead and he pushes the escaped hair back, matting it back into the grease that holds the rest of it in place.

Handing my schedule back to me, he says, "Take a seat there." He points to the desk in the center of the room. "For now, share a textbook with Tiffany."

A girl with light brown skin and tiny spring-like curls exploding from her head looks up from her phone, thumbs still busy on its keyboard.

"Put that thing away, class is about to start," says Mr. Tauras. And on cue, the bell rings.

I sit down in what has to be the exact center of the room. "Hi," I say, risking the possibility of being crucified or ignored by girl #3. And all before eight A.M. I'm hoping this one is slightly

47

nicer than blonde girl and Addison since I have to share a book with her.

"Hang on, almost done." Her thumbs cruise over the keyboard in a blur. "Okay, sorry." She puts her phone in her purse and looks at me. "Hi." As if in a toothpaste or mouthwash commercial, she flashes me a flawless smile with perfect white teeth.

I smile back, but I'm sure its unworthy of the one she's given me. "I'm Erik."

"Hi—I already said that—sorry, I'm Tiffany, but I bet you already guessed that—huh?" She fumbles in her bag and comes up with a book. "We're only on chapter two, so you haven't missed much."

Awkwardly, I move my desk towards her, unsure how close to go. She doesn't say anything when mine taps the edge of hers.

She puts the book between and leans into me, whispering, "So, how do you like the Home of the Patriots so far?"

"Are you a cheerleader or something?"

Her cheeks flush, and without it being possible, her smile brightens even more. "Yes." It's hard not to smile with her; its infectious. Then, with no warning, it falters. "Wait, why did you think that?"

"Just a guess," I say, and offer a noncommittal shrug and a cocked grin.

"I'm a huge fan of our varsity football team and I think they're going to be amazing this year. You should come see a game. Aiden, the quarterback, let's just say, well, he's incredible."

I'm finding it hard to simultaneously pay attention to Tiffany's chatter and Mr. Tauras' lecture. His arm streaks across the board scribbling illegible notes that somehow we're supposed to follow and comprehend.

By the time class ends, I've managed to fill five pages of notes on how Shakespeare influenced modern language.

"I can show you to your next class if you want."

"Sure, I'll take any help I can get." I hand her my schedule.

She studies it and then flips it over. "And, I can show you where your locker is, too."

I pick up my backpack and follow her out into the hall. Unlike Addison, Tiffany walks beside me. She looks at the locker numbers. "Yours is down here." A group of blue lockers line the wall.

"Must be hard to start a new school in your senior year," she says.

I shrug like it's no big deal and put the lie into words, "It's no big deal," leaving out the part that I'm starting school for the first time ever.

She looks at me, through me, through the lie, and out of pure decency, she smiles and says, "We have one of the best marching bands in Florida."

"Oh, that's ah...great," I fumble, thrown off by the quick change of subject, but thankful. We stop in front of a set of lockers and she hands me my schedule. I turn the dial and get it open on the first try.

"I've never seen anyone do that before." Her thin eyebrows rise and her eyes bulge in true astonishment. I hold in the chuckle at how easily she's amazed.

"Guess I was lucky," I say, shrugging off the simple task.

She taps her pink manicured nails against the locker. "For some reason, I doubt that."

"Hey, Tiff."

We both turn toward the voices. Blonde girl, a.k.a. Bitch, from parking lot, and her boyfriend are standing behind us. His arm is draped over her shoulder and he leans on her as if she's holding him up. The girls begin, stop, and start a dozen conservations. Talking over one-another in what sounds like a stream of incoherent tangents. I stand there feeling like an idiot, not sure of what to do. Confident I can find my next class on my own I turn to leave.

"I'm Aiden."

The only reason I stop and turn around is because I was raised not to be an asshole. I hear my mother's words in my head: *give him a chance*. So out of pure respect for my mom, I turn to face him; his hand is jutted out in the form of a fist.

"I thought I'd introduce myself to the guy who stole my parking spot." His face is hard with a thin line across his mouth that I can only interpret to be a smile.

I bump my fist against his. "Erik."

Blonde girl laughs at something Tiffany says and at the same time looks at me. I think if she could spit venom at me, she would. It's a fucking parking space—get over it, I want to say to her.

"Hey, Aiden, maybe Erik can try out for the team," Tiffany says.

"We already have enough players." He looks at her and then to me. "Sorry, man, tryouts were a couple of months ago, during the summer."

I shrug nonchalantly. "Not really my thing anyway." I look over Tiffany's shoulder and see Addison surrounded by people going this way and that, but she walks alone. Pointed-toed cowboy boots peek out from under her long white flowing skirt. She's so beautiful. Without smiling, she says hi to the group and keeps on walking.

Tiffany grabs her arm jerking her back toward us. "Addison, jeez, stop and smell the flowers once in a while."

"What's your problem?" Aiden asks Addison, and pushes her arm.

"Nothing." Addison's bag slides off her shoulder onto the floor. "Jerk." I bend down to pick it up and our heads collide.

"Ouch!" She puts her hand over her forehead.

"God, I'm sorry." I rub my head. Aiden doesn't try to hide his amusement; he points and laughs like he's in elementary instead of high school. Ignoring him, I ask Addison is she's all right and

50

hand her back her bag.

She puts the strap over her shoulder. "Yeah. Thanks." The look she gives Aiden could possibly be deadly. And I hope I'm never on the receiving end of one like it.

Tiffany breaks the uncomfortable moment and introduces us. "Addison, this is Erik. He just moved here and—"

"I know." Her tone isn't cutting, but it's not friendly either. She pulls her hair out from under the strap of her bag. "We've already met." I guess my introduction in the hall as I hurried after her was good enough. "I gotta go," she says. And at that, she walks away.

Tiffany picks her backpack up off the floor. "Okay then." The warning bell rings. "Erik, that's Candace and you met Aiden." Candace doesn't even look up from her phone as she grunts hi. "We gotta go, too. I need to show Erik where his next class is."

"What's up with Addison?" I ask when we're far enough away from Aiden and Candace.

"Her and Aiden don't get along too well. He's loud and has the tendency to be obnoxious and she's the quiet one." I try to piece together why she's comparing them when she continues, "He acts as her tormentor and her protector. My older brother would never treat me like that, but I guess it's different if you're twins."

Comprehension sinks in. Both have the same eyes; clear and light green. If it were possible to fall into them, you'd never find your way to the surface, or want to.

"Their eyes—"

"Exactly the same, I know." She nudges me down a hall. "They remind me of a piece of glass I found at the beach when I was little. You know the green ones that get soft and smooth from the ocean water? Not like my puddle-of-mud-brown eyes. They're the complete opposites. She's the artsy one and he's the jock."

We maneuver our way through the busy halls and out of nowhere she says, "Maybe she'll talk to you one day."

51

I don't say anything, and hope she's right. Addison might be a nice distraction for me for the next 252 days.

# CHAPTER 8

$\mathcal{M}$y backpack flops on the floor when I slump into the empty seat in the back row. Irritation walks towards me wearing striped purple and black stockings. She looks like a punked-out Wicked Witch of the West with her hooded goon trailing behind her.

"What's up," I offer.

"You're in my seat," says the girl. "That one's free." She points to a desk two over from where I'm sitting.

I get up and sit in the seat she pointed to. Dropping her bag next to her, she falls into the seat, red and black chunks of hair fall over her face. The hooded guy, as if made of goo, oozes into the seat next to her. I hear him say, "What's his deal?"

"He's ruined. You saw who he was hanging out with." She bends down and pulls at a loose thread on her stocking.

What the hell does that mean? Ruined. I love how they act like I'm not sitting two feet away from them. Ignoring them, I busy myself with getting a notebook out of my backpack. Before setting it on my desk, I read the foul words etched into the worn wood of its surface.

"That desk used to belong to Mike. He dropped out last year." I look up to hooded goon. He's leaning over the front of his desk, wires coming out of his head. "Dude was a total idiot."

I lay my notebook down, covering Mike's profanity. "Yeah, I can tell from his spelling."

He huffs out a laugh. "So, what's your story, dude?"

I don't give him the satisfaction of looking up, and answer, "No story."

The girl pipes up, "Everybody's got a story."

Goon ignores her comment and says, "You're new."

I nod. "Yep." These two must be part of their own group. I've seen their type in movies, outcasts like the girl in *The Breakfast Club* who dumps out the contents of her entire purse. By a quick calculation of their attitudes, I can tell they think everything is wrong in this world—except them.

He surprises me when he says, "I'm Rip and that's Ash."

The girl, Ash, looks at me and says, "Hey."

"Hey," I return.

Rip pulls his hoodie strings and puts his hands in the pockets. Screaming abruptly blares from his ear-buds. Ash slaps his arm. "What?" he says, extra loud.

She yanks on the cord and tears the buds out of his ear. "You're going to go deaf. You know that, right?"

"Whatever," he says and puts the buds back in.

She yanks them out again and says, "Class is starting."

"*Mudvayne* or Ms. Granger droning on about how screwed up our government is. Hmm…let me think about which I'd rather listen to." He dangles the buds in the air. "Take good notes for me," he says wiggling his eyebrows as he inserts the buds back into his ear.

"You suck," she spats.

"What?" He points to his ears. "I can't hear you," he mouths.

"He's not as useless as he seems," she says defending Rip.

"The thought never entered my mind."

The lights dim and I'm thankful she can't see the smirk on my face, but I wouldn't doubt if she heard it in my voice. The screen in the front of the class glows, diagrams and typed definitions become the room's focal point.

"Copy all that down," she points to the screen, "memorize it, and you'll ace this class. It's so brainless, I'm surprised we even get credit for it." She hits Rip's arm and points to the front of the class. He bangs on his air drums, ignoring her.

I look up to copy notes from the screen and raw violet eyes are staring at me. She doesn't say anything and neither do I. Her unsettling glare is full of unspoken words, or accusations, or even a possible confession. Black shoulder length hair halos her smooth pale face. Hoops hang from her pierced lower lip and nose. Seconds turn into long moments of being trapped by her hypnotic and frightfully beautiful face.

"Turn around, freak." Ash's voice hisses in the quiet room.

I'm ripped away from the grip of those violet eyes. I look at Ash; she's glowering at the exotic girl in front of me. I look back at her, only her purple eyes move when she bores into Ash. After a few seconds, with the ease of a serpent, she slinks around in her seat to face the front of the room.

"Just ignore her," Ash whispers to me.

The violet-eyed girl unsettled me, but empathy for her slithers around in my gut. *Freak.* I could relate to the feeling, but why was she staring at me like that with those eyes; unusual and striking, mysterious and unfamiliar, eyes. I didn't realize my heart was racing until I started to copy the notes again and notice my hand was shaking. Taking a deep breath, I try to calm my nerves.

As if nothing weird just happened, Ash whispers, "So, why are you hanging out with them?"

It's obvious who she's talking about, but I ask, "Them who?"

She rolls her eyes at me. "Class president and jock-head."

I'm in no mood to defend myself, but I understand why she's asking me. My unruly hair, piercings, and grungy outfit are a much better fit with her and Rip and even violet-eyed girl, than Tiffany's clean-cut crew. "Oh, you mean Tiffany?" I leave out jock-head and bitch girlfriend. "She was showing me to my class."

"I bet she never shut up."

She's right. I nod in agreement and can't help but smile.

"I seriously would rather listen to that shit he's listening to," Ash jerks a thumb toward Rip, "the sound of vocal cords being torn from their throats, than listen to her for more than five seconds."

~~~

I find a quiet spot for lunch—alone, as far from everyone as possible. As I take out my book and a sandwich from my backpack, a shadow falls over me.

"Why are you over here all by yourself?"

The rays set Tiffany's springy curls into glow mode when she steps directly in front of the sun. "Just trying to catch my breath."

She nods. "You actually read for enjoyment." I'm not sure if she was asking a question or not. I hold up the book and she reads the title. "Frankenstein." A "hmmm" sounds from her and her mouth does a kind-of-interested motion as it droops down.

"Never read it."

"It's a good book."

She puts her hands on her hips. "I kind of pegged you as an intellect." She shrugs. "Guess I was right."

"An intellect?" I can only speculate what that means—nerd. I stretch out my legs and cross my feet, waiting for her to explain.

"What I mean is, you won't catch very many people here reading something that's not required. And the ones that do are usually—" she stops herself before continuing.

I finish for her. "Nerds." She looks like she kicked the corner of the couch. I laugh. "Then I guess that's me, an intellect. A true rebel. A nerd." She laughs and nervously tugs on the hem of her skirt. I don't think she's sure if she wants to leave or not.

She gains some of her composure back. "All right, I'm gonna

go. I just wanted to see how you were getting along today."

"Thanks. I'm good. Your assistance this morning was invaluable."

"Yeah, right. But you're welcome anyway." She smiles and lets go of her hem. "I'll see you in class."

I take a bite of my sandwich and look at the book in my lap, intent on freeing my brain from reality for a while, but I only see a jumble of words, unable to concentrate on Mary Shelley's masterpiece. I chuckle. She brings back the dead. Maybe I should see what is on the required reading list.

"Hey."

I hold my hand over my eyes to block the sun, and look up to see Ash. She moves to block the rays of the sun and I take down my hand. Her army messenger bag hangs over her shoulder. I didn't notice before but her red plaid skirt matches the streaks in her hair. I wonder if she planned that. Rip slinks out of her shadow, buds still in his ears.

He kicks my boot. "Hey man, you're in our spot."

"Shut up, Rip," says Ash, elbowing him in the gut.

"Ow," he grunts and then a sly grin eases its way onto his face. "Hey man, heard what happened in the parking lot this morning, just trying to make a joke."

"You got me." I put down my book.

"Frankenstein. Great book," says Ash as she throws down her bag and sits down cross-legged across from me. Rip sits next to her. "How far are you?"

"This is my forth time reading it, but I'm three quarters of the way through it now."

She picks at her black fingernail polish and the flakes land on her shirt. "You're a bigger fan than I am. I've only read it twice."

I can't help but ask, "So, you're an intellect?"

"A what?" she asks, looking like I've just insulted her mother.

57

I wave my hand, dismissing the question and smile to myself. "Nothing."

"Why aren't you hanging out with the in crowd?" She shoots her thumb behind her toward Tiffany and her friends.

The three of us look at the bench on the far side of the courtyard. Aiden's arm is in its usual position suffocating Candace. Tiffany sits across from them, with a guy on each side of her. It's a scene from a sitcom. Addison isn't with them and I wonder where she goes during lunch.

I wait for Ash to turn around. When she finishes her scrutinizing glare, I ask, "Why do you care who I hang out with?" I try to soften the rough edges of my words, but they still come out jagged and sharp. Rip jerks his head up. He looks at her just as curious to hear her answer as I am.

"They all dress and talk the same, they're all in the same clubs or on the same teams...it's truly vomit-inducing," Ash says. She ruffles the back of her shaved head.

"That's not really an answer," I challenge.

She looks directly at me then. "I don't care. You just don't look like their type." She shrugs and her demeanor relaxes as she reigns in callous feelings. "That's all."

I realize then, she's right. Groups in high school do actually exist and they're even more divided than I could have imagined. Determined to stick to my own, I offer, "They're not so bad."

"You'll see," she says.

"Back off, Ash." Rip tugs on her shirtsleeve.

She slaps his arm away. "Shut up. You hate them as much as I do. They hide behind their popularity."

"So what," he says.

I want to tell her we all hide behind something: red-streaked hair, black lined eyes, clothes, friends, books. Whether we're cool or uncool, smart, stupid, over-weight, short, athletic, can bring back the dead...we all hide behind something.

"She's probably the most real of all of them." She points to Addison who's walking toward them.

I have a thousand questions about the beautiful mysterious girl, but I don't ask any of them. Ash wouldn't be the one to get answers out of anyway, especially about one of them. I take a bite of my sandwich and look up, behind the school, hidden from most of the people on the benches and in the courtyard, the girl with purple eyes leans against the building. "So, what's her story?" I point to her. Except her face, black sheathes her entire body, rendering her only a silhouette of a girl.

"You mean psycho?" asks Rip.

Ash coughs and I think she may actually choke on her granola bar. "Stay away from her," she sputters out.

Psycho, freak, warnings... "Why?" The disturbing glower she gave me in class should be enough to take their cautions seriously, but with the way I grew up, watching freak shows almost every night, my curiosity is now on fire.

"Her name is Naya," answers Ash. "She's a complete head-case. I'm serious, stay away from her."

Rip nods in agreement. "Dude, she's a self-contained creep show."

Creep show—they have no idea. "And?" I ask, pushing for more information. I take another bite of my sandwich, trying to add in a dose of nonchalance to my fevered inquiry.

"She moved here a few of months ago. The rumor is she was kicked out of her last school for breaking into some kid's house who was supposedly," Ash makes air quotes, "making fun of her and to retaliate, she smeared pig's blood all over his walls."

"Totally fucked up," says Rip.

"Here, though, she keeps to herself," says Ash, "well, at least until you came along." She fidgets with the zipper on her bag. Zip. Zip. Zip. Zip. Zip.

Across the courtyard, as if she can hear us talking about her,

Naya looks over at us— no, not us, me.

~~~

I walk into my last period of the day, physics with Mr. Ashford. Before I even have a second to look around the room, a man with thick glasses holds his arm out to me, palm up. "There are assigned seats in here, son." The gesture reminds me of Riley, the boy who held the butterfly, and my stomach sinks a little thinking how much my life has changed in only a few days. Blinking back to the present, I hand him my schedule, assuming that's what he wants.

"Mr. Davenport," he says. He points to the back of the room without looking up from my schedule. "There's a reason those seats in the back row are empty."

"Okay," I say, going along with some piece of logic I don't understand.

He grabs a book off his desk and hands it to me along with my schedule. "You can have a seat there," he says, and points to an empty desk on the far side of the room.

Turning, I trip over a backpack lying next to a person sitting in the front row, but manage to stay on my feet.

"Is this guy for real?" I say under my breath, not expecting an answer.

"Yep."

I look toward the voice as I drop my backpack next to the desk. Sitting a row over, and one seat back to my right, Addison is leaning over her desk. Wavy strands fall onto her desk. Her pen is constantly moving, not writing…drawing.

"You talk," I say, and regret the words as soon as they leave my mouth. She purses her lips, saying nothing else. Why would she after that dumb-ass comment? "Look, I'm s—"

"There'll be time to make friends after class, Mr. Davenport."

Humiliated, I turn around, and try not to think about the beautiful girl behind me.

60

As I put on my helmet, a flash of white catches the edge of my vision. Addison is walking across the parking lot. She's digging for something in the bag that hangs over her shoulder. Pulling out keys, she walks towards a red sports car. Figures, I think. Straddling my bike, I look back up to her just as she throws her bag into the back of an old black topless Jeep. Gathering her skirt in one hand, she uses the roll bar to climb in.

People start to gather around the car next to me. Aiden revs the engine repeatedly as if readying for a race. He gets out of the car and sits on the hood, his girlfriend right at his side. When I look at Addison, she's looking in our direction and shaking her head. Glancing in her rearview mirror, she backs out of the space. She has to pass me to get to the exit. When she does, our eyes meet. The roll bars of the Jeep frame her as if she's in a picture. I wave, and I'm not surprised when she doesn't return the gesture.

I start my motorcycle and follow Addison out of the parking lot. At the main road, she turns left, and I turn right.

Ten minutes later, I dump my backpack on the floor in the foyer. Through the living room's slider, I see CeCe in the backyard. She's leaning against the metal skeleton dissecting tiny flowers. "Hi."

Gus follows me out into the yard. He races off to catch a lizard crawling on the fence. I sit down next to her and prop my arms on my bent knees. "Why are you torturing that flower?" A small pile of petals rests on her leg; she twirls the naked stem between her fingers.

"They don't like me," she says in a little voice. The sun slips behind gray clouds and the long shadow of the old swing-set disappears.

"I wouldn't like you either if you were pulling off my arms."

She stifles a giggle, elbows my side, and says, "Not the flowers, silly, the kids at school."

61

My heart sinks into my gut at her pained words. "Impossible."

A soft warm breeze lifts up a curl from the side of her face, and a tiny tear sits on the edge of her eye. "There is this one girl." She wipes away the teardrop that threatens to fall. "Her name's Melissa. She was nice to me, but I don't think her friends like me."

"It's only the first day, give them a chance." I should be taking my own advice instead of trying to alienate myself. "I bet by the end of the week, you won't even to be able to count all your friends."

Finally, a smile touches her lips. "I can count really high, you know?"

Smiling, I say, "Yeah, I know." She's most likely the smartest one in her class. "What about your teacher, what's her name?"

She pulls another flower from the ground. "Ms. Jenkins. And she's about ninety years old."

"I'm sure she's not that old."

"She is! She has the longest, grayest hair I've ever seen, like a witch. And I'm pretty sure she could be Oli's grandma."

I laugh at that. "Is she nice?"

"Yeah." She pulls off the white petals and piles them near the others on her knee. "So, what about you?" Gus struts through the yard and makes his way onto CeCe's lap.

"I think he's trying to make friends with you so he can meet Scooter."

"You might be right. But I still love him." She pulls the cat to her chest and he doesn't fight the embrace.

"So?" she asks.

"What?"

"How'd your day go?" She sounds so grown up. I guess she's more mature than eight-years-old when understanding and talking to people older than herself; that's all she's ever really been around.

Not daring to tell her that I miss the way everything was only days ago, and I would do anything to have our lives back the way they were, I muster some false bravado and say, "It was great."

She looks up at me with squinty eyes. "You're lying." Her lips are pursed.

"No, I'm—"

"Yes, you are." She points at my face. "Your dimple is showing." She imitates my face, squishing up her cheek.

"I don't do that."

"Yes, you do." She pushes on my left cheek with her finger. "Right there, it dents in when you lie."

She reaches for another weed-flower next to my boot. A white wing peeks out from under my sole. CeCe nudges my leg and I lift up my foot. She picks up the dead butterfly with speckled white wings. "Oh, Erik, it's so pretty." I hold out my hand and she puts the delicate corpse in it. As she looks at me, I see the all sadness that has brought us to this point; it's because of my weakness that her life changed, too. "Erik, don't do it." The hardness in her voice can't compete with her begging eyes.

The simmering in my veins has already started and I feel the spike of energy rise up from somewhere inside me. I know I should be forcing the desire back down into the trenches of my being, but it feels too good, too familiar, like an old friend that knows every one of my deepest, darkest secrets. The release of energy leaves my body as I touch the dead insect.

A wave of dizziness accompanies the weakness that washes over me. CeCe is staring at me, not the butterfly and I offer her a smile. Then she looks at the insect. Its legs twitch and its delicate wings slowly begin to pulse into a rhythm that brings it once more into flight. Together, we watch it fly away. "Erik, you brought it back to life," excitement in her voice. Gus paws at the air after the butterfly. CeCe settles him back down onto her lap, petting his back and pushing down his raised fur.

"It's what I do."

"I know," she says quietly and hugs my waist. Her collection of dissected flower petals falls to the ground. And whatever the price, it was worth it to see her happy.

Lightheadedness and dizziness hit me as I get up and start for the house. "Don't tell Oli."

"Duh. What do I look like?" Her face is still lit with happiness.

"Come on, let's go."

I'm almost to the slider when she calls after me. "Erik." Her voice is small again. I turn around and she's working the petals off a new flower, a yellow one that sprouted from a weed. She puts the petals on her knee where the others sat moments ago. "Thank you." She never looks up, and I'm grateful she doesn't see the guilt on my face. I turn back toward the house and leave her alone sitting against the metal skeleton.

# CHAPTER 9

Thunder rumbles in the distance, waking me from a nightmare. Naya is the one haunting my dreams now. Surrounded by funhouse mirrors, a thousand of her beautiful violet eyes stare at me. Then, without warning, gaping mouths appear in each of the pupils screaming. Shattered pieces of glass crash to the ground around me.

Pushing the thought of her away, I lay in bed, tangled in my sheets dreading having to go back to school. Then I think of Addison. I can't say I'm dreading seeing her again. It's obvious she's uninterested, but the thought of her catapults me out of bed. Even though there's no real explanation as to why I'm drawn to her other than her looks, or a possible challenge, or for mere distraction, she enchants me and I want to know her. Underneath the attitude, there's just a girl with pale green eyes and secrets of her own who just so happens to wear cowboy boots.

~~~

The storm's dark billowing clouds ride my rear the entire way to school. I park a couple of spaces down from Addison's jeep just as the first drop of rain hits the ground, and I make a run for shelter.

Blackness edges its way into my view as I close the door to my locker. Naya. A sliver of a smile streaks her face. She's very pretty when she's not penetrating my soul with those eyes. I think back to my nightmare and a shiver passes through me causing me to take a step back.

Reluctance and curiosity are both tugging at me. And even though there's something unidentifiably haunting in her eyes, I decide to give in to curiosity.

"How's it going?" She takes a step closer to me. "I'm Erik," I offer.

"I know." Unlike her severe looks, her voice is soft and offers traces of a slight accent, reminding me of Serpentina's Czech one. "I'm Naya."

"I know."

Her smile widens. She never breaks eye contact with me and it's unnerving. Somehow, her stare is more intense and intimidating than the hundred, expectant stares I get when I'm performing.

"How was your first day?" She tilts her head, inquisitive and comical-looking like a dog.

I shrug and glance down the hall. "Fine. Just another day at school."

She creeps around to move into my line of vision and asks, "Wasn't it your first day—ever?" The scents of sweet berries and sandalwood drift off her; I've smelled aromas like that in Oli's shop before. It's incense.

Uninterested in giving explanations, I say, "Something like that. It was nice meeting you." I turn and start to walk away and she catches my arm.

"I'm sorry. That was rude." She lowers her head. "Not a good way to start a friendship."

Friendship? First, the death stares, and now we're going to be friends? Is she for real?

"You're a freak like me," she says, no doubt present in her tone.

Shaken by her word choice, but intrigued to know why she's chosen it, I ask, "Am I? And just how do you know that?" I swallow

66

nothing, feeling my throat constrict as I wait for her answer.

With concern on her face, her lips purse, and she shrugs one shoulder. "I just know." She touches my arm, leans to me and whispers, "As a friend, just be careful. The people here," she looks to her left and then the right, "well...they aren't very nice to our kind."

Our kind—what the hell does that mean? Stupefied, I manage a nod. "Um...thanks." I should have run the other way—damn curiosity.

Her violet eyes soften and the lines around her mouth smooth over. "I'll see you in class."

As she walks away, I glance around to see if anyone overheard our conversation. Aiden is standing at the edge of the lockers with a mock grin watching me. Of all people—fuck!

"Got a girlfriend already?" He shakes his head and laughs. "Man, you work faster than I do."

Refraining from giving him a crude gesture or calling him something obscene, I walk away. On my way to homeroom, Naya's words ricochet in my skull, reverberating off each other as I try to make sense of them. She seems nice enough, but there's a shadowy and mysterious—possibly dark—side of her lurking just beneath the surface, too. Until I figure out why she's given me the friendly warning, I intend to keep my new friend close.

Addison's seat is empty when the bell rings. I look around the room to see if she's sitting at another desk when the door to the class opens and she walks in.

"Ah, Miss Bailey, thank you for gracing us with your presence on this lovely morning."

"Actually, it's pouring outside," she retorts.

"Have a seat, Miss Bailey." The class laughs and Mr. Tauras demands silence.

As she walks by my desk on the way to hers, the loose end of her scarf brushes the paper on my desk and it falls to the floor.

"Sorry," she whispers.

"No problem." No problem at all, I think. I bend down to pick it up and smell her perfume; I close my eyes and imagine eating vanilla ice cream in the woods.

"I hope all of you are ready for a pop-quiz," announces Mr. Tauras.

The class groans, pens and pencils drop on desks in a frustrated clanking song throughout the room.

"Mr. Davenport?" Mr. Tauras says.

My head jerks up. "Yes?"

He combs over the loose threads of his hair. "I'm not usually a very patient man, but this being only your second day, you're excused from the quiz."

"No, that's okay, I'll take it," I say.

"You must be really smart or really stupid." The smooth edge of Addison's voice finds its way to my ears.

Precisely positioning its fall, I drop my pen behind me and to my right; it lands perfectly at her feet. As I bend down, she follows my movements and I look directly at her and say, "I think I can handle it."

"We'll see." She shrugs and looks back to the paper on her desk.

"Is that a challenge?"

An almost invisible smile slides over her glossed lips and then it disappears.

"Everyone, take out a piece of paper," Mr. Tauras says.

As soon as the bell rings, Addison is out of her seat and walking past me. I grab her bag, pulling her to a stop. "Hey." She looks down at my grip, and then up to me. I let it go.

"Don't you want to know?"

"Know what?" Impatience grows in the lines of her face.

"How I did on the quiz."

"I really don't care." She continues to walk to the door.

I reach for my backpack and see something glint under Addison's desk. A silver bracelet lay on the floor. Picking it up, I call out to her, "Addison."

After a few steps, she turns around, but says nothing.

"Is this yours?" I hold out the bracelet. A small red-jeweled heart dangles from one of the links.

She walks toward my outstretched hand. "Yes." Her fingers brush my hand as she takes the bracelet. A thrill rushes through me, and the touch shoots flashes of heat across my palm. It's so similar to the sensation I get when I bring back the dead, and I feel ecstatic and miserable at the same time.

"What's wrong?" she asks.

I can't imagine what my face shows. "Uh...nothing." I pull my hand back and shove it into my pocket.

She heads for the door. As she reaches for the handle, she turns around. "So, how'd you do?"

Only too happy that she's even speaking to me, I have no words and answer with a wink and a playful grin.

A repressed smile plays on her lips as she tugs on the ends of her scarf. She holds up the bracelet. "Thank you."

The feeling on my palm is still there, a faint tingling right under my skin. And, maybe I'm imagining it, but I don't care.

# CHAPTER 10

"So, how was your first week?" Oli asks.

CeCe drinks the last of her milk from her cereal bowl. "It's getting a little better. But I'm glad it's Friday."

"I couldn't agree more," I say.

"Well, I must say you both seem to have adjusted rather well. I know this move hasn't been easy." Oli gets up and takes our empty bowls to the sink. "CeCe, go finish getting ready and we'll leave in a bit."

I know she's trying to be strong in front of Oli, so after Oli leaves the kitchen, I ask, "Are you really doing okay?"

She stares at the floor watching her foot shuffle back and forth over the tile. "Yeah. But, I miss Mom and Dad. I mean—not a lot or anything."

"Hey," I say and she looks up at me. "It's okay to miss them. I miss them, too." I open my arms and she rushes into them.

"That makes me feel better. I thought I was just being a wimp."

I pull her away and lift her chin to look at me. "You are the farthest thing from being a wimp." I wink at her, and she tries to wink back, but only manages to produce a scrunched face and two closed eyes.

"Want me to show you how to wink?"

"I am winking, see?" She winks again.

I can't help but laugh. "Here." I take her hand and press her fingers to her right eyelid. "Open your left eye." She does. "Okay, now move your right hand away from your eye and try to keep it closed."

She moves her hand away. It opens a little, but mostly stays shut. "I'm winking!"

"You're almost there, little one. Keep practicing."

"Okay." She gets down from my lap. I watch her as she walks out of the kitchen, the whole way pressing and releasing her eye.

I pick up my backpack from the chair. "Guys, I'm going."

"Have a good day," Oli yells from her room.

"Thanks."

I have the door open when CeCe slams into the back of me, her arms wrap around my waist. "I love you."

I turn and hug her. "I love you, too."

She lets go of me, and holds her right eye down and keeps her left open.

I wink back and close the door behind me.

Getting on my bike, I think of how brave that little girl is. Braver than me, I think. I start the bike and put it in gear.

At the main road, I turn left instead of right. There used to be a road about a half-mile down that winds around the lake, bypassing town. If I'm remembering right, it should bring me a block or two from school.

When I turn down the road, it's exactly like it used to be. Homes, one after another to my right, and woods to my left. The houses end abruptly and then start up again. Between them is a beach. I thought developers would have built houses here by now, but it's exactly the same. This is where I used to come with my grandfather and Oli when I'd visit them in the summer. A thousand memories of fun come rushing back as I gaze at the shore. I get off my bike and walk through the path of wheatgrass, down to the shore. It's all the same except for a few more docks edging out from backyards and hovering over the lake. The water licks the base of a mass of boulders. I used to climb to the top of them and jump into the water. The rocks aren't intimidating like they were when I was younger. Now they're only a little higher than my waist.

"Hey!" I turn around and beam uncontrollable delight. "Are you planning to cut class?" Addison yells. She's pulled off to the side of the road and parked next to my bike.

I walk toward her and rest my arm on the door of the Jeep. "I will if you will," I suggest and shrug, unable to tuck away the grin on my face.

She smiles. "I'll see you in class." She puts the Jeep in gear and drives away.

Climbing on my bike, I forget about the lake behind me and follow the quiet, beautiful girl in front of me to school.

Fifteen minutes later, I walk into class and see Addison already in her seat.

"So, do you go there often?" she asks when I get close enough so that only I can hear.

I ease into my seat and lay my backpack on the floor. Turning to face her, I say, "I used to. You?"

Ignoring my question, she asks, "Did you used to live around here?" She plays with the loose hairs at the end of her braid.

I've never lived anywhere, but I don't say this and instead answer, "No." And before she has time to ask another question, I ask her again, "Do you go there a lot?"

"Sometimes. I live right down the street." She looks down at a notebook on her desk. "Actually, I try to go there whenever I get the chance. It's my favorite place to—" She stops abruptly and looks up at me. Her mouth is open in a perfect circle, as if she just received

72

an epiphany regarding who she's talking to.

"To what?" I encourage.

"Nothing." She looks back down and picks up her pencil.

Reluctantly I turn around, and for the entire class, I try to imagine what Addison was going to say.

When the bell rings, I turn to look at her, hoping she'll continue our conversation. She's standing by her desk, putting the strap of her bag over her shoulder. "See ya later," I say.

She looks up and then quickly lowers her head back down. "Yeah," is all she says and walks out of the room.

Tiffany picks up her bag off the floor and drapes it over her shoulder. "I told you she keeps to herself. But, she's letting you in a lot faster than anyone I've seen in a long time."

All through next period, Tiffany's comment leaves me to wonder; do I want to be let in? Things will only end up complicated. My goal isn't to find a girlfriend, but to get back on the road performing.

I walk out into the busy hallway and Naya creeps up behind me. "Hey," she says, nudging my backpack.

"Hi."

"Looks like you've survived your first week." Her black painted lips have a slight upward curve. She hasn't brought up any more crazy talk about how we're the same since Tuesday, and through our small talk, I still haven't figured out why she thinks we're the same. But, she's been nothing but nice to me, and as far as I can tell, I'm the only one she talks to. So, I continue to ignore Ash's warnings and just laugh when she starts in on the topic and find ways to change the subject.

"Piece of cake."

"Are you going to the game tonight?" she asks.

"No. You?"

"Do I look like I go to football games?" She doesn't wait for an answer and says, "I wasn't sure about you though. You seem

73

pretty close to Tiffany, not to mention the quarterback's sister."

I'm shocked she used Tiffany's name and not some smart-ass nickname. "Addison and I, close? Hardly."

"Well," she lowers her eyes and looks sideways toward me through long dark lashes, "if you don't have any plans, want to do something?"

"What'd you have in mind?"

She shrugs and hikes the strap of her bag higher onto her shoulder. "I don't know. Maybe we could go to the cemetery and raise the dead." The hall closes in on me as soon as the words penetrate my skull. I stop in the middle of the hall. She stops too, and a few people run into the back of us, but I hardly notice. When I look at her, those inquisitive violet eyes are staring back. I don't say anything in the hopes that she's going to start laughing. She doesn't.

"You're joking—right?" I say as calmly as I can, trying to inject a hint of humor.

Her face is deadpan. "Oh. I thought you'd be into that."

My gut feels like it's sinking into the floor. There's a sudden pain in my temples and I refrain from rubbing them. Forcing a laugh, I try to disengage the look of horror I can only imagine is smeared all over my face. "As tempting as it sounds, maybe we could get a bite to eat instead." The withdrawal has almost killed me this past week, but Naya, in less than thirty seconds, has managed to temporarily suck out every sliver of desire to bring back the dead. I take a deep breath and trap it in my lungs, waiting for the next blow to come.

She hands me a small piece of paper I didn't notice she was holding. "Here's my number. Text me when you get to class and then I'll have yours."

The jolts of shock are still shuddering through me as I nod. "I gotta get to class."

"Me, too." She hits my arm and starts giggling. "You know I was just kidding. Right?"

74

"Yeah." A choked-off cackle deteriorates in my throat. "Of course."

*Was* she just kidding?

~~~

Like a crowd running from zombies, students and teachers herd toward the gym for a pep rally. The cheerleaders are a synchronized blur of red, white, and blue as they run and tumble across the room and then fall into their choreographed routine that requires a lot of clapping and yelling. I don't see anyone I know, so I sit near the exit. The steel bleacher vibrates from pounding feet.

Silence takes over the room when a man's booming voice sounds from a bullhorn. "Put your hands together for this year's varsity football stars." And on cue, the football team smashes through the wide paper sign and stampedes into the gym. The audience erupts and is on their feet chanting, "Let's go Patriots."

I've had enough. The rowdiness fades the farther I walk down the deserted hall. When I open the door to the library, cool air wafts out along with the smell of books, new and old. Only a few others have decided to skip the afternoon fun and hide out in here. Scanning the room for an empty table, I see the tips of cowboy boots peeking out from under a table tucked away in the corner.

Addison's half-told secret is still on my mind. Curiosity again gets the better of me and before I can change my mind, I take a deep breath and walk towards her. She turns the page of the book she's holding and the swift sound ricochets throughout the library.

My hand is on the chair across from her. "Anyone sitting here?" What is it about her that draws me in the second I see her?

Addison looks up. She shifts the light gray sweater tighter around her shoulders. "No." She pulls her feet in and closes the book in her hands. But instead of laying it on the table, she leaves it in her lap.

As I pull out the chair the sweet smell of vanilla drifts pass me. "You're not a fan of your brother?"

She shrugs, "I'm not really a fan of the whole scene." Her eyes glance downward.

Tilting my head to the side I say, "Something else we have in common."

"What's the first?" she asks looking directly at me.

Her features soften, curiosity tearing down part of her heavily guarded wall. And while I take a moment to catch my breath and regain the coolness I had in place, her face never changes or crinkles showing impatience. "We both like that spot at the lake," I finally say. "I may have to start stalking you to find out what your mystery is about that place."

She looks up. "You'd do that?"

I laugh. "No. But I will admit, I am curious."

She smiles and rolls her eyes up to the ceiling. The gesture is more like an *oh-yeah* than a *you idiot*.

I don't want her to shut down again, and we have this private spot all to ourselves, so I drop the subject and ask, "What are you reading?"

Her demeanor shifts and she immediately builds back up her wall. Damn! "Nothing you'd be interested in," she says quickly and looks off into the library, holding the book to her chest.

I lean against the table, intertwine my fingers and ask, "And how do you know that?" She doesn't answer. Her eyes drop to the table and she tucks her lips in on themselves. "So?" I push.

She looks at me. And again, I'm trapped in her stare. More than anything I've wanted in a very long time, I want her to trust me. "What?" she asks in a hushed tone.

Keeping my eyes on hers, in a low voice I say, "You're assuming that I wouldn't be interested in what you're reading, but how do you know?"

Hesitantly, she holds up the book. It's a children's book.

"The Enchanted Forest by Ida Rentoul Outhwaite and Grenby Outhwaite." I tighten my lips and exaggerate a nod. "You

76

know, I can help you learn to read big people's books if you want."

She laughs and hurries to cover her mouth in the quiet of the library. "That's very generous of you, but I can read just fine." She looks back down at the book and runs the tips of her fingers over the cover. "I like the illustrations."

"Can I see it?"

She stiffens. "Why?"

"To see what you like." I hold out my hand, hoping she's gained enough trust thus far to put it in my hand.

"Don't you think that's a little personal?"

I can't help but laugh. "It's a book, not your diary."

Releasing an audible breath, she concedes and hands the book to me across the table.

I flip through it. Whimsical colorful creatures and fairies are depicted on the pages. One catches my eye, a slight delicate girl standing on a bat, her arms outstretched as they fly over a meadow. It's beautiful and haunting…tranquil. I close the book and hand it back to her.

"What? No smartass comment?"

I cross my arms over my chest. "Were you expecting one?"

Our eyes once again engage and something inanimate fills the empty air between us. This time, wonder gathers in each one of her pale green pools. Then without warning, it manifests, and something unidentifiable and primal passes between us. A rush of sprightly thrill scintillates my insides. Deep within the depths of my bones, a feeling I've never experienced before, more intense than the energy that courses through me when I raise the dead, shifts within me. Breaking the connection, she glances down at the book, and my bones instantly chill. I take a moment to collect myself, shaking my head to dislodge the unfamiliar feeling wedged in my gut. "Actually, I was going to say I think the drawings are genius."

Her head pops up. "Really?" A minuscule smile dances on her lips. She wants to believe me.

"Yes," I say without a trace of amusement. "I'm guessing your hobby isn't too popular with your friends."

"It's not just a hobby, it's going to be my career one day." Her fingers touch the cover and it's as if she and the book have their own connection. Without even knowing the story, I wonder for a brief second if Addison identifies with the little girl on those pages. "Ida Outhwaite is my favorite illustrator." She lifts the book and hides her face behind it.

"You okay?"

"I should go." She stands quickly and starts packing her stuff into her bag.

Without thinking, I reach over and put my hand on top of hers. "Don't go."

She stops and looks at our hands. Without moving hers away, she says, "It's just..." Easing back into the chair, she continues. "I've never shared that with anyone. It just kind of came out."

Reluctantly, I move my hand away from hers and readjust my arms to hide my thrashing heart and whisper, "I promise I won't tell a soul."

She lays the book on the table between us. A truce. "That's what I was about to tell you earlier today, when we were talking about the lake. It's my favorite place to draw."

I watch the deep breath she's been holding leave her lungs. "I can understand why."

Her eyes soften. "Thank you."

I want to reach across the table and touch her hand again. But I don't. "Maybe one day you'll show me your drawings."

"I don't know about that." She puts her drawing book in her bag.

Shrugging and still aching for her trust that she hasn't yet completely afforded me, I say, "Well, one can always hope."

We're quiet for a minute, and I figure I too owe her an explanation. "I used to go there with my grandparents when I'd visit them during the summer." The look she offers gives me the instant desire to tell her my truth, but it'd be reckless, and instead say, "I have a thousand memories I hope I never forget."

"That's really nice." Her glossed lips ease into a smile. "Maybe you can share them with me sometime."

I find myself suddenly wanting to kiss her. "Only if you show me your drawings." The corner of my mouth tilts upward, teasingly.

A light chuckle escapes her. Nodding, she says, "Ahh, bargaining. I see how this goes, show me yours and I'll show you mine."

"Something like that." Bewilderment and giddiness slide side by side down my spine. She was not in my plans.

# CHAPTER 11

"We're having pizza," CeCe says as soon as I walk in the front door.

"I'm going out, little one," I say, and pull one of her curls and let it bounce back into place.

"More for me," she singsongs and skips off toward her room.

I throw my backpack in the corner of my room and lay on my bed. Grateful the week is over, only 248 more days of this normal life to endure. My phone buzzes and I pull it out from my pocket. "Hello?"

"How do tacos sound?" Naya's voice on the other end is upbeat and excited.

It took most of the day to get her joking suggestion—to bring back the dead—out of my head. But what I can't shake is why she would even suggest that—of all things? And to me—of all the people on this planet? "Sounds better than going to the cemetery."

She laughs. "Although, if you have the desire to try the hot sauce, you might end up there."

"Then I'll stick to the mild."

"Wimp," she taunts. "I'm not the motorcycle type, so what time should I pick you up?"

It never occurred to me how we'd get there, and I didn't

80

think that we would be driving together. I was thinking it would be more of a I'll-meet-you-there kind-of-thing. "I have a few things to do first. Why don't you tell me where it is, and I'll see you around seven."

"What kinds of things?" Her voice is playful but curious.

"Things I need to do alone," I say lightly.

Naya doesn't persist. She gives me directions and hangs up.

CeCe is at my door. "So, where ya goin with your girlfriend?"

"She's not my girlfriend." I pat her head as I walk past her and go into the kitchen.

Oli is sitting at the table looking at a magazine and drinking tea. "Plans?"

Before I can answer, CeCe says, "Erik has a date with his girlfriend."

Oli's brows rise.

"I'm going to have tacos with a *friend*," I say, emphasizing the word friend.

CeCe makes kissing noises. "His *girl*-friend," she says and giggles.

"Tacos? I assume you're going to Rico's," says Oli.

"Yeah. You've been there?"

She nods. "Beware of their hot sauce."

"I've heard that." I lean down and kiss her cheek. "I won't be home late."

"Ow." She looks at one side of my face, then the other. "Are you sure you don't want to shave before you go?"

"It's not a date," I say and grab my keys off the counter.

Their laughing quiets as the door closes behind me.

The talk about the cemetery reminded me I hadn't been there in a while—not to raise the dead as Naya suggested, but to visit my grandfather. After the thought struck, the urge to visit his grave grew into a necessity. I don't tell Oli I'm going there, and I'm not sure

81

why.

I have a few hours before going to meet Naya. There's a convenience store on the corner of the main road of Oli's street. Plastered on the store's windows are advertisements for beer, cigarettes, lottery tickets, and beef jerky. The door buzzes announcing my entry.

I grab a bag of chips and a Coke and go to the counter. The guy looks over his shoulder and says with a smokers rasp, "Hold on, be right with ya." He comes to the counter; he's balding and anorexic skinny. "Sorry 'bout that, had to put more dogs on."

"No problem." I put the money on the counter. He slides it across the counter with a hand sporting a glistening coat of grease and filthy fingernails. I look at the hotdogs he's just put on the spinning metal cylinders and cringe internally.

"Are you hiring?" I don't know what makes me ask. I haven't thought about getting a job or doing anything other than school. But when I hear the words come out of my mouth, it feels right. I'm sure it's a minimum wage job, but free chips and sodas is a benefit.

"No, not now. It's dead in here."

My shoulders slack.

"My wife and me run this place on our own. We never get to see each other though. Who knows, that's probably a good thing." He laughs at his own joke; dry lips peel away revealing yellow crooked teeth.

"Alright, thanks," I say and pick up the chips and Coke.

Before I push open the door, he calls out, "I think Roy's looking for help."

"Who's Roy?" I ask.

"Roy Harris. He runs the grounds at the cemetery. Hear he's looking for someone to dig graves." He follows me out the door and lights up a cigarette, blowing out a cloud of smoke. "That job ain't for everyone. Digging holes for the dead. Eeshhh…gives me the creeps." He exaggerates a shiver.

Eating those hot dogs you just touched gives me the creeps. "Maybe I'll check it out, thanks."

A few moments later, after I sat on the curb and ate the chips and drank the soda, I pull into the cemetery. The ominous black iron gates are closed. Gold letters swirl and loop to form the words "Edgewater Cemetery." Staying on my bike, I clutch my fingers around the hot steely rods of the gate and stare beyond them. It's so familiar, and haunting, and comforting. Unlike the living, the dead are easy, un-wanting and un-needing. I want to drive down the center road through the graves, past the headstones and markers and tombs, and find a place to sit and think about nothing.

The grumbling of an engine behind me disturbs my moment of reverie.

"You waiting on someone, son?" A big man gets out of pickup truck, a ring of keys in his hand.

"No, sir."

"Then ya mind backing up so I can get these here gates open?"

I push my bike back and watch him unlock the padlock. He pulls the chain through one of the gates and lets it drape over the other one. I cringe as a penetrating screech echoes as he pushes open each of the gates to their respective sides. A "Help Wanted" sign I didn't notice before, hangs high on the right gate.

The man climbs back in his truck and pulls alongside me. "You coming in or what?"

I follow him into the cemetery.

Huge oak trees are scattered throughout the property, their massive reaching limbs shade thousands of graves. Headstones large and small dot the far off fields. Statues of angels and saints, carved from marble, granite, and stone stare down at me as I drive through their territory.

Dragonflies are everywhere. There must be water on the

property. And then I see it. A pond rests under the long limbs of a tree. They hover over it, diving down, touching its surface, barely making a wake.

The truck goes on ahead, and disappears around a bend. I creep along the road so slowly that I have to weave back and forth to keep from falling over. Parking my bike next to the pond, I walk through the manicured grounds toward my grandfather's grave. The plot next to it is empty—waiting for Oli? His headstone reads *Ewell L. Prebble, A gifted man who loved life*. It's situated in an open field with very little shade. The grass is soft under me as I sit down next to him and bring my knees to my chest and rest my arms on them. The past years without him have been hard, and now knowing we shared this gift, there's even more of a connection to him. God, if only I could bleed out everything that's happened and share with him all of my experiences and my love for bringing back the dead, and the dread from missing it, and how weak I've become. I want to ask the thousand questions that swirl in my head, even knowing no answers will come; hear his thoughts on something no one else could ever imagine. But instead, I just cry.

The sun slowly passes over me. In the past hour, calm has somehow found a way to spread through me. Rising to my knees, I touch my finger to my lips and with my other hand I trace the letters G-I-F-T-E-D on his headstone. I walk away with something I didn't have before; a strength and courage to endure the next several months.

I was so lost in the moment, I almost forgot to ask about the job. With no idea where to go or what Roy looks like, I straddle my bike and go in the direction the truck went earlier. Since it seems the guy in the truck is the only living person here, it's a good place to start. The road winds around. The man is standing by a golf cart; he looks up as I come to a stop next to him.

"Can I help ya, son?"

"I'm looking for Mr. Harris?"

Holding the straps of his overalls, he says, "Who's asking?" The man's southern accent seems too drawn out for this part of Florida.

"Erik Davenport, sir."

"Sir. Hmm, I like that. I'm Roy Harris. What can I do for ya?"

I push down the kickstand and get off my motorcycle. "I'm looking for a job and heard you needed help."

"From who?"

"The guy at the mini-mart."

He chuckles, and the word "Vern" comes out in the noise. "He's happy enough just putting them dogs on them rollers. They don't taste too bad, but there ain't nothing like a dog cooked on a grill. Mmmmm." He looks at his watch and says "Damn, it's almost dinner time, no wonder why my stomach's growling at me."

"Is the position still available?"

"Sure is. There ain't too many people cut out for this type of work." He looks me over, sizing me up. "You got a good build on ya. Let me see your hands, son." I hold them out and he takes them in his, turning them over and then palm up again. Feeling exposed as he examines my hands, I want to pull them out of his. "These ain't gonna look like this after you dig a couple of graves."

"I'm not worried about that."

He drops my hands. "Well, your girl might." He chortles.

"I don't have a girl." Addison's face sparks in my head, and for a flitting moment, I wish I could say I did.

"Now that there's a damn shame. But, no matter," he turns to the golf cart and then back around, "ya got time for that." He hands me a screwdriver. "Why don't you go and take down that "Help Wanted" sign off the main gate."

"Thank you, Mr. Harris."

He nods. "Call me Roy."

"What are the hours?"

85

He barks out a hard laugh, throwing back his head. "Whenever somebody dies, son." His barrel of a belly bounces. "You're pretty much always on call for digging graves. Never know when the Big Guy is gonna call on ya. But, in between, I can always use a helping hand maintaining these grounds."

Understanding, I nod.

"Pay ain't great, but you ain't doing brain surgery either." He climbs in the driver's seat of the golf cart and it whines, protesting the big man's weight. "We'll work out your hours around your schooling. That's more important than shoveling dirt."

"How do you know I'm in school?"

"Son, not much gets past me here in this town. I might look and talk like a redneck, but I ain't blind and I ain't stupid." He scratches the white scruff on his face, and adjusts his wide brim hat. "There ain't no ghosts, the dead don't whisper, you might get a creepy feeling once in a while, but nothing other than that."

"The dead don't bother me."

"Then you ain't got nothin' to worry about." He takes a toothpick out of his pocket and puts it in his mouth. He nods toward the tool in my hand. "Leave the screwdriver and the sign by the gate. I'll get them on my way out."

"Yes, sir."

"Come back in the morning. I'll get ya familiar on how we do things 'round here." And at that, he drives away leaving me there in the middle of a graveyard, my new place of employment. And I wonder if anyone plans to work in a cemetery; I'm thinking it's the kind of job you kind of fall into, like I just did.

# CHAPTER 12

Through an archway I see Naya, her usual black-on-black stands out against the burnt orange wall. She waves me over to a table for two in the back of the busy restaurant. Her high ponytail swings back and forth, while her short spiky bangs don't budge. When I get close, she seems almost shocked that I showed up; her face is partly smiling and partly contorted into a wide-eyed approximation of road kill.

After pulling out my chair and sitting in it, she seems to relax. "Hey." I probably stink and should have gone home to at least change my shirt. Oh well, too late now.

"Hi. Did you have any trouble finding it?" she asks in a higher than normal voice. I can't imagine she's nervous about us hanging out. I can't imagine her getting nervous about anything.

"Nope."

"Good." She hands me a menu. "I just ordered waters, and some chips and salsa."

"I guess you already know what you're having." Without opening it, I look over the menu at her.

She shrugs. "The usual, chicken burrito with black beans and rice."

I set the menu back down on table. "Since it seems you're a regular, I'll have the same."

"Good choice. You won't be disappointed."

When the waitress comes to take our order, Naya orders for both of us and I add a Coke.

She pushes back her chair and points to a bar in the middle of the restaurant. "I'm going to get the sauces and salsas."

I run my fingers through my hair and think how ironic it is that I got a job at the cemetery. Just after Naya suggested "jokingly" that we go there tonight. I haven't thought about it until now and I hope she doesn't bring it up again. And the fact that I'm employed there needs to stay out of tonight's conversation, too.

Naya comes back with a plate of at least ten small plastic cups filled with green, red, smooth, and chunky sauces.

"This one," she points with a black painted fingernail toward one of the cups, "is the one to stay away from."

"Then why did you get it?" I ask, chuckling.

"Because, it at least has to be on the table, and," she shrugs, "who knows? Maybe you'll get the urge to try it."

"I've been warned twice about that stuff, once by you, and then by my grandmother."

"Yeah, well, maybe your curiosity will get the better of you, or if you're dared." A devious grin spreads across her black lips.

Without another word, I pick up a tortilla chip from the basket and dip it in the sauce from Hell. Even before it reaches my lips, its peppery stench burns my nostrils. I can't back out now. Naya's face is scrunched as if waiting for a shot from the doctor. I shove the entire chip into my mouth. I don't have to wait more than a second before fire explodes on and around my tongue. Naya must see my suffering and hands me my glass of water. I gulp the cool liquid but it does little to ease the burn coating every cell in my mouth. She waves for the waitress and points to me. I think she mouths the word milk.

Stifling a snicker at Naya, the waitress sets a glass of milk in front of me. "Your food will be right out."

"Drink." Naya points to the milk.

Mexican food and milk don't go together. But, trusting her I pick up the glass and drink it. The thick white liquid lessens the pain, but by no means makes it go away.

The waitress sets our food on the table.

"Better?" Naya asks me.

I nod. "I'm glad you're enjoying this." I have to laugh. I can't very well hold a grudge against her for my ego showing off.

"I won't say I'm not." She laughs, too.

Naya points to another cup filled with a green sauce. "Seriously though, you should stick with that one. It's verde salsa, very, very mild. I promise." An innocent, coaxing smile appears, and her whole face joins in. She looks pretty.

We both take bites of our food. "Is it good?" I ask her.

She looks at me like I'm crazy. "You're eating the same thing." She points to my plate with her fork.

"Yeah, but I can't taste anything. I think I scorched my taste buds."

She laughs. "I'm sorry, I shouldn't have tempted you like that."

I can't help but ask her, "Why are you so nice to me?" The question has been on my mind since Tuesday when she approached me at my locker.

"What do you mean?" She takes a bite of her food.

"This?" I wave my arm the length of her. "You're always so standoffish at school and whenever we're alone, it's like this other person comes out."

Picking up a chip, she scoops up salsa and puts it in her mouth. Between crunching she says, "I don't know."

"I haven't decided if you're shy or you just like being creepy." My taste buds have yet to return to their full capacity and the bite of burrito still doesn't taste like much.

She shrugs. "Both, I guess. I never really thought about it."

"So, you admit that you're creepy?" I laugh.

"Intentionally, yes." Her smooth skin shuffles into an easy smile, and she lets out a laugh.

I'm not sure that I buy her answers, but it's easy conversation and we're not talking about raising the dead. "At least you're honest."

She puts down the fork and takes a sip of water, then says, "With most things."

"What's that suppose to mean?"

She ignores my question and says, "Besides, you haven't given me reason not to be nice to yet." She picks up one of the cups filled with salsa and pours it on her plate.

Still baffled by her bipolar personalities, I ask, "Why aren't you like this around anyone else?"

"They aren't like us."

"What do you mean by that?" Here we go, seeping into territory that also includes me in some way I have yet to understand. I guess I deserve it since I pushed her for explanations.

But again, she disregards what I asked, keeping her reasons to her herself. She looks away from me and glances around the restaurant.

"Maybe one day you'll tell me."

"Yeah, maybe…" She shrugs only one shoulder and her shirt slides down her shoulder revealing part of a wing inked on her upper arm.

"What's that?" I point to her shoulder.

She pulls down her shirt revealing the whole tattoo. Perfect black lines and shading grays create a kneeling fairy with tattered wings. The precise detail of her sharp angled eyes and pointed ears gives the impression she's evil, but the whole expression of her face is sad. It's nothing less than spellbinding. "She's…" I don't know what to say without sounding like an idiot.

"I got her when I was fifteen."

Zane and Lars would fall instantly in love with this girl—piercings, tattoo, swathed in black. "She's, um..." I don't know why I'm at a loss for words, but I am. Her stare feels like a wrecking ball coming at me as she waits for a response. I want to look up but I'm afraid to see her expression. And when I do, anger and regret is swimming in her violet eyes.

"What? Go ahead and say it." She pulls her shirt up covering the tattoo. "Sad, pathetic—"

"Mesmerizing. She's mesmerizing."

Naya doesn't let go of the hold she has over me as she slowly lets go of the grip on her shirt. The edge of it slips its way off her shoulder exposing the broken fairy again. For a long moment, we say nothing to each other. My eyes can't help but slide down to the tattoo.

"I was thirteen when I drew her." Her gaze falls to her shoulder too, and we both stare at the fairy as if waiting for her to say or do something.

"So, what's her story?"

"I don't know. Sometimes I think I'm like her," she says and picks up her fork and stabs at the burrito, dissecting its insides.

I need to cut through the thick and heavy emotions between us and bring us back to a lighter side so I say, "So, she's a self portrait?"

She rolls her eyes up to the ceiling and they stay there until she continues. Smiling now, she says, "Hell, who knows? She might be. Except for the ears." She touches her ears lined with piercings and laughs.

"So, you think you're a fairy?"

"And you think I'm mesmerizing."

"I walked into that one." I put another tasteless bite into my mouth. "A point for you."

"That's okay if you do." She smiles. "Seriously though, I wish I was a fairy. I'd wave a wand," she waves her hand around her body, "or dust myself," she says sprinkling imagined dust over her head, "and poof myself right the hell outta here." She lowers her arm and her animated face suddenly turns somber. "But unfortunately, I'm not a fairy." She looks at me, a sad smile on her lips. "Just broken."

I don't have a response. Her violet eyes are drawn to the floor, bleak and far away. She folds her hands under her chin and rests her head on them. I take a sip of the Coke.

When her eyes find mine again, she asks, "So what does the dragonfly symbolize?" She points to my wrist.

I didn't think anyone would notice the tattoo on the inside of my wrist with the leather cords worn over it. I shrug away the importance and insert a lie. "Nothing, just thought it was cool."

"And?" Naya pushes; she's not going to give up that easy.

In the short time I've known her, I know she's not stupid, but neither am I. "And what?" Nonchalantly, I focus on a sizzling plate of fajitas being delivered to the table next to us.

When I look back to Naya, her head is tilted and she's leaning back in her chair with her arms crossed over her chest. "Why a dragonfly?"

"I don't know. I like it."

"Uh-huh," she says, unconvinced. "Whatever."

"What are you doing getting tattoos when you were fifteen, anyway?"

"I could ask you the same thing," she says.

This one is easy, and I figure I owe her something of an explanation. "My parents are pretty easy going. Except for school. When it comes to that, my mom's like a frickin' piranha."

She laughs. "So is my mom. I can pretty much do whatever I want, except school. That's a priority."

We settle for a few minutes in quiet. When I look up from my plate she's looking at the family next to us. I glance at them, they look happy. Words I can hardly make out get lost in their laughter.

92

My heart aches for my family and I wonder if my dad's performing at this very minute. Naya and I meet each other's gaze across the table. Faint lines of sadness are etched around her eyes.

"Can I ask you something?"

"Sure," she says.

"Are your eyes really that color or do you wear contacts?"

She laughs. "I thought you were going to ask something serious or embarrassing. I don't wear contacts. They're very real." She bats her eyelashes. "I get them from my mom." She pushes her plate away. "I'm going to order a fried ice cream, want one?"

"No thanks."

She folds her hands on the table and leans in to me. "My turn to ask a question." I nod, and hope it's one that I can answer truthfully. "Is this your first time going to school?"

Sighing a breath of relief, I say, "Yep."

"Why? Did your parents keep you locked in a dungeon somewhere?"

"Not quite." I laugh. "My mom home schooled my little sister and me until this year. She started helping my dad more with work," I spread my arms out, "so here I am."

"Do you like it?"

"It's not as bad as I thought it was going to be. I hate getting up when it's still dark out."

The waitress set the dessert in the middle of the table with two spoons.

"I see you eyeing it. I'll give you a small bite, but that's it." She spoons out a section and faces it in my direction. "Ya see, being that I'm an only child and all, I don't like sharing, so this is all you get."

I take the spoon from her and put it in my mouth. The outer hot coating competes for space on my tongue with the cold smooth ice cream inside. "That's really good."

She rolls her eyes and picks up the other spoon. "Fine, have another bite."

"Thought you didn't share?" I say spooning another bite from her dish.

"There are always exceptions." She offers me that easy graceful smile. "And I'd say you're one of them."

# CHAPTER 13

"You got a job at the cemetery!" CeCe announces. "Gross." Scooter is on her hand eating part of her toast.

I take a bite of cereal. "I think I'm used to the dead."

"Yeah, bugs and reptiles, not people." She thrusts Scooter in my direction. "Mice. Not people," she repeats.

"I'm pretty sure I can handle it." I watch the field mouse. That small creature once lay dead in my hand, now he's eating from CeCe's hand. It's ironic and unnatural, and I miss it terribly. The teakettle screams breaking through my thoughts.

Oli comes into the kitchen and pours the steaming water into her mug. "Did I hear correctly?"

"Oli, you can't let Erik work in a graveyard," CeCe cries out.

"Let me guess…Roy Harris." She snickers.

"Yeah. What's so funny?" I ask.

The spoon clinks against the mug as she stirs in honey and cream. "That man has had a crush on me since grade school."

"Did you ever date him?"

She sits down at the table. "Once."

"And?" I ask.

She brings the mug to her lips and smiles into her tea.

"I've got to go." I put on my backpack filled with lunch and a

95

fresh shirt and tighten the straps.

"Oh, Erik." I turn to Oli's voice. "Have you seen Gus? He didn't come in last night."

"No. Maybe we can use Scooter as bait."

"Hey! That's not nice," CeCe says, holding the mouse tight to her chest.

Oli sets her mug on the table. "When he gets hungry, he'll show up."

As I turn the doorknob and step onto the porch, an eerie feeling settles over me and the hairs on my arms stand on end. Something isn't right. I don't know how or why I know that, but there's some instinctual alarm ringing in my head along with the disturbing icy sensation forcing itself through my bones. Something is on the brink. And it isn't good.

~~~

The gates are open when I pull up to the cemetery. I lean against the handlebars, debating whether to drive through them. Lowering my head to my arms I think of the irony…only a week ago I was bringing the dead back to life, now I'll be burying them. I laugh and lift my head. Revving the engine, I drive through the opened arms of the cemetery.

Roy is standing by the shed. "Morning,'" he says as I get off my bike.

"Good morning," I return.

"This being your first day and all, I wish I could say we're gonna take things easy." He puts on a pair of thick gloves. "But, that ain't gonna happen. Ole Bill Carter finally died." Roy looks over the low rolling hills of the cemetery.

"Finally?" I question.

"He was the meanest man I ever had the displeasure of meeting." He reaches into the shed, pulls out a shovel and hands it to me. "You got gloves?"

"No, sir."

96

He goes inside the shed for a minute and then comes back out. "Here, use these, you're gonna need them." He climbs into the golf cart. "Come on. What are ya waiting for? We got a hole to dig."

I put the shovel in the back of the cart and climb in.

"Cemeteries are broken into sections," Roy says. "A section is a piece of land that has a road going through it. For instance, you see that over there?" He points to a piece of land to our right.

"I see it."

"Okay. Now that there section is broken down into lots. Then on each of them lots, you got the actual graves, usually four to eight on each lot." He thumps my chest with the back of his hand and I look at him. "You getting all this?"

I nod. "Makes sense so far."

"Good. I'm telling ya this cause you seem like a smart kid. And I don't like being asked the same question twice."

I nod again, this time looking away from him to hide my smirk.

"Good. There's more. All those rows of headstones you see—those are called tiers. They're numbered from south to north." He stops the golf cart and holds out his gloved hand. "So it goes," he points with his pointer finger, "section, lot, tier, grave," assigning each to a finger. "Got it?"

"Yes, sir."

"I do like that, 'sir.'" He steps on the gas and we continue our travels on the one-way road through the cemetery.

I look out across the land and thousands of flowers, mostly fake from what I can tell, decorate the final resting place of grandparents, mothers, fathers, etc.

"Now, here in Florida the holes gotta be eight feet deep." I think of the shovel that's in the back of the cart. He has to be joking.

We pull off the paved road and stop. "Carter's grave is gonna be in here, section four." The paper flips up as he takes a clipboard down from the dash. "Section three, lot ten, tier twelve north. You got all that?" I repeat the location back to him. He grins. "I knew I did right by hiring you." We climb out of the golf cart. "Get that shovel and don't forget your gloves."

Over the crest of a small hill, a backhoe stands waiting for us, and I silently say a thank you. "I'll teach ya how to drive Bulldog another time." He pats the backhoe and climbs into the driver's seat. "For right now, just pay attention." He cranks the engine.

# CHAPTER 14

"Hi, Erik."

Addison's smooth voice breaches the dead zone I'm in. I lift my head from my hands to see her looking at me from the desk in front of me. "Hi." An immediate smile spreads across my face.

Long waves of her hair spill onto my desk. "Sorry." She hurries to tuck them behind her ear. The mood is stiff until she looks at me and finally there's a break in the awkward moment and the air around us lightens.

"How was your weekend?" She's still slightly blurred from rubbing my eyes, but even through the cloudiness, she's beautiful. I hardly know anything about her, but Addison has been in my thoughts since the first morning I laid eyes on her.

"It was good," she says. "Thanks."

I lower my voice to a mere whisper. "Did you have a chance to go to the lake and do that thing you love to do?"

Her cheeks turn pinkish and she lowers her head. When her eyes come up to meet mine, I am more awake than I think I've ever been in my life. She looks around the room, sneaks an animated smile as if preparing to divulge a massive secret. I laugh quietly watching her. She whispers, "Yes."

"I'm glad to hear that."

She clears her throat. "I actually came over to ask you for a favor."

Raising my eyebrows, curiosity eats away at any thought I may have had prior to her words.

"Do you mind if I borrow your notes? I think I'm missing a few things."

I hand her my notebook.

"Thanks," she says and gets up. She angles back around and says, "How rude of me. I never asked you how your weekend was."

I smile thinking the hottest girl in school is standing in front of me, and most likely, she's an angel that wears cowboy boots. "It was good, thanks."

She nods and the corner of her mouth tilts into a smile. "I'm glad."

I once knew a girl whose name was Raven. She had hair the color of the setting sun, fiery red, and a personality to match it. She was mean, nasty, and rude, but that was only half the time. The other half she was kind, funny, and patient; and that was the half I had a crush on. The bad thing was, I never knew which side I would get when.

Her parents were stilt walkers and travelled with us for a couple of months before they moved on. But, since this unwarranted half-time cruelty from a girl, I've always been careful to stay clear of girls. Addison may be an exception.

Even if a girl was not on my agenda.

"Here you go." Addison hands back my notebook fifteen minutes later. "Thanks. I missed a lot. You take good notes."

"No problem. Borrow them anytime."

Class begins boringly and ends just as mind numbingly.

"See ya later," I say to Addison.

"Thanks again. I'll see you in physics."

I follow her out into the hall and notice what she's wearing.

It's not like what most of the other girls wear; a long, light blue plaid oversized man's dress shirt with the sleeves rolled up, and a wide woven belt around her waist, cowboy boots on her feet, and her long tan legs in between.

Tiffany's arm links through mine and I'm positive I was caught gawking. She leans in even closer as we walk down the hall. "Okay, what's your secret?"

Baffled, I ask, "What are you talking about?"

She jerks me to a stop. "Addison hasn't gave anyone the time of day since tenth grade, and here you come," she coughs out a laugh, "and it's like you've tapped into the old Addison. I don't know how, I mean yes," she rolls her eyes, "you got the looks, anyone can see that, and you smell damn good—" she nods and holds up her hand, "yes—I went there. You're like a package: blue eyes, dark messy hair, mysterious hot new guy. But Addison," she shakes her head and waggles her finger, "Uh-uh, she's not that easily worked over. So?" Holding me with her stare, she waits for an answer.

My face feels as hot as the energy that courses through my veins, and I'm pretty sure my lower jaw is lying on the top of my boots. "Um. I got nothing," I mutter.

"Anyway," Tiffany says as she hikes up her backpack on her shoulder, "I don't know either, but I'm grateful. And I just wanted you to know." She reaches up, puts her arms around me, and steals a quick hug. And just as fast she releases me. "Listen, the bell's going to ring, but I wanted to invite you to a party we're having Friday night. I'll give you the details later." She pats my chest and walks down the hall.

I shake my head to clear the thoughts I have of her as we go our separate ways and head to second period.

"What's wrong?" Naya asks.

I look up from my notebook to see Naya. Still in Tiffany-daze and not sure what, if anything is wrong, I say, "Nothing, just

101

tired. I was up all night looking for our cat."

Naya's eyes narrow and concern fills her purple eyes. "Did you find it?"

I shake my head. "No."

Ash and Rip walk down the aisle towards their desks. Like a laser beam, Ash's death stare aims straight at Naya.

"Do you want me to come over after school and help you look for it?"

From the corner of my eye I see Ash and Rip; they're watching me and Naya's normal interaction and I wonder if they'll give her a chance by actually accepting she's human and a little less like a mutant blood painter. I kick Ash's desk and finally she disengages her torpedo-like glare. "Nah, that's okay. He'll show up." I hope.

"Anyway, how's your tongue?"

I stick it out to show her. "I think it's almost completely recovered."

Without being able to help it, I look over at Ash and Rip to see their reactions. I want to help them lift up their jaws that are practically lying on their desks. I laugh.

"I'm glad to hear that," says Naya. I would hate to have been the one responsible for a permanent injury." The bell rings and she turns around in her seat.

"Fucking sick," I hear Ash say under her breath.

"Chill out, Ash. Don't be so presumptuous," I tell her.

A minute later, a note lands on my desk. Unfolding it, I see bold red letters reading: *Naya is totally crazy! Stay away from her! ~Ash.*

When I look at Ash, she's staring at me, her eyes bulging out of her head. I can't help the grin that spreads over my lips. I think of Raven, her two very different sides, and realize Ash reminds me of her and I shudder.

Tiffany's words about Addison have me excited and scared.

And again, I find myself perplexed as to why I'm drawn to this girl and yet I'm not sure I want to be, but I'm virtually powerless when it comes to controlling these unfamiliar feelings surfacing inside of me.

~~~

"You listen for shit!" Ash is on me before I step foot inside the cafeteria.

I don't pretend to know what she's talking about. "What's the big deal? She's nice."

Ash grabs a chunk of her hair in her fist and waves her other one at me. "They're always nice at first. Then, when you're not looking, Mr. Hyde takes over and you're fucked."

"Ash, before you find a seat go wash that mouth out," Mr. Hankins says as he comes up behind us.

Ignoring him, Ash pulls out the chair at the closest table and I sit down across from her. She looks over her shoulder and then to me. "I guess you're a fan of bloody art."

She'd probably fall out of her chair if I told her I once traveled with a guy, I forget his name, but that's exactly what his medium was, animal blood. During his show he would brush and splatter the blood, creating "art," while the carcass lay at his feet. I laugh thinking about it now, but there was no humor when I watched him perform.

"Ash, you need to relax." I point to her shirt. "Besides, do you know how difficult it is to take you serious when you're wearing a t-shirt that has a kitten with a mohawk on it?"

She stifles a grin, reaches across the table, and slaps my arm. "You guys were having an un-freaky conversation this morning."

"See? Maybe if you just say hi without trying to petrify her with your eyes, she might say hi back."

"I don't do that!"

"You so do that." Rip comes up behind her confirming what I was about to say to her. She kicks his leg and he emits a yelp.

"Come on punky kitty, let's go." He holds out his hand, she takes it and eases out of the chair.

She looks back over her shoulder. "I'll try to chill out, but just a little." She follows Rip out of the cafeteria.

I take out my book and lean back, balancing on the back two legs.

"Hey there."

Startled, the chair falls forward and I bang my elbow on the table. I look up to see the mysterious and cryptic Naya. "Hey."

"You saving this seat or can I sit?" I wave my arm for her to take it. "It's lunch time—don't you eat food or do you just devour books?"

I take a PB&J out of my backpack and hold it out to her. "See? Lunch."

"Gourmet." She exaggerates a wink. "So, what are you reading this week?"

"*Metamorphosis*."

"What's it about?"

I take a bite of my sandwich and answer around a mouth full of food, "A guy who wakes up as a bug."

"Sounds interesting, and weird."

"Like you," I joke.

"Ha-ha. Let me see it." I hand her the book. She reads the back cover and shakes her head. "Where do people come up with this shit?"

"It's not shit, it's called fiction. And you know better than to insult that little world of mine."

"Yeah, I know." She hands the book back to me and reaches across the table to pick up the napkin left by whoever sat here earlier.

A mass of brown ringlets come up behind Naya. "Hey, Erik. After the game on Friday—" Tiffany stops in mid sentence when she notices Naya. "Oh…hi."

Naya wiggles her fingers with an embellished smirk on her face.

"What about the game?" I ask.

"Ah…nothing, I'll talk to you about it later."

Naya glances over her shoulder as Tiffany walks away. "Bitch," she says under her breath. She looks back to me.

"She's actually really nice."

Ignoring me, she says, "You're already getting invited to their parties." She puts her finger in her mouth, imitating a gag. "Impressive, and vomit inducing."

"Parties? What are you talking about?"

She rips off tiny pieces of the napkin, balling each one before putting it in a pile. "There's only a select few invited to their parties and it looks like you made the list." Her lips purse and pucker as she tears off each piece and rubs it into a ball.

"Is there something wrong with that?"

Her pile of paper balls is growing into a small heap. "Not if you're into that kind of thing."

"I didn't say I was."

She shrugs. "I guess I read you wrong. That's all. Whatever." She says the word "whatever" like it's more for her benefit than mine. She looks up from the napkin. "You're different from them."

"And how do you know that?"

"I just know." She gives no more of an explanation than that.

Of course, she's right; they're nothing like me. No one is. Not even Naya, who thinks we're the same—freaks.

She pushes back from the table, the chair shrieks as it scrapes across the floor and the tiny balls of paper scatter across the table. "Like I've already told you, be careful." She picks up her bag. "I'll see ya later."

~~~

As I walk to last period, knowing I'm going to see Addison, I think about what Tiffany said this morning. I really have no clue as

105

to why Addison talks to me, or in Tiffany's words, is 'letting me in'.

Tiffany comes up beside me and links her arm through mine. "So...you and Naya—huh?" She pouts out her lip. "And here I thought you liked Addison."

Without acknowledging my feelings for Addison, I pull my arm out from hers, and ask, "Let me guess—Aiden?"

"Well...he did kind of mention it. And you guys were having lunch together...alone."

"There's no me and Naya—trust me."

"That's your business. I was just hoping—"

I know exactly what she's hoping for. But I'm not ready to admit those feelings to anyone. I can barely concede them to myself. "Don't go there," I caution her, adding a laugh to my words to cut down the harshness.

She dismisses my warning and says, "Anyway, what I tried to tell you at lunch is after the game we're all going to the lake to party. Wanna come? It's a blast." She talks the entire way to seventh period. "So? What do ya think?"

"What does he think about what?" Aiden asks. He must have come up behind us.

She puts up her hand for him not to interrupt. "There's music, dancing, food, and drinks," she lowers her voice and says, "the good kind." And giggles.

I glance at Aiden and he's glaring at Tiffany. His face is so red it looks like he just got out of practice. Oblivious of him, she continues to invite the new guy to one of their secret parties.

I smile and say, "Count me in." I have no intention of going, but agree only to piss-off Aiden.

Then I reconsider—maybe Addison will be there.

# CHAPTER 15

"How are you coping?" Oli asks. We sway on the porch swing, like we did the first night I came to stay here, which seems like forever ago. So much has happened, and everything has changed. I'm different now. I'm afraid that I'm losing the core of who I really am and what I'm capable of doing. It's like I'm in between worlds; the one where "normal" people live and I'm trying to fit in, and the one where I realize I do fit in, but don't want to.

"Hanging in there." I haven't brought anything back from the dead since the butterfly on the first day school. It's becoming almost automatic to cram the energy that begins to rise to the surface back down into the trenches where it nestles in the crevices. The constant battle between holding back the writhing energy that aches to be released, and greedy need to grow stronger is punishment alone, but I've come to realize it's necessary. And, I feel stronger than I have in a long time.

She nods. "You knew this wouldn't be easy."

"I know."

Night creatures rustle under the porch. "Possums," she says. "A whole family, maybe two, harmless, but loud as hell." She stomps on the wood planks and it quiets under our feet.

"It's not as bad as I thought." I look up at her and she's smiling, and I realize that I am, too.

She bumps into my arm. "Come on, what's her name?"

"Wh—nothing." I shake my head. But I can't stop smiling.

"Addison."

"And?"

"I don't know." I hunch my shoulders, and it dawns on me that I really don't. "She's different from any of the people I've met here." My heart thumps faster just thinking and talking about her. "She doesn't give a crap what anyone thinks. I mean she wears cowboy boots with dresses."

"Have you asked her out?"

"No."

My shoulders sag and I think the truth aloud. "As long as I don't ask her, I can still think that she might say yes."

"Erik, that's no way to live. You of all people should know that."

"I do." I don't tell her I hate my feelings for betraying me. Or mention the countdown until I can start performing again, and how Addison doesn't fit into that plan. I look out into the night; the black sky poses as a backdrop for the scattered pinpricks of light.

"We'll see." Do I ask her and hope that she says no? Or do I ask her in hopes she says yes?

~~~

I close my eyes and try to ignore the good morning chatter around me. Holding my throbbing head, my brain rattles in my skull as books slam on desks and backpacks drop beside desks. Sleep eluded me most of the night and I'm paying for it now. And the moments I do sleep, nightmares consume them.

"Rough night?"

"Not rough. Not enough sleep," I say.

Taking the pencil out of her mouth, Addison says, "I can relate to that."

When our eyes meet, I lower my voice to a whisper and say, "You look like you got all of your beauty rest to me." Stupid. Stupid. Stupid. Why can't I keep my mouth shut?

Instead of shunning me, she surprises me with a half smile.

108

"Thanks."

Our eyes stay locked, and in this exact moment I want to tell her my secret, the reason that I'm really here, how drastically my life has changed in such a short time, how at moments it takes everything I want to ask her why I have this overwhelming need to know her, to be close to her. Does she see any of those things as she stares into my eyes?

The bell rings and the rest of the class comes into focus.

Tiffany turns around in her seat, and as usual, her smile is as bright as a headlight. It must be a prerequisite for cheerleaders. "Erik, you're still coming to the lake tonight, right?"

Addison is so close and I wonder if she's listening to our conversation. I want to look at her for a signal; a wink, a nod that says, please go, it'll be fun, and we can hang out. But I don't look at her.

"It's a great way to end the week and to start off the weekend." She doesn't wait for an answer and asks, "Do you need directions?" she says.

"I think I passed by the entrance the other day. I'll find it."

~~~

Moving as silently as I can, I walk through the guided path of the pines toward the lake. I sit by the mouth of the trail, at the edge of the wheat grass. The swaying blades camouflage me from the crowd on the shore. The gathering is smaller than I thought it'd be, maybe only twenty or so people.

They surround a small bonfire, talking, dancing, all with their red plastic cups probably filled with whatever they could get their hands on to catch a buzz. I recognize a few people.

Behind me, I hear a rustling noise. Before I can turn around a body slams into me. A puff of warm breath trails along my neck. A girl's muffled cry follows. I reach around to help her; our faces are very close, and my heart tightens at the sight of her. My hand is on her waist. She moves slightly and my fingertips feel the thin material

109

of her dress.

Addison's breath catches. "Sorry."

"Are you alright?" I taste something sweet in the air between us.

"I think so." Her hands are on my shoulders. "There must be a stump or something and I..." she trails off. Using me for leverage, she pushes herself to her feet. My hand slides from her waist down her side and the smooth fabric feels almost nonexistent under my touch.

"Why are you sitting up here all by yourself?" She brushes sand off her dress. "If you join me, I won't be all by myself."

She sits down. "Just for a bit—and only because you saved me from falling on my face." Our bodies are close, but not touching.

I laugh. "Glad I could be here."

She glances toward the shore. "So, you're watching the popular kids get drunk and act stupid."

"Something like that."

"Ah, so you're into voyeurism. That's good to know." She knocks her shoulder lightly into mine. The insignificant nudge forces tremors to rise up from my core and expose themselves as tiny chill bumps on my arms.

Our laughs mingle with the shifting blades of the wheat grass.

She looks at me, the smile still saturating her mouth, and asks, "So, what are you really doing here?"

I break off a blade of grass and twist it around my finger. Lowering my voice, I answer, "It's kind of a secret."

Her eyebrows rise. "Oh really?"

"You first," I tease. "I didn't think this was you're kind of thing." I wrap my arms around my knees. My arm brushes hers. Her skin is soft and cool.

"It isn't really. I usually don't come to their parties, but once in a while...I mean they're still my friends—you know?" She plays

110

with her braid. "I don't know…I just thought maybe…" she trails off.

"Maybe what?"

"Nothing." She picks up a stick and draws in the sand.

"So you have a secret of your own?" I ask.

Her face turns serious. "Don't we all?"

"Yeah, I guess we do." And like this morning, the feeling to divulge mine to her is overwhelming. "You know, secrets are one of the most versatile things, they can be anything in the entire world. Absolutely anything. But, they're also one of the most fragile; they can only exist as long as they're kept safe."

She brings her knees to her chest and rests her chin on them. "So, why'd you come?" The grains collapse on top of each other as she draws in the sand.

"The truth?"

"Always." The word is stiff but full of feeling.

I'm afraid the truth will scare her off, but if I lie, she'll know. I look at her, take a deep breath and hope she doesn't get up and leave. "I was hoping to see you." She ignores my truth—or maybe tucks it away for later—and looks at the sand, continuing to draw.

It's quiet for a few minutes. And at any second I know she's going to get up, but she keeps drawing in the sand. "Is it true this is the first time you've ever been to school?"

"Yes."

"Were you home schooled?"

She still hasn't looked at me. I want to put my hand under her chin and turn her to face me, but I don't. Instead I say, "Yes, by my mom." Since I told her one of my secrets, slivers of relief wedge their way into the uncomfortable mass between us, and I don't regret that I told her.

The music is loud by the water and a familiar song finds its way to us. "Where'd you move from?"

"All over," I say.

"Is your dad in the military?"

I laugh. "No, quite the opposite."

The air around us lightens. She puts the stick down, and tilts her head finally looking at me, and she's smiling. "Let me guess, you're from a family of gypsies and you travel from city to city selling magic potions and promises you never plan on keeping."

My laugh sounds like a combination of chuckle and a gag. "That's a bit closer." I hope she doesn't notice the nervousness that surrounds my words.

She touches her bracelet. "It must be difficult for you."

I want to tell her school is the easy part of this transition. Holding back and swallowing the urges to bring back the dead, that's the ultimate challenge. "It's been an adjustment, but not too bad."

"I don't know if I could do it."

"I'm sure you could. You just have to watch a bunch of movies about high school, then you act like you know what you're doing." I shrug. "That's what I did."

"You're joking?"

"Yeah." I grin.

She shoves my leg a little and laughs.

"I see you got your bracelet fixed." I touch the small heart resting on the inside of her wrist.

"Yeah, it was my grandmother's. She passed away a few months ago."

"I'm sorry."

"Thanks." She nods and purses her lips. "The clasp was loose and I kept putting off getting it fixed. It's the only thing I have from her." She looks at me. "I don't know what I would have done if you hadn't found it."

The moment is perfect to lean in and kiss her. And I badly want to put my hand on her cheek and bring my lips to hers.

She looks at her wrist, my fingers still there. "I should go," she says shattering my thoughts.

112

I slide my hand from her wrist, along her palm, lingering on her fingertips with my own. Looking up into her eyes, I ask, "Are you sure you want to?"

She meets my eyes. "No." Her voice whispers the simple word I was hoping she would say. "But they're expecting me down there." My stomach aches when she starts to get up. "Thanks for catching me when I fell." She brushes the sand off her dress and walks through the wheat grass toward the shore.

"It was my pleasure."

I have no reason to stay and I get up to leave when I hear, "Who's that?" The words echo off the shoreline and I turn to see Aiden in his sister's face while pointing in my direction.

Without giving him an answer, she pushes him out of the way. Tiffany waves her over to the fire and pats the sand next to her for her to sit. Addison looks back to where I'm standing. The fiery orange glow shines on her face, a sad smile lingering there.

I look down at the blurred swirls and lines Addison drew in the sand. A dragonfly.

# CHAPTER 16

Another nightmare wrenches me from sleep. The clock on the nightstand says it's only six. Tired of lying in bed still exhausted but restless, I get up and pull on jeans. Sneaking through the dark house, I step out onto the porch, closing the door behind me as quietly as possible. The wood plank creaks under my foot, and I purse my lips and try to lighten my steps.

The morning is perfectly still, and I think of the carnival the way it is before anyone wakes to scurry and prepare for the day's events. A thin layer of fog shrouds the front lawn. The moist air leaves a damp layer on my bare chest and I fold my arms over it.

A light cluster catches my eye on the porch swing. Gus is sleeping on the red pillows. He's lying on his side; his head rests on his front paws, his tail wrapped around his body. Took him long enough, but at least he knew how to find home. The unruffled gray fur looks as if he just returned from the groomer instead of a week lost and eating who knows what.

I sit on the swing. The chain groans under my weight. The cat doesn't look up, or even stir. Stoking his fur, his body is stiff and cool under my touch. Lifting his eyelid, the eye is milky and dead. Picking him up and setting him in my lap, I don't see any scratches or marks. I know he wasn't very old. Oli just adopted him a few years ago. Could he have died in his sleep? How else would he look this unharmed and this peaceful?

CeCe can't see him like this, and as soon as my head wraps around the idea it's too late to stop the lava spilling from my veins. A current of energy, enough to illuminate an entire city, grasps the edges of the trench and seeps into my fingertips. The feeling is exhilarating, powerful, and more than anything else...alive.

Gus folds into a perfect ball and then stretches out into his full length over my lap. Watching him, the vivacious and buzzing sensation still flows through me. He yawns the perfect cat yawn, wide and long and rubs up against my chest. I pull his now warm body against me and hug him tight. His whiskers tickle my chest.

Thrilling excitement replaces the subsiding heat and energy. The exhilaration dies a fast death as the sudden faintness and dizziness strikes me. I grab onto the swing's chain to keep from falling forward. Gus jumps down from my lap, his nails clawing through my jeans and scratching my leg, a minor pain to offset the sudden evacuation of energy. Training my eyes on the potted plant across the porch, I focus on breathing and calming the disappointing after effects, the ones that got me here in this fucked-up situation to begin with.

The front door opens and Oli steps out onto the porch. My heart freezes. Gus weaves through her legs, caressing his head against them. Oli licks away the sliver of a smile and purses her lips as she looks at me. I can only imagine the emotional agony she sees drawn on my colorless face.

"Look who came home," I manage to say and force an insignificant smile.

She reaches down and picks up her pet, wrapping her arms around him. "He looks perfect." She lifts her eyes to me. "You wouldn't have anything to do with that, now would you?" Cocking her head, disappointment concocted with joy in her voice. She strokes the cat's head.

"I don't know what you're talking about." I get up and walk

past her and she grabs my arm.

"How do you feel?"

I give her a smile the size of Texas. "Great."

"You're a horrible liar."

~~~

Oli and I don't talk about what happened this morning again. CeCe was ecstatic when she woke up and Gus was sleeping at the foot of her bed. She kept asking what happened and where he was, but there was nothing to say, I didn't know. Oli just gave me "the" look. I just looked away, feeling the sizzle still in my veins, and went to get ready for church.

What I did know was Gus didn't end up on the porch swing by himself. And that was disturbing.

The small white church looks like it came right out of a movie. A towering steeple is perched at the highest part of the roof. The last time I was here was for my grandfather's funeral, and it hasn't changed a bit. Before the service begins, people gather on the wide steps that lead to the double doors. They shake hands and hug, make small talk and catch up on gossip.

Inside is bright and colorful from the sunlight filtering through the high stained glass windows. CeCe and I slide into the pew while Oli mingles with the other churchgoers. Glancing around my eye catches the long golden brown hair that captured me the first time I saw it in Student Services. Addison is sitting in a pew a few rows up and on the other side of the isle. She's cradling her head in her hand and she looks upset.

Rising, I want to go to her. Aiden comes into my view standing between a woman and his sister, and I sit back down.

"What are you staring at?" asks CeCe.

"Ah—nothing." I reach for a bible tucked in the pocket in front of me. Opening the book, I flip through the thousand or so pages. CeCe stands up, craning her neck in Addison's direction.

The second Aiden sits Addison comes back into view.

"Ooohhh…." CeCe grins. "Not a what, but a who." Her wicked smile puckers, and she makes kissing noises.

"Cute. You can sit down now," I hiss.

For the next hour, my brain fights over thoughts of the amazing and still vivid feeling from this morning and Addison. Things are getting complicated—not good.

After the last prayer and amen are said, we stand and begin to file out of the pews. I wait for Addison to pass; she's one of the last to leave. Her hand still cups her head. "Addison."

Startled, she stops and looks up. Her gaze is distant, and darkness circles her eyes. "Oh, hi."

Aiden crashes into the back of her. "Shit, Addison. What the—" He stops in mid-rant as soon as he sees me.

We stand eye to eye and he looks like he wants to hit me: nostrils flared, eyebrows scrunched together. "Aiden," is all I say as a gesture of merest acknowledgement.

He doesn't say anything and continues past Addison and out of the church. We look after him until the door closes. "Don't mind him, he's a jerk," she says.

I reach out to touch her arm, decide not to and drop my hand back to my side. "Are you okay?"

She moves her hand away from her head. "Yeah, I—"

"You're pretty." CeCe says wedging herself between Addison and I.

Rolling my eyes, I realize my sister has just hijacked the few minutes I'd have with Addison. "Addison, this is my sister, CeCe. CeCe, this is Addison." I tuck my hands into my pockets.

"Hi, CeCe. It's nice to meet you and thank you for the compliment."

"Is CeCe short for something?"

"Celeste. My parents thought it would be cute to name me after—" I bump her with my hip. I'm not ready to divulge that she was named after Celeste Evens, a famous magician who would fill

117

the stage with flying doves, and escape from straitjackets. CeCe gets it and continues. "Anyway, they got a little too creative with that one, so I go by CeCe."

"Celeste. I think it's a beautiful name."

CeCe's head lifts and her face transforms from annoyed to delighted, bouncing on the balls of her feet. "You do, really?" she asks as if Addison is someone to be idolized.

Addison nods. "Really."

"Are you my brother's girlfriend?"

As soon as the words leave her mouth heat crawls up my throat, and I can feel blood tinting my face. "CeCe why don't you go see where Oli went." I nudge her away.

If her searing evil eye could melt you into a blob, I would be oozing under her feet right now. Reluctantly she says, "It was nice to meet you, Addison. I hope I get to see you again."

"Nice to meet you, too," says Addison.

"I—" we say at the same time.

"You first," I say.

I didn't notice the dark-haired woman approaching us until she says, "How's your head, dear?" She puts her hand on Addison's shoulder.

Addison stiffens and she closes her eyes for several seconds before answering. "Better."

I don't know what's wrong with Addison, but if she looked any worse than she does now, I'd be very worried.

"Who's your friend, dear?"

An audible breath releases from Addison's lungs and she says, "Erik, this is my mom, Mrs. Bailey."

"Nice to meet you, Mrs. Bailey." If I didn't have performing experience that includes keeping eye contact, I would have looked away from her severe face and judging eyes.

She tilts her head and nods slightly as if she's an heir to a throne. Boredom sketched with curiosity spreads into a smooth pink sliver over her mouth. "Are you new to the area?"

"Yes, Ma'am. I recently moved in with my grandmother, Ms. Reeds." I turn and point toward Oli.

Mrs. Bailey looks around me, "Ah, Olivine. Lovely woman. I visit her shop often. She has the best candles and oils on this side of the state."

I would love to crawl out of my skin right about now and creep right out the door. Mrs. Bailey asks, "Are your parents passed?"

"Mom!" I watch red coat Addison's cheeks.

"It's alright." I force a laugh to lighten the mood. "No. They are very much alive. They're traveling." This woman's demeanor is so sharp and over-bearing, I'm pretty sure she could intimidate an entire hockey team into joining the girl scouts.

"I see." Smoothing out her bright pink skirt that doesn't need to be smoothed, she says, "Well, you must be something special."

Before I can clamp my mouth shut, "Excuse me?" pops out.

After a brief moment lasting only a few seconds, which feels like the earth is completing a rotation, she says, "My girl doesn't talk to just anyone." There has to be a response to that, but whatever it is, it is completely eluding me. I don't say anything.

She looks at her gold watch, its face circled with diamonds, and touches Addison's arm again. "Come, Addison, you need to rest."

The muscles in Addison's jaw tighten. She doesn't look at her mother when she says, "I think I'm old enough to know when I need to rest...or not."

Their exchange is quiet and private. Addison's retort seeps into a crack fracturing Mrs. Bailey's perfect façade. Quickly fixing her pristine disposition, she says, "I'll be in the car." She looks at me, offers a curt nod and walks away.

The second she disappears, the air shifts and settles, and probably the flowers open to the sun and the fairies come out of their hiding places.

"Can you please show me the closest rock to crawl under?" Addison supports her head again. "And I wonder why I suffer from migraines."

"Come on, I'll walk with you." I put my hand on the small of her back. "Migraines, huh?"

"Yeah. Sometimes they're painful but bearable, and other times they're excruciating and unbearable."

I push open the door, and the high noon sun blasts my eyes. Addison quickly turns her head and buries it in my shoulder. She grips my shirt and holds her other hand over her eyes to block the glare. "Brightness is not the best thing for a migraine."

I put my hand around her waist and guide her to the side of the church. "It's okay. You're in the shade now."

Trusting me, she eases away from the safety of my shirt and looks up at me. "Thank you." She tries to smile, but it barely touches her lips.

"You're welcome." Watching her in this much agony and not knowing how to help her, I feel powerless.

"Light is my enemy on days like this." She reaches in her purse and takes out a pair of sunglasses. "Forgot to put these on." In the shade, her eyes are dark green and look drained of life. "I almost didn't come today. But I'm glad I did," she says, sliding on the glasses.

My hand is still on her waist. And neither of us makes an effort to move it. "Me, too." I lean in a fraction of an inch and a horn blares. We both jump.

"I have to go." Addison slips away from my hand and it falls to my side. "I'll see you tomorrow."

Pocketing my hands, I nod and smile sparingly, giving her only a fraction of the enormous smile hidden in my chest.

# CHAPTER 17

Posters cover the walls of the main building announcing a Halloween party in the gym. One of the orange flyers, like the ones littering the floor, is shoved into my hand as I walk to my locker. I ball it up and toss it on the floor with the rest.

"Guess you're not interested?"

I turn around and see Naya. "I don't dance."

"Me neither," she says, "but we could always dress up and no one would know it's us." The bell rings. "I got to get to class. I'll see ya later." She turns and walks away.

Musty vanilla envelops me before I see Addison. "Hey." She stops at my locker. "I just wanted to thank you again for yesterday."

"No problem. How are you feel—"

Her smile drops off her face. "Oh my God," she whispers and lowers her head.

"What's the matter?" I ask baffled.

"Thanking you," she huffs, "that's like all I seem to do." She hikes up her bag as she looks down at her fingers, ticking them off. "First you find my bracelet, next you catch me from falling at the lake, and then you save my brain from getting scorched at church." She runs her hand through her hair and part of it falls over the side of her face. "Maybe I can make it up to you sometime."

121

"Not necessary." I take a book out of my locker, and glance around the open door. "But, I will admit, I am curious how you would plan to do that."

"Expectations?"

"Absolutely none." Addison is not the typical girl, and she's not one that you place expectations on.

"How about pizza…Friday night?"

"No way am I turning down pizza."

She lowers her head and laughs. When she looks at me her mouth is curved up and is slightly open. "Great."

As I watch Addison walk away, a hand lands hard on my shoulder. "Hey, Derrik," Aiden says. Two of his buddies from the football team stride up behind him. Both of which I've only seen him without a couple of times.

"It's Erik," I correct him.

"That's right, Erik." He slaps my shoulder again as he glances at his sister. He lowers and shakes his head. Pursing his lips, he says, "Not a good idea."

"What's not?" I push his hand off my shoulder.

"I think you know exactly what I'm talking about." He crosses his arms over his chest.

"Actually no. But, I have a feeling you're going to tell me."

"She likes you."

Though they're not intended to, his words hollow out my gut and I'm beaming on the inside, but I manage to keep a serious face. "Yeah, well," I shrug, "I guess I'm just a likable guy." Then I give him the cheesiest smile I can muster.

He shakes his head. "No, you're not."

I lean into him. "You got me all figured out, don't you?"

"Yeah, I do."

I get in his face. His football friends gather in closer. I lower my voice and whisper in his ear, "You don't know shit."

He throws a punch and I duck. His hand smashes into the

locker. "Fuck!" he yells. His friends come at me but a teacher walking toward us tells us to move along, and they back off.

"I'd stick to throwing balls," I say slinging my backpack over my shoulder and walking away.

~~~

My motorcycle is on its side in the parking lot. Aiden.

When I get home, I don't go in. I throw my backpack on the porch and sit on the swing. A dragonfly lands on the armrest of the bench. I swat at it and with lightning speed it flies away. It returns and perches itself on the same spot. I ignore the bug and put my head in my hands.

"You look like you could use a friend." Through a blur, I recognize the black silhouette of Naya's thin body. She walks up the few steps, stopping just before the overhang of the porch. How does she know where I live? A light rain begins to fall.

"Why don't you get out of the rain?"

She steps onto the porch. "I heard what asshole Aiden did." She sits down next to me. "Does it still run?"

"Yeah, but it's scratched to hell."

"What are you going to do about it?"

"Nothing, it'll only make things worse."

"I told you they don't like our kind."

"Why do you keep referring to us like that, 'our kind'? You act like we're a different species or something."

"Aren't we?"

I ignore her question. I'm in no mood for her perplexing antics.

"You can try to fit in and be something you're not, but it'll never work. They see right through you. The same way I saw you for what you are…a freak."

Even though she's starting to piss me off, she might be right. In only a few weeks, I've gotten so involved with people who me, Lars, and Zane would sit around after our shows and laugh at or

123

insult. Naya keeps herself distanced from everyone but me, and this continues to baffle me. "How come I'm the only one you talk to? Maybe you'd have more friends, if you talk to people." She's very close, and I feel her body go rigid.

She lifts her feet and brings her knees to her chest. "I don't want friends." Her voice is hard and unforgiving.

"Naya, stop being so goddamn cryptic." I get up from the swing and it sways back and forth. "I got to get ready for work."

She reaches out and grabs my arm. "I'm sorry. It's just I'm not good with those kinds of people. I just want to be friends with you."

I pull my arm from her grip. "I know, and I can't figure out why." Turning my back to her, I open the screen door.

"I've seen you perform." Her stone voice has cracked and shattered into a million pieces of sand, fine grains of words fall out of her mouth, and I barely catch them. "It was a few years ago, but out of the hundreds of freak shows that I've seen, yours was the most amazing and unforgettable."

I let the screen door close without going inside. *"No one's going to recognize you. Don't worry about that,"* Dad had said. He was wrong.

"It's not an act, is it? It's real," she says answering her own question.

I don't turn to look at her. I can't, invisible restraints bind me exactly where I stand. "It's—" I stop myself before I say something I'll regret. I wasn't prepared for a confrontation about my past or future.

Without another word exchanged between us, I hear her get up. The chains of the porch swing shake as it slows to a stop, and the wooden steps creak as she walks out into the rain.

~~~

I try to read before going to sleep, but Naya's words keep haunting me. Over dinner, I almost told Oli about Naya seeing me perform, but decided not to. I need to deal with this, I'm just not sure how yet. Naya isn't going to let this drop. Maybe she just has a thing for freaks. She did say she's seen hundreds of them. The only thing I know for sure is why she's labeled me a freak, because she knows for a fact that I am, and that I can't deny.

Keeping Naya quiet is vital. I don't need the entire school to know my little secret. I'm not ashamed of it, but if more people know, it'll only serve to make my life more difficult. I need her to realize that. And if she doesn't, the outcome isn't going to be very good for her or me.

# CHAPTER 18

"Someone's giving you the evil eye over there." I look up to see Addison. My stomach flips at the sight of her. The blackness is gone from under her once again light green eyes. Behind her, Naya is staring at me from across the courtyard. For the first time I notice how rough the tree trunk is against my back.

"She's mad at me." Naya wasn't in second period and I haven't gone out of my way to find her. I'm dreading any conversation with her, cause I know where it's going to lead and I'm not ready to go there.

"I've seen you hanging out with her. You're nice. Most everyone else stays clear of her and calls her freak or creep show." She sits down, her skirt flows out and around her and she tucks it under her legs. It's quiet for a few beats, and then she says, "I heard what my brother did to your motorcycle yesterday." She pulls at a piece of grass and tears it down the center. "Here." She hands me one of the halves. "A peace offering."

I can't help but smile at her intentions. "Why would I be mad at you?"

She tucks loose strands of hair behind her ear. "How can you not be?"

"Hey." I wait for her to look at me before I continue. When she does, her face is etched with remorse and shame. "I don't think I could ever be mad at you."

She looks at the blade of grass she's holding and ties it into a knot. "You shouldn't say that, you hardly know me."

"I know. But I'm working on that." I hand her back the blade of grass and it too is tied into a knot.

She takes it, looks me in the eyes and smiles. "I'm glad."

I want to lean into to her and kiss her. Fall into those green pools in her eyes and stay there forever. I feel an instant of fear as my countdown pops into my head. She is not in my plan and I hate my feelings for betraying me. I glance over her shoulder and Naya's violet eyes are still boring into me. My truth in this normal world sucks.

She turns around and looks at Naya. She puts her hand on my knee. "Do you want to talk about it?"

At this very second I think I could spill everything. Maybe that'll chase her away and I can go back to concentrating on healing and performing again. I consciously relax my shoulders and shake my head. "Maybe another time." I have to make this right with Naya.

"There's another reason I came over." She hands me a small note. "My number. You'll have it for when we meet Friday."

Every thought of Naya, freak shows, and everything disintegrates as I unfold the piece of paper.

~~~

"Naya, wait up." I run to catch her in the parking lot after school.

She stops, but doesn't turn around. I come around to face her. "You never gave me a chance to explain."

"What's there to explain?" She looks over my shoulder like she's trying to ignore that I'm two feet away from her.

"Oh, I don't know? Maybe the fact that you think I can bring back the dead—for real." My voice is a strained whisper. People pass us and eye the freak show right here in their school parking lot.

127

I hunch even closer to her.

She shifts her eyes directly to mine and says, "I know you can." There's no humor anywhere on her face.

Her words and the intensity in her eyes scare the shit out of me. My heart is pounding a thousand times over in this minute. I take a deep breath. "I'm not denying I was a freak in a freak show, but it was an act."

She slowly shakes her head without ever taking those violet eyes from mine. "No, it wasn't," she whispers.

"Okay, even though you have no idea what you're talking about and what you think you saw, can you please keep—" I lower my voice even more, "this whole situation to yourself?"

"And why should I?" She puts the tips of her black nailed fingers over her mouth. "Oh wait! I know...so little miss perfect won't find out you're a freak?" She lowers her hand. "We can't have that now can we? Do you honestly think you can have a normal life in this shit hole? Put up your pretty boy front, say hi to the girls, maybe ace a physics test here and there, and poof, you're fucking normal?" She points a finger at me. "I'm telling you right now, it doesn't work that way. Believe me, I know." She lowers her hand. "I tried to tell you that, but you didn't want to listen."

I'm getting nowhere and my frustration is reaching the dizzying heights of Mt. Everest. I want to grab her shoulders and shake her. But, did I really think she would just say, "okay, sure." I roughly run my hand through my hair and take a deep breath. "What now?"

She shrugs. "I don't know." She kicks at a pebble with her boot. "We did plan to hang out on Friday. I told my mom you were here in town, going to school and she can't wait to see you...again. Why don't you come over for—"

"How does your mom—never mind. I can't, I already have plans."

She huffs. Looking at me, she raises pencil thin eyebrows.

"You're not making this easy."

"I can say the same about you." I let out a breath. "Listen, this…" I point back and forth from me to her, "whatever you think we…" I can't finish the sentence.

"I know. That's not what I'm looking for. I know it may have come off that way." She finally backs down. "I'm sorry. I came on stronger than I meant to and all I ended up doing is pushing you away." She takes my hand in hers. "The only thing I want is for us to be friends." She smiles. "I swear."

Even though her smile is unsettling, I feel relieved. I have to stay in control of this situation. She could ruin me, not just here, but in my world with the freaks. I pull my hand from hers. "What if we have lunch tomorrow and you can tell me about how you got to see so many freak shows?"

"Sure." She kind of smiles and walks away. I walk in the opposite direction to my motorcycle.

"Trouble in freak paradise?" Aiden says as I walk toward him.

This is not the time to piss me off. And after what he did to my bike and just for being a douche bag, his face looks like the perfect punching bag. But I think of Addison and keep walking. "Shut up, dick."

His fists tighten at his side and he starts toward me. I walk past him without stopping. I don't look behind me. The blow never comes. I kind of wish it did, to take out all the bitter frustration built up inside me.

It begins to rain.

~~~

I'm drenched when I walk into the house. The cool air rushes me and chills cover my arms. I want a hot shower to wash away everything.

"He just came in. Okay, I love you, too." CeCe hands the phone to me. "Here, it's Mom."

129

I take the phone. "Hey, Mom."

"Hi honey, I miss you."

"I miss you, too." I hear the life of the carnival in the background and a pang of what I gave up hits me. I want to slam the phone down to stop the torture.

"How are you feeling? I spoke to Oli earlier and she said you were feeling good, stronger."

"Yeah, I feel great." Physically anyway. I leave out all the other shit. She asks me about school, friends, and my job, and I tell her enough to satisfy her. When she disconnects, the carnival disappears with her voice.

"Erik, you have guests," CeCe yells from the front door.

When I walk into the family room, Ash and Rip are standing there.

"Hey, what's going on?" I tuck my hands in my pockets.

"We're here to do an intervention," says Ash.

~~~

Rip shrugs. "Dude, this is all her idea." He throws a thumb toward Ash and she elbows him in the ribs.

"Ouch," he says rubbing his side.

I cross my arms over my chest. "And what exactly are you intervening?"

"Oh, I don't know. Let's see here…" She taps the side of her head. "Oh yeah! Maybe the fact that you're hanging with all the wrong people."

"Is this about Naya?"

"And Addison," says Ash folding her arms over her chest. Her hair is teased and wide beyond her head, and I wonder what the occasion is.

"Guys, I really appreciate you trying to look out for me and having my best interests in mind, but I think I'm doing okay."

"Really? Then how come it's all over school that you and Naya are an item and you and Addison have a thing going on, too?"

Ash sputters.

"Dude, how do you get them to talk to you? I mean really, the only two girls in school who don't talk to anyone...ever, the most popular one and the freak, and they both talk to you, only you." He's shaking his head and grinning.

Defense mode kicks in. "First off, Naya and I are not anything...except friends." I hate how I hesitate. "And Addison..." I trail off.

Ash shifts from her left foot to her right and taps the wood flood, the sound reverberating throughout the room from her heavy boot. "Whatever! Just go get your damn shoes on."

~~~

The back seat of Ash's environmentally non-friendly, black, big-ass boat of a car smells like old socks and gasoline. "Where are we going?" I ask.

"My brother's in a band and they're playing tonight," Ash answers. She parks the monster car on a side street and we get out and walk toward the alley.

"Why aren't we going in through the front door like everyone else?" I ask.

"Because we aren't everyone else," Ash says

Rip drops back to my side and whispers, "Because we're not twenty-one." I grin. "Dude, speaking of age restrictions, how'd ya talk your parents into letting you get inked?"

We walk into the mouth of the alley. It reeks of garbage and shit. "I didn't. I showed up with it and there wasn't anything they could say about it." It was somewhat of a half-truth.

"Man, my mom would kill me. She went ballistic when I came home with my ear pierced."

I look back over my shoulder without knowing why. Across the street, Addison is staring into a shop window with her mom. "Hey guys, I'll catch up in a few." I take out my phone and dial her. I watch as she takes her phone from her pocket and answers.

"Hello?" She sounds guarded.

"Turn around," I say. She does and her eyes lock onto mine. She takes the phone away from her ear and a few seconds go by. I stare at my phone display and see the call was ended.

"Erik, come on, what are you doing?" Ash yells.

I look back to Addison. She's talking with her mom and it looks like they're arguing. I turn towards the alley. "Nothing."

"Erik!" Addison's voice is close. I turn around to see her running across the street toward me. "Hey stranger, I missed you after school." She tugs on the front of my shirt.

Not wanting to tell her about Naya, I say, "I was trying to beat the rain."

"And did you?"

I shake my head. "Nope. It pounded me the entire way home."

Her smile shines under the streetlight. "Next time, wait for me and I'll give you a ride."

"Thanks." I say, as I silently pray for a monsoon tomorrow, and the next day, and the next.

She looks over her shoulder. I glance in that direction, too; her mother is glaring at us. "I have to go." She rises on her toes, and without any rush, kisses me on the corner of my mouth. The control not to grab her and pull her to me takes everything I'm made of. "Call me later," she says and runs to meet her mother.

"Come on, lover boy." Ash grabs my hand and pulls me down the alley. I look over my shoulder. Ms. Bailey's face is smeared with pure hatred. Mine, I'm sure looks just the opposite.

~~~

Ash knocks once on the metal door and a few seconds later, it opens. A guy stands in the doorway, tattoos covering his arms. "Hey, Ash. I didn't expect to see you on a school night." His long black hair falls to his lower back.

"Hey, Devon," she says.

132

"Hurry, come on, before someone sees you." Devon waves his arm gesturing us in. "Hey Rip, how's it goin'?" They pound knuckles.

"Hangin'." Rip points over his shoulder at me. "Dev, this is Erik."

"How's it going?" I ask, and follow them in and down a tight hallway.

"Hurry up, curtain's getting ready to go up," Devon says.

"You don't have a curtain," Ash says.

"It's just a bloody expression my dear, Ashlynne."

As the lights dim, I close my eyes and imagine that this is my performance, that's my stage, and this is my audience.

An electric bass guitar strums; the cord bounces in a deep rhythmic sound. The stage lights power on illuminating four guys. The one singing winks at Ash. The smile on her face radiates its own convulsive energy and reminds me of CeCe's when I'm performing.

At this very second I want nothing more than my old life back. I feel sick with a desperate hunger. I crave to once again have control over my audience, their relentless admiring eyes on me, the oohs and ahs falling out of their gaping mouths. But most of all, I want the heat of writhing energy to race through me, to feel the surge of it in my fingertips, and to see the life I'm able to give back fly away.

I can't take it. I push back my seat, and almost fall over but catch myself on Rip's chair.

"Dude! You okay?" he asks.

Ignoring him, I maneuver around the crowded room until I reach the exit. Fresh air welcomes me when I push open the door. My lungs burn as I run down the sidewalk and when the club is out of sight, I stop to catch my breath.

My phone buzzes in my pocket. I take it out; it's probably Ash wanting to know why I lost it at the club. What the hell would I say? I know it won't be the truth. But, when I look at the display it

133

reads, Naya. I don't know what possess me to answer it. "Hello."

"Hi." She sounds startled that I even answered. "I was wondering if now would be a good time to talk."

# CHAPTER 19

The Round House is a small coffee and pastry shop. It's a couple minutes after eight and the place is dead. A guy in a suit is tapping away on his computer in the corner, and a girl with a shaved head is reading and drinking something out of the biggest mug I've ever seen. This looks like a Naya kind-of-place with the dark lighting and eclectic furniture.

I order a Coke and huddle at a table in the corner by the window. The nerves under my skin are still jumping, and no matter how many deep breaths I take they won't calm. The Coke tastes too sweet and the sugar coats my tongue, leaving a horrible after taste in my mouth. I don't want to be here and should have never told Naya I'd meet her, the last thing I feel like is talking to anyone right now. I get up to leave.

Too late, the black outline of Naya walks into the café and I slide back down into my chair as she walks toward me. "Were you getting up to get something?" She sets her bag over the back of the chair.

"Yeah," I lie and suck down the enormous idea to bolt out of here.

"Well, I'm already up. I'm gonna get a coffee, want one?" Her attitude seems less defiant than earlier; maybe I can talk some sense into her.

"Sure." I'd rather have a hot chocolate but agreeing to the coffee takes less effort.

She motions towards the counter. "Their chocolate filled croissants are incredible. Want one?"

I shake my head. The thought of eating anything makes my stomach turn. I lower my head into the crevice of my folded arms. What is wrong with me? What happened in that bar? I didn't realize how much I miss my life as a performer until the lights dimmed and the stage was like the only place in the room where I belonged; I'm not living unless I'm bringing back the dead.

"You okay?"

Her lighter than normal voice startles and I pop my head up and clear my throat. "Yeah, fine."

She rolls her eyes, unconvinced, and sits down, sliding my coffee to me. "I brought some cream and sugar, not sure how you like it."

"Just cream, thanks."

"Ever been here before?" she asks.

I shake my head and pour the cream into the cup.

She puts her hand on mine. "Erik, what's wrong?"

"Nothing."

She takes her hand off mine and inhales so deeply I think she may explode. On the exhale she says, "Listen, you and I need to come to some kind of a truce. I'm not a bad person, I'm just trying to be a friend and I don't have much practice."

Thoughts of performing, my feelings growing for Addison, school, Naya—all of them convulse and bang around in my head and I feel like I don't know anything anymore. I pick up my coffee and glance at my dragonfly tattoo peeking out from under the leather bands and the words vomit out of my mouth. "I was just at a music gig with Ash and Rip and I fucking lost it."

"Why? What do you mean?"

136

Grasping fistfuls of hair, I rest my head in my hands. "I don't know." I'm not ready to go there with her yet.

She waits a few moments, and then asks, "Want a bite?"

Naya always has a way to detour the conversation. I'm grateful for now, but that detour always leads back to the original route. The air is sweet as if the wrapper of the richest chocolate was just peeled away releasing its intoxicating perfume. I look up. The croissant on the plate is cut in half, chocolate oozing from its middle. "I thought you didn't share."

"And I thought we already established you were an exception."

I take the bite off the fork. For the smallest moment the warm chocolate and sweet bread nullifies any other thought.

She cuts a bite for herself and puts in her mouth. "It's amazing, right?"

"Much better than the hot sauce, but equal to the fried ice cream." I take a sip of coffee and look out the café window.

"So, you want to tell me why the dragonfly?"

"You're relentless." I look at the inside of my wrist and know I have to lie again, but this time it has to be believable. "I got it when I offered to volunteer at a friend's tattoo/piercing show." Without telling her the whole truth, I resort to the facts. "Did you know dragonflies have three stages of life?"

"I wish I could be so lucky."

"It's actually a little depressing. The egg stage, then the nymph stage—this is when they can live under water for up to two years—and finally their adult stage, when they can fly, and then they usually only live for about three months, just long enough to find a mate."

"That's depressing." She cocks her head and lowers the fork with the piece of croissant still on it. "And?"

"I just like them—okay?" I try to force a laugh.

"Fine. I guess I'll just have to settle for the dragonfly mini-

137

course." She holds the fork up to me again and I take another bite.

I lean back against the chair and ask her, "So, how is it you've seen so many freak shows? Are you like a freak show groupie or something?"

"I guess I was. But not by choice." She doesn't look at me, but stares out into the street. Her thoughts look far away, somewhere in the past.

"What's that mean?"

She eats the last bite of the croissant. "My mom was in the show. She's a psychic." She huffs. "Actually, she was a psychic act. People paid her to tell them lies." Naya shrugs. "She looks the part and she's good at reading people."

"So you traveled with her?"

"Yeah. She's all I got. My dad left when I was a baby."

"Did we ever travel together? Is that where you caught my act?" I regret the questions as soon as they fall off my lips. I didn't want to talk about what I left or me; or, especially the fact that she believes the truth.

"No. We just ended up in the same city together once."

"When?" I want to know, the need to understand why she's so enthralled with my performance.

"It was a couple of years ago." She looks toward the guy still tapping away on his computer. "It was right before my mom stopped performing and we moved here."

"The traveling and shows get old after a while." I take a sip of the coffee. "Why'd you move here?"

"Cause my mom grew up here and this is where she wants to be. So, why'd you stop performing?" she asks and reaches in her bag and pulls out Chap Stick and slides it over her lips.

"Just for that reason. Non-stop traveling and being on the road gets exhausting."

"I don't believe you." She leans on the table and rolls the tube of lip balm back and forth between her fingers. "When I watched

138

you perform, you were captivating. Living it, feeling it, and everyone in the audience held their breath until the very end. No one dared to blink when you where on that stage. I watched you at every one of your shows that weekend."

How could I have not noticed her?

She continues, "I couldn't get enough. I have no idea how you do what you do but it's like nothing I've ever seen before."

I'm already raw, and I want her to shut up. I want to cover my ears and squeeze my eyes closed to shut out her words and face. "Naya, stop," I say as nicely and quietly as I can.

"What?" She looks at me like I've just slapped her, insulting her as she raves about me.

"Please just stop." I have spent the last few weeks stuffing down the need…the want to bring back the dead; cramming it into crevices and trenches I've dug into the depths of my soul. And, especially now after almost collapsing when I brought Gus back and realizing how weak I still am, every one of Naya's words scratches away at the feelings I've tried so desperately to protect.

"Oh my God, it's something I'll never forget." She puts her hands on either side of her head. "It was mind-blowing—I mean the madness and craziness of what you can do is—"

"Shut up!" I slam my hands on the table. Sweat beads gather on my forehead, my hands begin to shake, and vomit threatens to garnish the table.

She jumps. "Shit! You scared the crap out of me." She looks around the café and I follow her gaze. The few people in the café are looking at us, at me. When her eyes stop on me, she asks, "What the hell is wrong with you?"

"Nothing." I put my head in my hands. "You believe the hoax, the scheme that was manufactured for en-ter-tain-ment-pur-po-ses-on-ly." I say each syllable as if they were their own word. "I can't do anything—okay? Will you please just stop talking about it?"

"Fine." I hear her take a sip of her coffee. "Just know, that I've seen all sorts of shit while on the road with my mom—real and fake—and most of them are probably unsuitable for a little girl's eyes." Her voice is low and intense. "So, you can feed everyone else your bullshit that what I watched you do is just some hoax, but I know exactly what I saw."

I get up to leave and she thrusts her hand out. I move mine before she can touch me. "All right, I'm sorry."

Remembering I don't have a ride, I ease back down. Naya's smile returns, and it's unnerving. I could go back to the bar and meet Ash and Rip but I don't feel like explaining myself. Hell, they might have already left by now.

"Listen, I can't promise I won't ever bring it up again, but will you just answer me this?"

"What?" I close my eyes and take slow easy breaths.

"How come you don't like to talk about it?"

She seems sincere and without any reservations, I whisper the truth, "Because I miss it."

She doesn't say anything and I'm grateful. I hope she took what I just admitted, that I miss performing, and not bringing back the dead. But, when I look into her eyes, I know precisely how she took it and my truth just fueled her; it was exactly what she wanted to hear.

"I know I'm a pain in the ass, but thanks for meeting me tonight."

"I won't argue with you about that."

Her face scrunches like she's mad, but then she laughs. The mood between us is better. She starts tearing off tiny balls of the napkin.

"Is that a habit?"

"What?" she asks.

I point to the pile of tiny napkin balls. "That."

"Hmmm. I guess it is. I've never paid attention to it."

140

The jazzy music in the background fills in the quiet space between us until Naya says, "Hey."

I look at her, into those light purple eyes and I see a pity there, pity for me that I don't want. "Don't ruin it."

"I wasn't. Jeez." She tears at the napkin. "It's just…I know I can be kind of a bulldog with things, you know, biting into something and not letting go, until—"

"Yeah, I kind of got that." I finish my coffee.

"I was wondering…"

"What? You're not going shy on me, are you?" I ask.

She shrugs. "My mom wants to know if Sunday would be good for you to come over for dinner."

"Sure." I shrug. The sooner we get this over with, the better.

"Cool." She smiles. "I gotta get home."

The lack of a ride pops into my head again. "Me, too. Do ya think you can give me a ride?"

Twenty minutes later she stops in front of my house. She turns down the radio. The front porch glows in the overhead light. I open the door and climb out. Leaning down, I say, "Thanks for the ride."

"My pleasure. It's not every day I get to drive around a celebrity." Her voice is high and saturated with a forced giddiness.

"You're hilarious."

"I know." She looks past me and takes a sharp inhale of breath. "Is that your cat?"

"Yeah, why?"

She cranes her neck watching Gus climb the porch steps and sit by the front door. Bewilderment, confusion, and contentment all pass over her smooth features. Then, she smiles. A set smile neither warm nor nice but rather laced with something possibly very devious and cold behind it.

"Are you alright?" I ask.

She relaxes against the seat and huffs out an awkward laugh.

141

"Yeah. Yeah. Sorry I just spaced there for a second." Ruffling her short bangs, she adds, "You didn't tell me you found him, that's all."

"Ah, yeah, he came home Sunday." I close the door and the noise seems to be echoed times a thousand.

"That's great."

"Yeah. I'll see you tomorrow."

~~~

The house is quiet inside. CeCe's nightlight glows from under her door as I walk by. I'm half expecting her to hear me and come out, but she doesn't. These sleepless nights have sucked every ounce of life from me. I take my phone out of my pocket and turn it on. Six missed calls and seven texts from Ash, ranging from *"What the hell happened to you?"* to asking if I'm okay; two missed calls from Rip; a text from CeCe that reads, *"Goodnight, I love you,"* and finally a text from Addison saying *"I'm going to sleep, I'll talk to you tomorrow."*

I toss my phone next to me and curse under my breath. "Dammit, how could I have not called Addison?" Naya, that's how. I'm not good at this balancing act, and I sure as hell don't want to be. Picking up my phone, I key in a text to Addison: *"I'm sorry."* I hit the send button; sorry is all I got, pathetic. Staring at the display hoping for a response, nothing comes for a minute then my phone buzzes. I grab it, eager to see Addison's message.

Naya: Thanks again for tonight. BTW I won't tell anyone.

Fuck. My. Life.

142

# CHAPTER 20

Addison's Jeep isn't in the parking lot at school. As I get off my bike, the smell of pollution blasts me before Ash's big black Lincoln comes into view. I weave through the lot to avoid her. She sees me and pins me in place with her finger.

Rip gets out of the car before she does and starts in my direction. "Dude, just warning you now, she's in a bitchy mood."

"Shut up, Rip, I am not," Ash says as she comes up behind him.

"See what I mean?" he asks.

I don't say anything; I'm not going to start this conversation about how and why I lost it. "What happened last night at the Raw Iguana? Where the hell did you go?"

*The Raw Iguana.* I didn't even know that's what the place was called. "Nothing."

"That wasn't *nothing.* You practically fell on your face trying to bolt outta there," Ash says. Her eyes are lined even darker than they usually are, matching her dark mood.

I shrug. "I got sick, alright?"

"Sick? What kind of sick?" She crosses her arms over her chest.

"The puking kind. You didn't want me throwing up everywhere did you?"

Why does she care so much? "Okay, now that you got that lie out of the way, let's try the truth. Did you run back to your stuffy girlfriend?"

"Be careful, Ash," I say.

I watch Naya walk toward us. Her head is high, she looks confident, not like usual when she walks through a crowd. Ignoring Ash and Rip, she says, "Hey, Erik."

"Hey. What's going on?"

"I just wanted to thank you again for meeting me last night."

My head falls in defeat. Thanks, Naya.

Ash turns on me so fast. "Really? Ditching us—" She nods her head in Naya's direction, "for her? And here I was trying to be nice." She pulls her bag over her head and rests the strap on her shoulder. "It would've been better if you left to see the other one."

"What's that suppose to mean?" asks Naya.

"Now, now, ladies," Rip says easing in between the two of them.

"Ash, let it go. You don't know the half of it," I say.

"So, why don't you explain it to me?" She puts her hands on her hips.

"Oh, trust me, you'd want to know," Naya says. "It's some damn good shit."

"Naya," I warn. This whole situation is so out of control.

"What? It's true, isn't it?" she asks.

Ignoring her, I shake my head, turn and walk away from all of them.

~~

Addison's seat stays empty the entire first period. I text and call her after class ends, but she doesn't answer either.

I take a chance and sit outside near the tree at lunch, far away from everyone. My phone buzzes and when I look at it; it's a message from Addison. *Did you and Naya enjoy your lattes last night?*

144

Fuck. Can this day get any worse?

I type back: *Where are you?*

Addison: *Home. I have a migraine.*

Erik: *Can I come over?*

Addison: *Not a good idea.*

Erik: *Why?*

Seconds tick by and Addison doesn't type anything back.

Erik: *Are you there?*

Addison: *Yes.*

Erik: *I want to see you.*

Addison: *I'll see you at school tomorrow.*

Erik: *I'll call you later.*

This day cannot end fast enough. I lean back against the thick trunk of the tree and close my eyes. The weather is starting to cool down, giving the humidity a much-needed vacation. A breeze rustles the leaves above my head, leaves that will stay green through winter.

"Hey," someone says as they kick my boot.

Holding my hand over my eyes to block out the sun, I look up. "Hey, Rip. How's it going?"

"It's goin'."

He sits across from me. "Everything okay?"

"It's all right."

He nods. "Girls are crazy as hell, aren't they?"

"Yeah." I look across the courtyard and see Tiffany talking to Candace, Aiden's girlfriend. Aiden, surprisingly, is nowhere near.

"You goin' to the dance?" he asks.

"No. You?"

"Yeah right. It's not really my thing, but the only crazy chic I'd want to go with anyway—would never go."

I laugh. "I knew you had a thing for Ash. Man—"

He throws his hands up. "You don't have to tell me! Dude, Ash lives by her own set of rules and she has since grade school." He laughs to himself as he reties the laces on his boots.

"Wow, you've known her for a long time. And you haven't killed her." I laugh. "Kudos, man, kudos."

He leans back and crosses his legs at his ankles. "We hated each other at first— fought constantly. But then something happened in ninth grade and she's been my best friend ever since."

"That's cool," I say, simultaneously thinking Rip must thrive on being bossed around and abused.

"Most of the time." Defending the love of his life, he says, "Ash really is a good person, she just has a weird way of showing it."

I laugh and shake my head. "Still, must be hard for you to be around a girl all the time who thinks she's always right."

He huffs. "Which makes it even more important that us guys stick together."

"You got it." He knocks his knuckles against mine.

I look at the tattoo of the dragonfly on my wrist. He catches me and asks, "What's it mean? I mean why a bug?"

I move the leather bands so its entire body is visible and touch the tattoo's blue and green wings. Ignoring his question, I ask, "Did you know they're predators and they snatch their prey right out of the sky?"

"Really? Cool."

I never tell him why it's significant. And he wisely doesn't ask again. "What's Rip stand for?"

"Rupert." He points directly at my face. "But, if you ever call me that I will kill you."

I hold up my hands in mock self-defense. "Dude, chill. You got my word."

He lowers his hand. "Listen, I don't know what the hell happened to you last night—and I'm not even gonna ask, that's your shit. But, they're playing again this Friday if you want to go."

I watch Tiffany; her hands are in non-stop motion as she carries on about something. Candace nods her head and laughs.

146

Their faces are animated and happy. "Thanks, but—" The rest of the sentence freezes in my throat as I watch Tiffany collapse, her head hitting the bench seat on the way to the ground.

"Holy Hell! Did you see that?" Rip yells. I jump to my feet to watch the horrific scene. Screams and confusion slowly spread across the courtyard as people realize what just happened. "Dude, is she dead?" Rip asks.

Candace kneels next to Tiffany, shielding Tiffany from my view. She yells to the boy next to her to call 911 and then points to another person to get a teacher. Everyone is yelling, "get help," but no one moves, they all stand frozen staring at Tiffany's body on the ground. The crowd around her thickens and I can only see slivers of her through the mob of people surrounding her. From the main building, Principal Tacker runs toward the scene. He and some of the teachers try to gain control of the chaos surrounding Tiffany. They thin the crowd, sending students into the building. Some remain, forming a circle around Tiffany, Candace, and Principal Tacker.

"I don't know, maybe she just fainted," I say.

Sirens wail in the distance. Everything is happening in slow motion, the moment is terrible and surreal.

"She's dead." Rip and I both turn to see Naya. Her face is drawn inward and her eyes squint through the brightness to the shocking display.

"How do you know?" I ask.

As still as a statue in the cemetery, she says in a low and ominous voice, "I just know."

The paramedics rush across the field pushing a gurney to where Tiffany lay. They work fast, taking out instruments and machines from their bags.

"They're wasting their time," Naya whispers.

For the next five minutes the paramedics work on Tiffany. They paddle her chest. Tiffany's legs jerk and then still. Paddle. She jerks and then stills again. They lift her onto the gurney. One of her

147

arms falls from her side and the female paramedic sets it back on the gurney, at her side. The male paramedic looks at the woman and they shake their heads in unison. Even from this distance, I can tell their expressions are grave. As they push Tiffany on the gurney toward the ambulance, the woman pulls the white sheet over her body and then over her face. Screams erupt.

Candace cries out, "No!" Her shrieks dominate and pierce the gasps and cries of the others in the shocked crowd. Aiden holds on to her as she tries to run toward the gurney, her arms reaching out to it.

Instantly, I feel the spine chilling craving that death has over all of us. I have seen a lot of shit at all kinds of creep and freak shows, but watching someone die is the ultimate creep show. I pick up my backpack and toss it over my shoulder.

Rip says nothing; we don't even look at each other until we hear Naya's haunting voice, "I told you," she whispers, then turns and walks away.

~~~

Tiffany's death has hit hard. Irreversible grief has painted itself over every face in school, even the people who didn't know her. She was an icon here, the captain of the cheerleading team, head of various groups and clubs. She was the first person who was ever nice to me here. And it's her death that has replaced all of our invincible thoughts and reminded us how fragile we are.

Principal Tacker's somber voice sounds from the loud speaker. "Students and faculty." He clears his throat. "Due to the tragic event that happened moments ago, dismissal will be early today. Please stay in your seats until the bell rings. Thank you."

No cheers or hurrahs at what would be, under different circumstances, happy news. Soft cries and sniffles are the only sounds around the room. When the bell rings, there's no rush to the door. We leave the classroom and slowly file out into the hall.

The sun has disappeared behind bulging gray clouds. They hover over the stifling parking lot; no one is leaving. I walk by groups of people huddled together, catching pieces of their conversation: who saw what, those who witnessed the tragedy filling in the blanks for those who missed it, others inventing details and adding their own drama—like any is needed.

I straddle my motorcycle, take out my phone, and call Addison.

"Hello?" Her voice sounds sleepy.

"Hey. How are you feeling?" There's no way to even try to put happiness in my voice, even though I'm glad Addison answered and is feeling better.

"Better, thanks." A pause. "Shouldn't you be in class?"

I imagine her forehead scrunching and her eyes knitting together in confusion. "We got dismissed early." And then I tell her the tragic news.

She takes a sharp breath. "Oh my God. Are you sure?"

"Yes. I'm so sorry to be the one to tell you. I know she was your friend." I hear tears streaming into her words. And I want to hold her, comfort her, and make the pain of it all go away.

"I just can't believe it," she whispers. "It doesn't seem possible." She's quiet for a beat then asks, "Where you there?"

"Yeah. I was sitting in the grass under the oak when I saw her collapse in the courtyard. It was pretty bad."

An odd laugh, one I've never heard from her comes out before she says, "I've never been thankful for migraines, but I don't think I would have been able to watch my friend die."

I don't want to talk about it anymore and ask her, "Can I come see you?" I want to see her, need to see her.

"I feel like I should be doing something for Tiffany right now." I can hear she's trying to control her crying.

"There's nothing for you to do right now."

"I know. You're right." She sniffles. "I have something I was planning to do today."

"Do you want some company?" Silently praying she does,

not caring what it even is.

Addison lets out a breath. "I don't think what I'm going to do will interest you."

Cradling the phone between my shoulder and ear, I drop my arms over my motorcycle handlebars. "You're not even going to give me a chance?"

She doesn't answer. "I'll call you when I'm done." Her voice is soft and final.

"Okay." There's silence between us. "Listen, about last night—"

"Don't," she cuts me off.

I feel like I owe her some sort of explanation. "Addison, I just want you to know there's nothing—"

"I know. It doesn't matter." She does a weird little laugh. "It's not like we're dating or anything." I hear rustling of pages turning in the background. "I'll call you later," she says and hangs up.

Reluctantly I refrain from pushing the redial button and put my phone away. The smell of coming rain wafts by me and I should be getting my bike in gear and hightailing it home. But, sitting at home, consumed by the memories of what happened today and moving ten steps back with Addison. No thanks.

# CHAPTER 21

I'm not scheduled to work, but I find myself driving toward the cemetery. Roy's truck isn't here, and I remember it's Thursday, his day off. Parking my bike, I walk through the grave markers and headstones. The curling, blackening sky is a deterrent for visitors. Since I've started working here, I've noticed that the older graves rarely have visitors. It's a chore for the living to visit the dead. Once the dead are buried and people pass the mourning stage, the dead are often left here alone with each other, and the statues.

The statues of angels and saints peer down at me. They seem less ominous without their foreboding shadows falling on me as I walk under them. Their blank eyes and outstretched arms welcome all while they look over and protect the dead at their feet. One of the angel statues, I forget her name, Roy's told me, but I think I purposely blocked it out because she gives me the creeps. Her frozen form arches downward as if offering a helpless child a piece of candy only to lure them into her world where only stone exists. I do my best to stay away from her.

The clouds release a mist of cold rain. I jog toward the shed and get a bright yellow raincoat to drape over me. I hang the hood on my head and tuck my backpack under it to keep it dry. The mist turns into fat drops and is loud in my head as it pelts the plastic.

I walk back through the rows of graves, reading them as I make my way to my grandfather's. The grave markers for Harold James Bailey and Josephine Bailey catch my eye and I think of Addison—her last name is Bailey—and wonder if they're related. I whisper her name repeatedly to feel the way it comes out of my mouth and crosses the threshold of my lips. The D's vibrate between my tongue and the roof of my mouth and I say it over and over. I sit under the huge oak tree with moss hanging over my head. Richard Moore's grave is closest to me. The words on his grave marker tell that he was a loving father and beloved husband. And I wonder if he really was.

Rain splashes and plops, filling the crevices of the engraved letters. I pull my legs under the raincoat and think about all the shit that's happened in the last few weeks. My whole universe has tilted onto its side, like a turtle stuck on its back. It's been as if I'm in a pool of glue grasping for the surface only to breathe in more of the sticky gooey stuff, the thick liquid sticking to my lungs. I start crying. Today's awful event broke through the emotions I've kept boarded up; feelings that have been begging to escape, now fall down my face in tears.

I look up to the dark sky and let the rain mask my tears. I'm cold inside and out. The rain slows to a drizzle. The crickets begin their song and my emotions begin to get into check with themselves, finding calm once again. I take down the hood.

"Erik?"

Her voice is unmistakable. Shit. I don't want her to see me like this, but it's too late now. I turn around. Addison's face is blotchy and her eyes are red. I stand and want to wrap my arms around her, but she looks guarded so I stay where I'm at.

"Hey. You stalking me?" She's holding a clear umbrella that comes down around her and makes her look like she's in a bubble. In her other hand she's holding a bouquet of flowers. Dark clouds still decorate the sky. The rain isn't done.

"Hardly," Addison says. "You okay? Not many people I know hang out in the cemetery…in the rain." One of her best friends died today and she's asking how I am.

"I'm probably not like most of the people you know."

"No, you're not." She smiles. "Mind if I join you?"

"Only if you share your umbrella."

A small smile touches her sad face. "Sure." She sits crossed legged on the wet ground, tucking worn gray Converse under her faded jeans. She lays the flowers next to her and puts the umbrella she's holding over us both. I scoot a little in her direction to have the protection of the umbrella and…to be closer to her.

"Can you hold this?" She hands me the handle of the umbrella, and she zips up her black hoodie.

She takes the umbrella back. "Have you been crying?" she asks.

Our personal space is breached to its limits. "And if I say yes?"

She nods and smiles ever so slightly. "So have I, it's been a rough day." She's looking at me: sadness, hurt, pain, all swimming in those pale green eyes.

"One of the roughest." There's no hesitation when my mouth begins spewing. "Since I've moved here my life has changed so drastically. I mean, if you knew what my life was before…and then today—" I put my balled fist to my mouth and squeeze my eyes shut fighting the tears. I feel her lay her head on my shoulder.

"I'm sorry," she says. I lay my head on top of hers and we sit nestled together underneath the umbrella in the middle of a cemetery. The rain starts to fall harder and we press against each other.

"I'm really sorry about Tiffany. Do you want to talk about it?"

She shakes her head against my shoulder. "Thanks. She was a good person." Wordlessly we sit, huddled together and warm. I

153

watch each drop of rain stream down the clear umbrella and puddle at our feet. Refusing to let this moment with her pass with only depression and sadness, I ask, "So, you like to hang out in the cemetery, in the rain, too?"

She chuckles. "I guess so."

"Ha! Another thing we have in common."

She laughs, the tinkling harmony barely heard over the rain. "Who are those for?" I point to the flowers.

She lifts her head and looks at me. The softest smile forms across her lips; even her eyes seem to grin. A tear spills onto her cheek, and I cup her face and wipe it away with my thumb. "My grandma," she whispers. "I try to come every week."

"That's really nice." While twirling the bracelet on her wrist, I touch the heart that dangles from the center link. It's quiet for a long time. "So, is this what you were planning to do that you thought I wouldn't be interested in?"

"Yes."

I nod, respecting her choice to come here alone. "You know, I've worked here for the last couple weeks—"

Her head pops up, but she leaves our hands together on the bracelet resting in her lap. "Here, in the cemetery?"

"Yeah. Does that gross you out?"

"No. I just didn't know." She sounds hurt and now I feel bad I didn't tell her.

I shrug. "Yeah, well, I'm not ashamed, it's just not the kind of job you go around bragging about." I lace my fingers through hers, lift my free hand, and cup her chin tilting her head toward me. "You are so beautiful." Embarrassed, she tries to lower her head, but I tilt it back for her to look at me. "Addison." I love the way her name sounds as it floats away from my lips.

"Yeah?"

"Would it be terribly morbid if I kissed you right now?" I ask, hoping the rain falling against the plastic doesn't drown my words.

A smile, ever so slight, crosses her lips. "Maybe a little, but I don't care."

Her eyes don't leave mine as we lean into each other, and the short distance to her lips feels like I'm crossing an ocean. Only our breath is exchanged between us. I push strands of her hair away from her face. The glossed silky surface of her mouth grazes mine. I close my eyes and inhale deeply smelling the sweetness of her lipstick. Her eyes close. Our lips move together as if we've practiced for this moment all of our lives. I slide my hand from her chin along her jaw line, through her hair to the back of her neck. She unlaces our fingers and her hand wraps around my neck. My hand moves to her lower back bringing us even closer together.

Thunder cracks its angry whip and the blast from the noise disrupts the moment. We both jump breaking contact. She smiles and I can't help but do the same. I tuck her hair behind her ear. Lightning zigzags behind her. "Let's bring those to your grandma before we get electrocuted."

Our hands are linked. I'm now holding the umbrella over us as we walk to Josephine Bailey's resting place. She lays the flowers over the grave, bows her head and whispers silent words to herself, the whole time never letting go of my hand. When she's done, she looks up to me. "Thank you."

"You okay?"

Through a sad smile she says, "Yeah, let's go. Why don't you leave your motorcycle here, and I'll drive you home."

We race through the storm to her Jeep and climb in. It feels like the thunder and lightning are going to come crashing through the canvas top of her jeep.

"Do you want to go get a quick hot chocolate or something?" I ask.

"Sure," she says, putting the Jeep in gear. We go to the closest drive-through at a fast food restaurant.

155

"Their hot chocolate is so good. Cheap and instant, but delicious." She orders two hot chocolates and I hand her money. She parks in the parking lot and we sit in silence for a few minutes. I set the cup on the dash and take both her hands in mine.

"Listen, I don't want to ruin our time together, but I want to talk to you about something that happened today, and I need to tell you something that's going to happen in the near future."

"This sounds serious."

"Not serious, just weird. And I want to be open with you."

She stares at the lid of her drink. "I'm listening."

"It's about Naya," I throw out the words before I lose my nerve. If anything is to come out of this, I need to be open with her.

"Okay." Her face is without judgment, but concern is written all over it.

"When Rip and I were frozen in place watching everyone panic while Tiffany—" I stop myself before I say more. "Out of nowhere Naya is standing next to us and all she says is, 'She's dead.'" I run hand through my hair. "I mean—how the hell did she know that? No one else did. And then when the rest of us knew Tiffany was…" I think back how bizarre the moment was.

"I don't know what to say." Tears well up in her eyes.

"I'm sorry, I don't mean to keep bringing it up, it's just something I need to talk about. I think all I want to know is, if Naya had anything to do with her dying."

"I don't think so."

"How do you know?"

"Tiffany had a lot of medical problems. She looked healthy on the outside, always happy…but on the inside she was very sick."

"I know I haven't been around for long, she never looked sick and I've never seen her anything but happy."

"I think I may be one of the few that knew she was sick. I think Candace knew, too. I only found out because we were in the emergency room together a few months ago. Even as one her closest

156

friends, I didn't know. My mom had insisted I go when I had one of my unbearable migraines, and Tiffany was there. She told me she was very sick when she was born and she was always in the hospital for treatments or something. She never talked about it. And I think she thought if she didn't, then she felt like she wasn't really sick." She huffs.

"What?"

"She laughed about it." Addison looks far away remembering their conversation. "It was so normal for her to deal with being sick all the time, she would just laugh about it."

I reach across and take her hand. "Not that I wanted Tiffany to be sick, and I'm very sorry you lost a friend, but it makes me feel better knowing Naya had nothing to do with it." I shrug. "Maybe she knew she was sick."

"Maybe, but I doubt it."

We sit in the quiet space of her Jeep. She takes my hand in hers, holds it open, and traces the lines of my palm. The sensation is overwhelming and I feel the warmth starting to heat as it writhes under my skin. She touches the tips of my fingers; she rubs each one lightly and then moves to the next. I want to pull my hand away, it feels so personal, intrusive, but so good. So I leave my hand in hers.

"What else did you want to tell me?"

I blurt it out, "Naya's path and mine have crossed before."

Addison's eyes widen and she lets go of my hand. "Oh."

I grab hold of her hand. "No, nothing like that." I watch her posture relax as she exhales. "The thing is, Naya told her mom I was in town, and she wants me to have dinner with them. I told her I would on Sunday. I just want to be honest, there's nothing going on between her and me, we're just friends."

"It's okay. I understand," says Addison without any edginess attached to her words.

"Thanks." I kiss her lightly on her lips.

"It stopped raining, do you want to get your motorcycle?"

"Yeah, thanks."

The iron gates to the cemetery are closed and locked for the night.

"I'll give you a ride home and after school tomorrow we can come get it."

"You know—" I lean toward her. We're not touching, but I'm close enough to see her expression in the dark and to smell remnants of hot chocolate on her breath and rain on her skin. "I would like to say that I orchestrated this whole afternoon just to be with you tonight. But I can't take credit for any of it."

"Do you believe everything happens for a reason?"

I trace a finger down her face. "Not until today." I kiss her gently on the cheek where my finger just left, then I kiss her other cheek, and finally her mouth. She tilts her head accepting my attentions. Her lips part slightly, inviting me to take more, and I sink into the moment, into her, and I forget everything as I kiss her and she kisses me back. I pull her tighter to me, leaving no space, or air between us. This is the closest I've felt toward filling the void left by not bringing back the dead. I want to hold her until a dead creature sits in my hand and I'm strong enough to bring it back.

I pull back, just a little. "Mmm…you were right, they do have delicious hot chocolate."

She grins and puts her forehead against mine. "I should get you home."

"Isn't that supposed to be my line?"

"Yep." She smirks and puts the Jeep in gear. "If you were in the driver's seat."

We pull up to my house. Addison says, "I'll pick you at seven."

"I like this, my own personal chauffer."

"Yeah, well I hope you have an extra helmet, cause next time you're driving."

The instant thought of her arms around my waist sends the

158

dragonflies in my gut into flight.

My phone chirps. I ignore it.

"Aren't you going to get that?"

"No."

"Why?" she asks. Her brows knit together, and her mouth dips into a frown.

"It's not you." I reach over the console and put my hand through her hair and pull her to me. I kiss her now smiling mouth. Reluctantly I pull away to open the door.

"I'll see you in the morning," she says.

I close the door and watch her drive away. Taking my phone out of my pocket, I look at the display.

Naya: *Sunday at 6?*

Erik: *K*

Naya: *:)*

Nothing could ruin the feelings flooding through me. Not even the enigmatic Naya.

# CHAPTER 22

When Addison picked me up the next morning, my "girlfriend" high was still in full effect. But, as we pulled into the school parking lot, my mood dropped a few degrees and the overcast sky didn't help the somber atmosphere. Tiffany's death was still evident on everyone's face. Healing from the tragic incident would take time. After the morning announcements, the melancholy atmosphere plunged deeper into the trench of grief. Principal Tacker provides the details for Tiffany's funeral. He also indicates that there will be counselors available to any student who feels the need to talk. She was really dead and no matter what happened she wasn't coming back.

Edgewater Cemetery is where Tiffany will be buried. And I will most likely be the one to dig her grave. The thought makes me sick to my stomach.

Addison stops at my desk when class ends. "Ready?" Her eyes are red and glossed over.

"Yeah." I get up, take her hand, and once in the hall I wrap my arm around her. She tucks her face into my shoulder and I hear her muffled cries and feel the soft shakes of her body against mine.

I pull away when we're standing outside her next class. "You gonna be okay?"

She nods.

"Listen, I understand if you don't want to do anything tonight."

She sniffles, wipes her nose, and takes a deep breath. "I feel guilty, like I should be doing something for Tiffany, but I don't know what."

I kiss her forehead and pull her into me. "I'm not sure there's anything you can do, but I understand."

"I think it'll be a good thing if we go out tonight, take our minds off of..." She doesn't finish, she doesn't have to. She pulls a bottle of water from her bag. "I'm going go to the office and help Ms. Perks for the rest of the day. I'll see you after school and we'll go get your bike." She rises on her toes and kisses my cheek.

When I turn around, Aiden is standing only a few feet away from me his arms crossed over his chest, his eyes hard and glaring at me. I walk past him and he catches my shoulder. "Be careful, freak boy."

I step out of his grip. "Don't. Touch. Me. Ever. Again."

A threatening grin lights up his entire face. "That's nothing compared to the touch I'll give you if you keep hanging around my sister."

I don't say anything and turn away.

~~~

Addison drops me off by the shed in the cemetery. I don't share the encounter I had earlier with her brother. His threat is the last thing I'm worried about. Although I don't doubt he'll follow through on it, I don't care. Addison is worth it. Besides, his jock head is a hell of a lot bigger than his muscles.

"I'll pick you up at seven." I lean into the driver's side window and kiss her.

She offers me her slow easy smile, the one that makes my knees go a little funny. "And I'll be dressed in my finest," she says and drives away.

"I see you got a girl." Roy's gruff voice is tinted with flecks

161

of humor. He's gripping onto his suspenders and tilted back on his heels.

"Her name's Addison," I say, unable to keep the grin off my face.

Roy chuckles and shakes his head. "Ah, I do miss that young love."

"I'm sorry about leaving my motorcycle here the whole night. I came yesterday and it was pouring—"

"Don't worry 'bout it, son." He adjusts his wide brimmed hat and climbs onto the golf cart.

"Thanks. You need anything while I'm here?"

"No, I'm going take one last go-a-round and close up. But in the morning, we got a grave to dig."

"I know. I watched her die."

~~~

I can feel Billie Joe's amused stare at me from the *Green Day* poster hanging on my wall. He's grinning as I pull on hole-less jeans. "Yeah, yeah. I know, just say it...I'm whipped." Pulling on my boots, I glance at my church loafers—*not a chance,* I think.

My hands are sweating as I roll to a stop in front of Addison's house. Our first official date, and the first time I'm meeting her dad and seeing her mom again. Her words still echo in my head, *"Well, you must be something special."*

I rub my sweaty palms on my jeans and push the glowing doorbell button. I hear a familiar melody of chimes in a jingle I can't place. The door opens interrupting the "What's That Tune" thought in my head. A man that I assume is Addison's dad stands on the other side of the threshold. I feel as I'm being dissected, stripped of all my ego, and warned by his intense eyes that if I so much as look at his daughter in a disrespectful way, I will be hunted down, beaten, and killed.

"May I help you?" he asks. His slick dark hair glistens under the foyer chandelier. A black button down is tucked into matching

162

dress pants, and a striped necktie is straddled around his collar hanging over his chest.

"Good evening, sir. I'm here to—"

"Daddy, let him in!" Addison comes to my rescue, yelling from somewhere inside the house.

He steps back and opens the door wider for me to enter. I wipe my feet on the "Welcome" mat before stepping onto pristine white carpet. Who puts white carpet at the front door?

He closes the door behind me and I hold out my hand. "I'm Erik."

"I know. I'm Dr. Bailey." Doctor? Addison never told me her dad was a doctor. He shakes my hand and I feel a slight sliver of acceptance in that small gesture. I look past the entry into a very modern room. A red couch is positioned in the center, and it's obvious it's not for sitting on. Waves of glass are perched on a pedestal separating the unwelcoming couch from a fireplace. Above the mantel hangs a huge painted family portrait.

Dr. Bailey guides me through a short hall that opens into a kitchen that overlooks a family room. A wall of French doors leads out to a pool with a waterfall. Some women's reality show grabs my attention on the biggest TV I've ever seen. Long pink nails claw at my peripheral vision. I turn my full attention to them; they decorate a delicate hand choking the stem of a wine glass. I watch Addison's mom swirl the golden liquid and after a few moments, she tears her eyes from the television and looks at me.

"Hello again," she says, and then tilts the glass to pink bulging lips and empties its contents.

"Nice to see you again, Mrs. Bailey."

"Hmmm, I guess you really *are* something special if you're here." Her tight unwrinkled face barely moves as she talks.

What does she expect me to say? Anything? I abandon her question and Dr. Bailey comes in for the save and asks if I would like something to drink.

"No thank—"

"I would like a refill," Mrs. Bailey says cutting through my words. She rises from the couch with perfect smoothness and grace. Her husband already has the wine bottle in his hand before she reaches him. She thrusts out the glass and he pours more wine into it.

She glances in my direction and gives me a dry smile with lips that look fuller than the first time I met her. I've come to the conclusion that Dr. Bailey is a plastic surgeon and his wife is his personal guinea pig.

"So where are you two off to tonight?" Addison's mom asks. Her eyes gaze over the top of her glass at me as she takes another sip of wine.

Addison dashes around the corner breaking through the awkward moment for me, and I let out the breath of air that's been trapped in my lungs since I walked in. "To have fun, of course." She kisses my cheek; heat instantly webs its way to my face and I feel myself blush.

"Of course," Mrs. Bailey says, hammering in her disapproval even deeper. I notice the slightest cringe and know they would rather have Addison being courted by some football jackass than me.

"Ready to go?" Addison takes my hand and as she holds it in hers, she pecks both her mom and dad on the cheek and says, "Bye." Between her excitement and my desperate need for an escape, I take a deep breath to calm my nerves. Without waiting for an answer, she leads me to salvation.

We're almost to the door when her mother says, "Don't forget curfew, Addison."

"I know, Mom." Addison looks at me. "Besides, I'm in good hands."

"Yeah, well that could mean a couple different things," her mom says as she smirks before taking another sip of wine.

"Very funny," Addison says, not letting her mom get to her.

When the door closes behind us, I want to scream. I think

that experience possibly made it to the top five worst moments of my entire life. But, then I look at Addison and know that it was completely worth it. I feel my hand in hers as she pulls me along; her white sweater sleeve brushes my hand, tickling my palm.

"Hurry, I didn't tell my parents that you were picking me up on your motorcycle."

Her jeans are tucked into black knee-high boots. Her hair is loose around her shoulders and when she turns to look at me, her pink lip-gloss glistens from post lights in the yard. She's beautiful.

"After pizza are ya up for a little game called Putt-Putt?" she asks.

"Are you ready to get beat?"

"Ha! You think so, huh?"

"Oh yeah." We laugh and she leans in a little and I take that to be my cue and meet her the rest of the way until our lips are touching. I break the kiss remembering we're still in front of her parents' house.

"Perfect. But, you have to promise to take me to get some hot chocolate when we're done. After eighteen holes of mini golf in this weather, I'll be freezing," she says.

"You're joking. Freezing, really?"

"Hey, I'm a Florida girl, remember?"

"Oh, yeah. Anything below eighty degrees calls for a jacket. I remember now." I lean in to kiss her. "I'll take you anywhere you want to go."

Addison climbs onto the back of my motorcycle and wraps her arms around me, just like I imagined, but even better. Her laughs and giggles vibrate against my back. The blurring lights rushing by and the wind blasting my face are the only things reminding me this moment is real. I could drive across the country with her holding on to me like this.

When we pull up to the restaurant, it feels as though only seconds have passed.

"Have a seat there and I'll be with ya in a sec." The waitress points to a table for two by the window.

Addison's face is beaming. "What are you so excited about?" I ask.

"A few months ago, I applied to an art school. I didn't tell anyone, not even my parents. I figure this is what I want to do and it's my life—right?" She doesn't wait for me to answer. "So, today, I got a letter saying that I was accepted and I start next fall." The seat squeaks and shifts as she bounces up and down.

"That's awesome! Congratulations."

Her beaming face falls a bit when she says, "I'm so nervous to tell my mom and dad."

"How could they *not* be proud?"

"Huh, you don't know my—"

"What can I get cha?" Addison and I both look at a girl who's no more than five feet tall. Freckles dot the bridge of her pug nose.

"Coke?" I ask Addison. She nods. "Pepperoni?"

"Perfect."

"Two Cokes and a large pepperoni pizza."

After our waitress leaves, and Addison continues. "You don't know my parents. First off, they totally think Aiden is going to be this great pro quarterback some day." She throws her arms up. "And, since he's the star, I should follow in his footsteps to whatever college *he* decides. That way we'll both be at the same school and that makes their life easier."

"So, basically, you live in his shadow?"

The waitress sets our Cokes on table and tosses a couple a wrapped straws next to them. "Yup." She picks up her Coke and takes a sip. "Let's talk about something different."

"So, what's the topic?"

"You, of course."

My stomach clenches. Practically every second of the day,

especially the moments I'm with Addison, I feel like my past is this giant squid wrapping its tentacles around me, threatening to squeeze my guts until I explode and start spewing out the small fact that I can bring back the dead, and that I'm counting the days until I can do it again. Once she knows the truth, I'm sure she'll run, fast and far. And maybe that's for the best, I don't know.

"You are a complete mystery."

"Nah." I put my straw in my glass and take a long drink.

"What was it like being home-schooled?"

I let out the breath I was holding; an easy one. "Tough as hell. My mom was like a sergeant in boot camp when it comes to school. We had two days off a week, but never consecutively, and we were up at seven thirty on school days."

Our waitress sets our pizza down between us on the stand and serves us each a piece.

Addison picks up a knife and fork to cut her pizza.

"Tell me you're joking." I laugh.

"What?" Clearly baffled, she looks down at her pizza.

"Listen, let it cool a bit, then pick it up, fold it down the center and take a massive bite."

Her mouth opens to say something and then closes.

"Come on, like this." I do exactly what I just told her. "Trust me." She picks up the pizza, folds it and takes a bite. "Way better than hacking it up—right?"

"Mmmmmm...I didn't know pizza could ever taste this delicious," she says with a full mouth sprinkled with drama and sarcasm.

"You can make fun all you want," I point at her with my pizza, "but you know it tastes damn good like that."

"Okay, so now I know how you eat your pizza. What's your favorite dessert?"

"By far, elephant ears." And just the thought of them brings back a thousand memories.

"Like at the carnival?"

"Yup, loaded with cinnamon-sugar."

"Delicious, but that doesn't count." She takes a bite of her pizza.

"Why not?"

She's laughing and shaking her head. Her left cheek fat with pizza. "Because that's not an everyday dessert, it's a special occasional dessert…cause it's not like there's a carnival to go to any time you want."

She's right, not anymore. "Fair enough, then I'd have to go with apple pie a la mode."

"That is a good one. But, for me, it has to have chocolate." She takes a sip of her drink. "Okay, next question. What's your father—"

"My turn." I cut her off, not ready for her to take me there yet.

~~~

"Ugh! I can't believe you won. I was so close to victory." Addison raises her arms to the sky and mocks a growl that only makes me laugh.

"I tried to tell you that you didn't have a chance, but you wouldn't listen."

"Yeah, well if it wasn't for that lucky hole-in-one at the end, I could've taken you down," she says.

"You sound like a wrestler," I say, and she roars again to emphasize my comment. We laugh so hard we're both bent over at the waist and gasping for breath. She stops laughing and looks up at me. "What is it?" I ask.

"I just had a memory-flash about Tiffany and I feel guilty for having a good time."

I put my arm around her, pull her close, and whisper into her hair, "Let's go get some hot chocolate?"

She bumps my hip with hers, and moments later we're

168

pulling up to The Round House. I order two hot chocolates with whip cream and a chocolate filled croissant. "I'll get this, go find us a seat."

She puts her finger to her lips and says, "Hmmm…oh the choices I have." I smirk at her sideways comment. The place is empty, except for a couple sitting at a table near the window. Addison weaves her way through the tables to the one in the back corner.

Sitting down across from her, I slide a hot chocolate over and then the dessert. She puts a bite in her mouth and says, "Oh my God, this is the most amazing pastry, ever."

My curiosity is killing me and I ask her, "What kind of doctor is your dad?"

"A dentist."

"A—oh…I, never mind," I say in a dumfounded voice that sounds stupid even to my own ears.

"What?" she pushes.

"Nothing, really," I say trying to forget I even brought it up.

She takes a sip of her hot chocolate, biding time for me to suffer and says, "Let me guess."

"Guess what?"

"You thought my dad was a plastic surgeon because of the way my mom looks?"

"I—well…the thought did cross my mind." She got me, and I have nowhere to go except to admit my thought aloud to her.

Her face drops into sadness, or embarrassment, I'm not sure which, and her eyes fold down from mine and she looks at her hands that are now in her lap. This is not how I wanted the night to end up.

She comes up with the biggest grin on her face and bursts out laughing. Here I was ready to start apologizing for hurting her, and now the joke's on me. She catches me by the arm and says, "I'm sorry, that was mean, but I couldn't help it. The look on your face looked as if you just raised the dead."

I almost choke on the piece of croissant in my mouth. My heart starts pounding so hard that it collides with my rib cage. I honestly think that for a nano-moment of time I will be scraping the bloody thing off the floor. My body's instant reaction to those words is so obvious that I need to hide. I push back my chair, mutter something about the restroom, and excuse myself. "Erik, are you—" I close the door before I hear another word.

I splash cold water on my face and take deep breaths. I face the person in the mirror and remind him that she meant nothing by what she said. She was simply making a joke. I recoup some of my calm and self-control, and feeling only slightly still off kilter, I go back and join Addison.

She puts her hand on my knee and asks, "You okay?"

"Fine," I say. And by the look on her face, I haven't convinced her. I kiss her cheek and say, "Really, go ahead," I prompt her.

Hesitantly, she continues. "Anyway, after seeing my mom and knowing my dad is a doctor, it's obvious you would think he's a plastic surgeon. I mean, who wouldn't?" I chuckle a little, not ready to let my guard down. "Erik, really it's all right," she says thinking she's trying to ease my dismay for being wrong; I let her. "I mean look at the woman, she's a walking mannequin." She picks up her fork and takes a bite. "Although, my dad did do her lips, dentists can do Botox," she shrugs and says. "She came home right after she got them done, and I as soon as I saw her, I had to run to my room so she wouldn't see me laughing. And later that night, I told my dad if he made them any bigger, he should buy stock in lipstick."

As easy as she threw me into my abyss, she pulls me out and away from the secret that I'm not ready to share. As I focus on her smile and animated words, my guard slowly dissolves and now I'm truly laughing.

We both turn as the bell on the door dings. Aiden and Candace walk in. What little smiles they have on their faces fall off

170

as soon as they see Addison and me.

"Let's go," says Addison. She starts to get up.

"What's up, Sis?"

Addison eases back into her chair. Without looking at Aiden she says, "Not much."

"Hi, Addison," Candace says.

I watch Addison's chest rise and then fall. "What are you guys up to?" she asks.

Aiden wraps his arm around Candace. "Not much, just keeping an eye on my little Sis."

It's Candace's turn to take a deep breath, she stays quiet, but the disappointment is smeared all over her face.

Addison stands up, looks up to Aiden. "I think your Lil' Sis," she air quotes her title, "can take care of herself." She moves her hand before he can swipe it away. "And it would be really great if you started to realize that." Her cheery tone is tucked neatly within the folds of sharp, biting sarcasm.

There's no way to hide the smirk on my face.

"What are you laughing at, freak?" Through pursed lips he tries to redeem his esteem. "I guess your freak girlfriend was busy tonight, sacrificing a baby or something, so you call my sister for sloppy seconds?"

My fists ball and I want to hit him as hard as I can. But out of pure respect for Addison, I step back without falling into his trap. I scratch my head and look up at the ceiling. "Today's Friday." I look at Aiden and say shaking my head, "No...sacrifices are scheduled on Wednesdays, but only during a full moon, and," I tick my fingers, "oh yeah, and only in the months that begin with L."

Confusion paints itself all over Candace's face. "Uh, there aren't any months that start with L."

I wink and lower my voice as if she's the only one there. "Aren't you a smart one?"

Addison chuckles and turns her head to the side. She takes

my hand and pulls me to leave. I wrap my arm around her shoulder. She stops. "Wait." Turning around, she shuffles back to our table and grabs our cups of hot chocolate. Scooting past Aiden and Candace, she says, "Excuse you."

We sit on the curb and finish our hot chocolates before it's time to take her home. "By the way, his little sister is older than him by three minutes."

As I walk her to the door, I wrap my hand around hers, not wanting to leave her. "We made it, it's one minute until midnight." I kiss her on her glossed lips, and briefly smell chocolate on her breath. "Thank you for an amazing night."

"You're welcome. I'll call you tomorrow." She walks into her house and before she closes the door, I see her reach up to cradle her forehead.

# CHAPTER 23

We stop at the—her gravesite, and it takes everything I have to get out of the golf cart.

"It was the worst thing I've ever seen. She was the first person who was actually nice to me on my first day. And she always had something good to say and she was always happy." I realize I'm rambling as I stare at the patch of grass where she'll be buried tomorrow. My hands are pushed deep into my pockets. Tomorrow I'll be in this exact spot again dressed in a suit and tie. "She was very sick, you know. Yeah, Addison told me that." I can't stop talking—must be nerves, I'm not sure, but I continue droning on about a girl I barely knew. Roy doesn't comment, or ask questions, he only listens. "It was so bad watching her fall, like it was slow motion or something. And I think a part inside of me knew she was dead but wouldn't except it. Then, when the paramedics..."

"Why don't you sit this one out?" Roy says, putting a hand on my shoulder.

Nodding, I silently thank him. I've never felt so grateful in my life. I drive the golf cart around the grounds and pick up fallen branches, and look for anything that needs to be fixed.

A couple hours later when I get back to the site, the hole is dug. I hand him a bottle of water as he climbs down from Bulldog.

"Thanks, Roy." He pulls off his wide brim hat, takes the rag from his pocket, and wipes his brow.

"No problem, son." He takes a long swig of water and puts his hat back on. "When I just started working here, my brother died—he was only fifteen. And the last thing I wanted to do was watch him be put in a hole, but digging it…" He grunts and looks off over the short hills. "My boss at the time told me to start digging, that it'd help me grieve. The damn fool sat in the shade and watched me dig my little brother's grave."

"That's rough." I want to ask him how he died, but I don't.

"I'll never forgive the bastard for that. Cruelest thing I was ever forced to do in my life, but we needed the money." Then, Roy starts laughing. "No matter, he got his," He nods his head. "I worked my tail off, got promoted to his job—became his boss and fired the lazy bastard."

I help him set up the canopy for tomorrow's service. "Most of the school will be here in the morning."

"I'll get here early, and son," I shield my eyes and look up, "if you need me, come find me."

"Thanks."

"And when this passes, I wanna hear 'bout that girl of yours. I haven't seen a woman put a smile on a man's face since my late wife plastered one on mine, and that was almost fifty-four years ago."

"You got it." I slide the last piece of plywood over the grave so no one falls in, and stop midway through. "Wait! Do I really look that whipped?"

Through a gruff laugh he says, "Son, do you ever."

~~~

We sit down for dinner and Oli asks, "How was work?"

"It was all right." I shrug. "We had to dig Tiffany's grave and…"

Oli lays her hand over mine. "It's okay."

174

I take a deep breath. "Anyway, Roy's a good guy, you should give him a chance."

"Ah. Yeah…well, that's a topic for another day." Her cheeks turn pink. "Let's change the subject to one that a little girl I know is dying to talk about."

"My birthday is in two weeks! Can you believe it? I'm gonna be nine years old. This is the last one before I get to double digits." I watch my little sister shovel a spoonful of mac-n-cheese into her very wide and smiling mouth.

Oli continues. "And we were thinking of having a party."

"With a bounce house, pony rides, cotton candy, and snow cone machines!" CeCe can hardly contain her excitement.

"Simmer down, baby girl, I was thinking more along the lines of a bounce house and cupcakes."

"Here?" I ask.

"Yes. So, CeCe and I have a favor to ask."

"Oh, you guys are smooth," I say wagging my finger at them. "You'd like me to get rid of the metal skeleton in the backyard?"

"Please! Please! Please! I'll help!" says CeCe.

"For you…anything."

She jumps up and wraps her arms around my neck. "Thank you! Thank you! Thank you!" She pulls back. "Can Naya come?"

I had to have misheard her. "Naya?"

"You know: black hair, black boots, black shirt, black pants, and purple—""Yeah, I know her. But how do *you* know her?" I ask in the calmest voice as I can manage, tossing in a little huff of a laugh.

"She was walking home from school and I was walking home from school—we were both going the same way and she introduced herself and we just started talking."

"When did all this happen?"

"A couple of weeks ago. She walked me home from school all last week. She's so nice—"

175

"She did what?" The control I was trying to hold onto just slipped completely away.

"What's the big deal? She said you know her, you guys are like best friends, and that you guys used to work together in the shows at the carnival so it wasn't like she was a stranger or anything. I love that we met someone who knows where we came from—you know…not having to explain anything or make up some stupid story. How come you never told me about her?"

"I don't—"

"Oh my God, and she has the prettiest eyes I have ever seen, and you know how purple is my very favorite color."

Dazed and outraged, I'm speechless and beyond shocked. Why is she hanging around CeCe?

"So? Can she? Please." Her hands are flat against each other in front of her chest.

"Can she what?"

"Come to my party, silly. Haven't you been listening?"

"Uh…I'll talk to her about it." And that's not all I'll be talking to her about. "I'm having dinner with her and her mom tomorrow tonight." My shock turns into terror. "Did you tell her about our show? Or what I—"

CeCe hops down from my lap, goes back to her seat, "I didn't have to tell her anything," she puts a fork full of food in her mouth, "she already knew."

~~~

I fight the urge to get on my motorcycle, go to Naya's house and ask her what the hell she thinks she's doing going behind my back. I pick up my phone, find her number, but hesitate pressing the call button. I take a deep breath and let the air slowly blow out through my mouth. How much harm can she be causing? CeCe seems to like her—a lot. She can relate…the both of them can. I'm overreacting. It's not a big deal. My worry is what CeCe is telling her if Naya tells her it's real and they've built a relationship, an "I

176

won't tell" kind of relationship, the trusting kind of relationship, the ones that can get you into trouble.

I fall onto my bed in emotional and physical exhaustion. My phone chirps.

Naya: *See you tomorrow at 6*

I turn off my phone, close my eyes and hope sleep comes easy tonight.

Tomorrow will be Hell.

# CHAPTER 24

¶ haven't put on a white button down dress shirt since my last show when I ended up on the floor. My stomach growls, but I can't stand the thought of eating. In passing, I look in the mirror in the hallway, and stop. I look different. Even with the lack of sleep, the dark circles under my eyes have completely disappeared. I look healthy again.

Oli and CeCe are waiting in the den when I come out.

"Hey, your scruffy face is gone," CeCe says.

Oli walks over to me. "And here I thought I was going to have to help you tame that hair."

I run my fingers through my hair that's pushed back from its usual position of falling past my eyes and lying on the side of my face. "Okay, now that you both have approved my appearance, can we please go and get this over with?"

"Almost." Oli lifts my collar and places a necktie around my neck. "I haven't tied one of these in years, so let's see if I still got my touch." She wraps, loops and pulls the tie, then pushes the perfect knot into the hollow of my throat. "There." She smiles. "Yup, I'd say I still got it." She hands me her keys. "Here, handsome. Do you mind driving?"

"Not at all." I open the front door. "After you, ladies."

178

~~~

I've seen a thousand dead things, touched a thousand dead things, this should be easy...right? I see the silk lining of the casket and as if death is calling me, a twinge of electricity sparks somewhere in my core. I push down the sensation that I've learned to harbor, but ignoring it completely is impossible—it's still very much a part of me.

In death, Tiffany looks very young. Staring at her, I was so wrong, so very wrong. There's nothing easy about this, and I was a fool for believing it would be. My body responds in such a natural way, and I want to touch her, but of course, I refrain. Her spiraling curls frame her smooth face. Part of them are tucked back and held by a small clip. Her lips are painted the same color as the light pink dress she's wearing. Frustrated and sickened, I turn away from her, no longer wanting to feel the mortification of what death looks like, especially when it's been all dolled up as if ready for a date. Death is supposed to be ugly. Reversing it is what makes it beautiful.

A hand slips into mine and before I turn around, I know it's Addison. The scent of her perfume surrounds me and the smoothness of her skin as it slides against mine ignites tiny volts of current just beneath the surface of my palms. I love the feel of her body next to mine. I bend down and kiss the side of her head. She leans into me, and I wrap my arm around her waist as we walk down the center isle to find a seat in the pews.

Prayers echoed with sobs and kind words said with tears fill the church during the remembrance of Tiffany. When the funeral concludes, Addison drives with her family to the cemetery and I drive Oli and CeCe. In the rear view mirror, I see Ash's massive car behind us in the procession. I'm surprised she came.

There are so many cars and people attending the service that when we arrive Tiffany's casket is already in position to be lowered into her grave when the last prayers are said. The finality of it all is so severe.

179

My friends, sister, and Oli stand behind Tiffany's parents and relatives. Almost the entire school is here. Some are close friends, others only acquaintances, or people who are here to support others. She was supposed to graduate this year and was planning to go to college—wanted to be a journalist they say. Now, none of that will happen. We bow our heads for the final time and say our last "Amen."

"Call me after you leave Naya's tonight," Addison whispers.

"What did you just say?" Ash says.

"Nothing. She said nothing." I pull Addison off to the side and hold her in my arms. "I'll call you when I leave."

"Addison, you're letting him go to that psycho's house?"

"He's a big boy. I'm sure he can handle it." She kisses my cheek. "What's the big deal?"

"You're just as crazy as—"

Rip pulls Ash away from us. "Come on, Ash, let's go."

She yanks her arm out of his grip. "Fine." Ash looks over her shoulder as she walks away, and says, "Don't say I didn't warn ya."

I watch her climb into her tank of a car, and Rip gets into the passenger seat. When she cranks the engine a black cloud billows out from the exhaust into the air.

"I have to go," Addison says. I look over her shoulder and her parents are waiting for her. "I'm going to tell them about my acceptance into art school today."

"Do you want me to be there? For support."

"No, that's okay." She lays her hand on my chest. "You got enough going on. And it's probably better if I do this alone. Thanks, though."

"Okay. Is it alright if I kiss you?"

She looks over her shoulder to see her parents facing each other and talking. She reaches up and puts her arms around my neck. I wipe away the wetness on her cheek with my thumb. "Definitely kiss me. Cause, after I tell them, this might be the last time you see

180

me outside of school."

I hardly know her parents, but from what I've gathered, I don't think I'd put it past them to ground her until graduation or until she surrenders and follows her brother's dreams. "Please, tell me you're joking."

An insecure chuckle falls from her mouth. "I hope I am." Taking my hand, she pulls me around the big oak. Standing on her toes, she wraps her arms around my neck. My arms lace around her thin waist and after a subtle hesitation our lips touch and slowly meld together. Everyone and everything around us dissolves into nothingness as I hold her in my arms.

"Good show, sis, making out at a funeral." Addison jerks away from me. "I mean really, can you be any more embarrassing?" Holding the back of his hand over his mouth, Aiden scoffs from behind me.

My hand slides away from Addison as I turn towards him. "I suggest you mind your own business."

"You're making it everyone's business as you grope my sister in the middle of the cemetery." He opens and closes his fists. Balls them until his knuckles are white and then releases, stretching out his fingers wide. "It's really sad how low your standards are, sis. You do realize you're kissing the guy who dug the hole your friend just got buried in, don't you?"

I step closer to him. My balled fists match his, ready at my side. Another step. Slight pause. Step. No more than ten inches of angry space is between us.

"Another time, boys," Addison's dad says as his arm comes between us breaking through the wall of angry tension.

"Yeah, another time," Aiden growls, his jawbones grinding against each other.

"I look forward to it," I hiss, and back away from him. Rolling my neck, the muscles in my neck loosen, and I flex my fingers feeling the blood circulate through my hands.

181

Addison pulls me to her and kisses me lightly on my cheek. "Call me later." And she walks off to join her family.

CeCe and Oli are waiting for me by the car. Most everyone has left.

"Everything alright?" Oli asks. I don't know what or how much she saw, or if it's just the look on my face, which still feels tight with anger at Aiden, but she knows something's happened.

Debating whether to answer sarcastically, sinfully sweet, or cleverly to avoid the truth, I decide to fall back on a simple, "Fine."

"Mm-hmm," is all she says. And I wonder if she would have preferred one of my smart-ass answers.

"I can't believe you stand on dead people all day," CeCe says hurtling right into the strain of the moment with one of her eight-year-old comments, and conveniently tearing it apart.

My lungs release the pent up air and I look at Oli and offer a half smile. "Let's go get the tools to take down the metal skeleton to make room for a bounce house?"

"Yay!" CeCe squeals, claps, and jumps up and down.

I back the car up to the shed. "Looks like your old friend is here, Oli." And on cue, Roy peeks his head out around the open door of the shed. As I climb out of the car, he comes out from the shed.

"Oh, goodness, hide me now," I hear Oli whisper from the passenger seat.

I laugh. "Too late. You know it'd be rude if you didn't get out and say hi."

"Hey, son, you coming to get them tools?"

"Yes, sir." I turn around when I hear the car door open; CeCe and Oli are getting out of the car.

CeCe stops in front of me. I put my hands on her shoulders. "Roy, this is my sister, CeCe."

"It's nice to meet you, young lady. I hear you got a special day coming up soon?"

CeCe's never been the shy one, and she answers in her sugar

coated matter-of-fact voice, "Sure do. I'm gonna be nine."

"The big nine, huh? That's something alright." Roy pinches his suspenders between his fingers.

"Roy, this is my gr—"

"I know exactly who she is." His smooth drawl—void of gruffness, which I've never heard before—suggests he's trying to make points. "How ya doing, Olivine?"

Oli looks like she may possibly curtsy, or run as fast as she can in the opposite direction. I bite the inside of my cheek to keep from laughing or blurting out something that would most likely be inappropriate. "Good. It's been a long time," she says, her voice also smooth and unfamiliar to my ear.

"Too long," he says.

And within ten minutes, they've managed to get reacquainted and arrange to have dinner out as friends, tonight.

~~~

It's 5:00 when I finish dissecting the old swing set. That leaves me an hour to get ready and drive to Naya's house.

On my way out, I watch Oli fiddle with her bracelets and adjust her skirt. "So, where's Roy taking you?"

She sighs, a long "what am I doing" breath of air. "Someplace downtown, a little hole in the wall he swears has the best seafood in town. I'm dropping CeCe off at her friend's house and I'll pick her up on my way home. She'll be fine and she has my number if she needs it. I won't be late anyway, in fact I'm sure I'll be very, very early," she says barely catching her breath.

I walk up behind her and put my hands on her shoulders. Our faces stare back at us from the mirror in the foyer. Hers; anxious. Mine; full of humor. "Oli, first off, Roy is a great guy, second, try to relax and have a good time, and third, don't forget to breathe." Her nervous giddy laugh is low and full of uncertainty.

"I'm goin' out. I won't be late." I should probably tell her if I'm not home by morning, call the police, give them Naya's address, and tell them to check the basement. The second the morbid thought drives across my warped brain, my teeth latch on to my bottom lip until the dark fleeting image passes. Forcing a smile, I say, "Have fun, Oli." Then I kiss her cheek and head out the door.

# CHAPTER 25

*1294 Knoll Rd. The third house on the left with the psychic readings/tarot cards sign in the front yard.* Those were Naya's exact words and directions.

I pull into the gravel driveway. As I get off my motorcycle, I study the rundown house. It looks like Oli's, but old and uncared for. The sign in the front yard reads, "Madam Selena, $25 Psychic/Tarot Card Readings, Walk-ins Welcome."

The wooden planks on the porch creak with every step I take, each one screeching at me to turn around and leave. The doorbell button is cracked and surrounded by peeling paint. I push it. Nothing: no ding-dong, no dog barking, no footsteps. I knock. After several clicks and clunks, the door opens. The scent of incense wafts out from the house.

Naya. Her long dark hair is pulled to the side, very straight and loose. The inked fairy kneels patiently on her bare shoulder. No black pants, shirt, or boots. Tonight she's wearing a tight, short dress. Very different than anything I've ever seen her in—probably anyone has ever seen her in—and it's almost the same color as her eyes, but a deeper hue. She smiles. And I begin to wonder why Naya really invited me here tonight.

"You came?" Her voice is shades of surprise, happiness, delight, but mostly it's filled with amusement.

"I told you I would." I feel like I'm cheating on Addison with

Naya dressed like this. I think I'll leave this part out when Addison asks me about how all this went.

"I know." She shrugs and looks down at the ground.

Her shyness is very unlike any aspect of Naya that I've yet to encounter. Awkwardly I say, "I think I'm a little under-dressed."

"No, you're perfect." She turns and says, "Come in." I follow her into the dark house that seems to be lit by only candles. The tiny flames are everywhere. Their glow shimmers on the back of her long legs that end in high heels which clack on the hardwood floor.

She looks over her shoulder. "I hope you like spaghetti."

"Who doesn't?"

We pass through a living room of sorts. I look around presuming to spot a crystal ball or Ouija board. But, only a round deep-seated chair, a small television on a table, a short bookshelf with a few books lining its shelves, and a side table with a picture of a woman and a little girl fill the room. The walls, that look as though they've been stained the color of dried blood, are just as sparse; only a poster of Madam Selena in a gaudy gold frame hangs on the far wall. "Is that your mom?"

Naya pauses and looks at the framed billboard. "Yeah."

Even though it's an animated picture made to mimic the old style freak show posters and ads, the woman doesn't look familiar. "Where is she?"

We walk into the small kitchen. "Actually, she's not feeling well, so it's just going to be us for dinner." She picks up a wooden spoon and stirs the contents in the pot. "Have a seat." She points to the table, set for two. "But, she still wants to see you. She's resting now, but we'll go see her after we eat."

I feel like I've been tricked into coming over so Naya can have me all to herself on her own playing field. "Naya."

She continues to stir, and without turning around she says, "Hmmm?"

"You know I'm with Addison and no matter how you dress

186

or how good your spaghetti is, that's not changing."

"I know." Amusement ricochets in her tone. The fact that she's not trying to get in my pants is all that's keeping me from getting up and leaving.

Not that I'm counting seconds, but it's been quiet for too long and the silence has fallen over the edge into uncomfortable. I spurt out, "How come you didn't go this morning?"

"Were you looking for me?" She glances over her shoulder, and a crafty smile takes up all the real estate on her face.

Without falling into her game, I answer, "I just noticed that you weren't there." Why is she making this so awkward? I'm not sure where to bring the conversation now or where she intends it to go.

She turns back to the stove. "My mom needed me to do a few things. Besides, I don't think I would have been very welcome."

"The service was nice."

"I'm sure it was." Her voice is stiff. She takes bread out of the oven. "Everything's done."

"It smells good." I didn't think I really had an appetite, but all of a sudden, I'm starving and my stomach growls.

She sets a bowl of salad, an enormous plate of spaghetti and sauce, and garlic bread on the table. I'm not sure whether to, out of politeness, serve her, or just help myself. Saving me, she picks up the salad tongs, grabs a claw-full of salad, and drops it in my bowl. And then continues to serve each of us.

"Hold up your plate," she says.

Now I feel weird with her serving me. "You don't have to serve me, I can get my own."

"You're my guest, and my mom raised me right," she says with pride.

"Sounds like our moms would get along well." I shrug. "At least, I think she raised me right," I say without trying to sound conceited.

She laughs. "I think you turned out okay. And you're right, they'd probably be great friends."

She loads a pile of spaghetti on my plate that's enough for both of us. "Do you have a doggie bag?"

"You're a big boy, I'm sure you can handle it." She puts a piece of bread on my plate and sits down across from me.

"So, you've met CeCe?" I ask stuffing a forkful of pasta into my mouth. I wasn't going to bring it up, but I haven't been able to get it out of my head since CeCe told me.

Delicately she winds the long strands of pasta around her fork. Without looking at me, she says, "Oh, yeah. I forgot to tell you."

Lie.

"She is so cute," she continues.

True. "She really likes you. It seems like you guys got a little bond thing happening."

"I know." She smiles. "We hit it off. It's like we're long lost sisters or something."

Or something.

Through eating and laid-back conversation, I relax and try to remember this is Naya, my friend who doesn't share, and the one who saved me with a glass of milk.

She stands, picks up our plates, and brings them to the sink. "Chocolate cake?"

"Is that a trick question?" I'm so full, I could possibly throw up right now, but I can't say no.

She cuts two slices of cake and brings them to the table. Thick fudge icing drips onto the plate.

I pick up my fork and take a bite. "This is delicious, did you make it?"

"Yeah. Well, kind of..." She rolls her eyes and wobbles her head. "It's from a box."

"That's homemade to me."

"And that's the closest I usually get to homemade."

"Why do you hide behind the black and the scariness? I still haven't figured out why you don't let everyone see this Naya." I wave my arm the length of her.

She gives me another enormous smile, adding wickedness to it this time. "Do you like this Naya?" She bats her long eyelashes and her light purple eyes glisten behind them.

I opened the door...now walk through it. "Yes."

And then, she kindly let's me off the end of her hook, freeing me to swim back through the door I should have never opened, and asks, "Wanna help me clean up?"

"Sure." Together we clear the table, pack up leftovers, and wash and dry dishes.

"We kind of have a constant battle going on," she says grinning, and hands me a wet saucepan.

"What are you talking about?" I ask baffled. The only battle I ever considered myself in is the one with healing and getting stronger so I can get back to performing.

She turns off the water and turns to face me with her hand perched on her cocked hip. "When you tell me why the dragonfly, I may tell you why I shy away."

"*May* tell me?" I laugh throwing my head back. "You're downright perplexing and even frustrating at times. You do know that—right?"

"Undeniably, yes." Now we're laughing together.

She makes a tray for her mom: broth, juice, and a sliver of chocolate cake. "It's her favorite."

"Can you blame her?"

She picks up the tray. "Come on, her room is down here." Closed doors are on both sides of the thin hallway. And at the very end there's another room, and another closed door faces us. "Can you get the door?"

I ease past Naya and put my hand on the knob. I feel like I'm

189

intruding on her mother, especially when she's not feeling well. "Are you sure she won't mind I'm here?"

"Trust me, she's fine with it. Like I said she wanted to see you."

I turn the handle and push open the door.

The smell of sickness hits me hard, the kind that's rotting and close to death. "Let me just set this tray down and turn on a light."

A click and light ignites the grotesque scene in front of me, and horror fills every cell of my body.

Naya's mother lies silent in the bed. Her eyeballs bulge under lids that look like they have never opened. Pasty gray skin lies over her bones like a thin blanket. Small clear hoses and wires weave around and across her body. A tube of liquid drips into the crease of her elbow, another is inserted in her nose, and another seeps something into the top of her hand. They all lead back to the beeping machines, drip bags, and tanks of oxygen positioned next to the bed.

"I...I—"

"I know, the music right? It's the same song all day long, but it's the only one she wants to listen to, so it stays on replay the entire day, over and over and over." Naya's laugh is raw and unnatural.

I shake my head. Music? No, not the fucking music! Is she seeing the same sight I am? The one I so desperately want to look away from, but can't. The repulsing scene in front of me of a woman who lies in a bed waiting to die, who probably wants to die.

"It's alright, come in." I take a half step into the room.

Naya walks over to her mother, pushes the few strands of hair away from her face. Her high cheekbones protrude under thin pale skin. "Hey, Mama, Erik's here. Say hi."

I don't think the woman in the bed is capable of saying anything, until she does. Without opening her eyes, her lips open and she rasps a barely audible, "Hi."

Naya looks at me, she looks so happy. "See, I told you she was excited to see you again."

190

Now I'm the one incapable of talking. I grasp for the doorknob and trip; the door opens to its fullest and bangs into the wall.

"She has cancer." Naya picks up a washcloth from a bowl of water on the side table. She wrings it out and wipes her mother's forehead. I watch her perform the simple movements with such precision and kindness. So quietly and without any question she says, "You have to be here when she dies."

Slowly, very slowly, I look from Naya's mother to Naya. Her amused tone is gone and has turned into something frightening and desperate. Then finally, finally when realization slams into me, I'm thankful I'm leaning against the solidity of the door. "Wh—what did you say?"

"You have to bring her back, Erik." Her whispered words slither across the space between us. "She's all I have." Naya's looking at me now, and her face doesn't look as pretty as it did moments ago.

The shock of what she's asking—no expecting—me to do stands out in everything she's done until now.

"Will she be sick when she comes back or healthy again?"

My own shock transforms into anger and resentment. Still facing her, I walk backwards, away from Naya's sad world. The scene shrinks as I get farther into the mouth of the hallway that opens into the living room. When the air feels different, lighter, breathable, I turn and force myself not to run to make my way across the living room to the front door.

Clack. Clack. Clack. Clack. Naya's heels crack on the wood floors. I pull open the door and Naya grabs my arm. "Erik—"

I yank it free from her gasp. "What the hell is wrong with you?"

"Please, she's all I have." Hysteria licks forth from her wounded words. "There is no one else. I have no one else." She falls to her knees.

191

As much as I hate that she tricked me, I can't hate her. She's desperate and my heart breaks for her. I pull her to her feet. Tears stream from her eyes. "Naya, look at me." When she does, I'm pulled into her violet eyes, and I want to hold her, to give her something, anything. But the only thing she wants, I can't give her. "I'm sorry, I can't." How familiar those four words sound, the same ones I told Sophie, the little girl who after my show asked me to bring back *her* mother. I turn and walk out onto the porch, the steps creaking again.

Her hysteria is magnified and she's screaming as she follows me down the steps and through the yard. "I saw you! I saw you! Please, I don't want to be alone."

I turn and grab her arms. She's still on the top step and we are exactly face-to-face. "Naya, look at me!" She does. "There is nothing I can do." I release her and keep walking.

She grabs my shirt still begging and blubbering, but I fight her grip, unable to be slowed. "I'm sorry, I didn't mean to hurt him. I didn't want to do it, but I had to know."

Her words are meaningless until they register and slam into me barring me from taking another step. I spin around. My skin crawls with invisible bugs and slithering creatures up my arms, around my neck and down my spine.

"What did you say?" I ask, praying I'm wrong, and if I'm not—Holy Hell.

She slinks back, hunching over on herself. I grab her before she falls to the ground, holding her up by her arms. "I know what I saw, and you didn't believe me," she whispers her sick motivations as tears fall into her open mouth.

"You didn't just hurt him, you killed him! You left him on the porch swing like some kind of trophy." Ferocity like I've never felt roars through me, pounding its way into every opening.

"I know. I know." She looks at me now and smiles, it's quivering and caught between revolting and kind. "But you see, you brought him back to life just like you can bring my mom back."

Pushing her back, I turn as if I'm fire and sprint for my motorcycle a few yards away.

"Then please, tell me how to do it. You could show me." Her voice is high now, excited like she's found the perfect solution. "Erik!" she screeches and screams for me to please help her.

Nauseated and furious, I put my helmet on hoping to shield my ears from her cries but I still hear her like she's in my own head, penetrating my skull. I start the motorcycle and the engine roars, drowning out her pleadings and apologies. Twisting the throttle, the motorcycle jerks forward. She grabs hold of my shirt and I almost lose my balance and fall on the sugar sand patches in the yard. Naya's hand slips away and I'm able get control of the motorcycle. My tire shrieks as I pull out onto the street, escaping Naya's contrived Hell.

# CHAPTER 26

The motorcycle's engine screams as I push it harder and harder until I shift into the next gear. It screams, I shift; an endless cycle until I pull into my driveway. No one is home yet, except Gus, who lay sleeping in his favorite spot on the porch swing; irony at its finest. My stomach aches, and I imagine the undigested spaghetti bathing in a sea full of bile and chocolate cake. I lean over the railing of the porch and retch into the bushes.

Spasms rock my entire body until I'm left dry heaving. Weak, exhausted, my stomach left in agony, I sit down next to Gus and wipe my mouth with the back of my hand. Propping my elbows on my knees, I rest my head in my hands and let the quick sharp inhales of breaths assault my lungs. The stench of death is still on my cloths, and I want to throw up again.

Finally, I'm able grasp onto a breath and inhale long and deep. As my body calms, the wrath of the last two fucked up hours begins to siege my brain. Naya's well-thought out plan—contrived from despair, fear, and desperate hope—sickens me, and simultaneously conjures the deep-seated need to bring back the dead and I hate her for it.

What if in some sick demented way, her ghastly plot—from her blatantly deceitful friendship to killing our cat to scheming to getting me to her house to watch her mother dying—is some kind of cosmic karmic punishment for all the thousands of people I cheated, ambushing them into believing I was a fraud. This thing that lives and breathes inside of me; I thought I was gifted, but now I'm beginning to see without fail, I'm cursed.

For the very first time in my life, I question the one thing I've always known, the one thing I'm destined for. But, not performing, not bringing back the dead would be like not breathing, and the thought is inconceivable. Uncertainty and doubt are eating me alive from the inside. My world seems to be filled with nothing more than unfamiliar feelings and an obscure future.

I'm terrified.

# CHAPTER 27

¶ ignore the vibration in my pocket until it becomes intolerable and I fish out the device. The most recent text is from Addison asking how dinner was. What do I say? Fine. No, it wasn't fucking fine. It was bad! Really, really, bad! So, I do what I'm good at…faking the truth. I type the first thing that comes to mind: *It was bearable. Just got home.*

The other sixteen texts, four missed calls, and three voicemails are from Naya. I delete them without reading or listening to them.

Addison: *Can you come by?*

The tips of my fingers hover over the letters waiting to get a command from my head, torn between wanting to see her and crawling into my bed and hibernating for the next 226 days.

*I'll be there in 10*

Addison is sitting on the bottom step of her porch when I pull up. She cuts across the lawn and stops in front of me. Her face is blotched with red patches and wet smears. Without any words, I pull her into my arms.

Through tears she says, "They're so mad." She pulls back and looks at me. "But after all the yelling and fighting, they said they would support me. But, I know they don't want to." She shrugs and huffs out a long breath. "I didn't follow their plan." Staring at the ground, she shuffles a brown leaf from side to side with her foot.

I lift her chin and look deep into her jade eyes. "Hey, the only plan you have to follow is your own. And even if you don't know what it is, you'll find it, or it'll find you. That's just the way the world works." I kiss her forehead and take her into my arms again.

I leave out the hard part—whether you're ready for it or not. And like a fire sweeping through me, my own words brand themselves into my core and I jerk back away from her. The future, my future is coming whether I'm ready for it or not.

"What is it?" she asks.

Afraid to say anything, I shake my head and force a smile. She folds back into my embrace and holds onto me with so much hope and courage, and it's only with her borrowed strength that I don't crumble to the ground. And I want to have her all to myself for a while. "Do you want to go for a ride?"

A grateful smile touches her lips. "Let me get my jacket," she says and runs toward her house.

When the door closes behind her, sudden anxiety rakes my nerves and I'm scared that she won't come back. But a minute later, the door opens and she runs toward me and straddles my motorcycle. Her thigh is pressed against mine and I rub the length of it. She rests her head against my back and grabs ahold of me.

A foreign feeling courses through me, as deep as the melting heat that prickles under my palms with enough power to raise the dead. Chills spike over my entire body and my gut thuds as if spirited wild horses are running through it. I don't dare say the word, the one that may be the culprit for the bizarre sensations I've never felt before. But is this what it feels like? An all-of-a-sudden, all consuming power that lays its giant hand upon you and possesses you to do anything for the person it bonds itself to, and refuses to release you from its grip? And to think…it does all of this without your permission and regardless of whatever may be going on in your head or your life.

Dismissing the inexplicable horses and chills, I put the motorcycle in gear and pull out onto the street.

Minutes later, we're walking hand in hand into the mouth of the pathway that leads to the lake. When we reach the shore, I sit down on the sand and lean back on my arms. Addison sits in front of me, her back resting against my chest. The ease and comfort we have with each other is so natural; it's as if I've known her my whole life, not mere weeks.

The deepening purple sky is speckled with a million tiny flickering lights.

"I wish we could stay here forever," I say. Addison's body is so relaxed against mine as we gaze out over the calm lake. The water looks less like something fluid and more like a piece of glass laid across the ground.

"Me, too," she says. "Right here, away from the real world, away from the expectations and demands—"

"Hey! This feels pretty real to me," I say.

She reaches up and swats the top of my head. "You know what I mean." Her head rolls onto my arm. "I'm happy here," she looks up at me, "with you."

I tuck her hair behind her ear and cup her face in my hand. She turns her body toward me and I kiss her. She kisses me back and we stay like that until the night completely sets in, embracing and mindless of everything else around us…both content for the moment.

# CHAPTER 28

"Can I come study with you?" Naya's voice is hushed and braced for rejection in the quiet of the library.

It's been a week and a half that I have successfully avoided her. I've ignored her written notes, which I've thrown into the closest trash can unopened; her endless calls and voicemails deleted without ever being heard; and the countless texts containing apologies and threats.

Without looking up from my English notes, I say, "Not a good idea." The venom in my voice is undeniable and I hope it's enough to make her leave. But black still edges in on the brink of my vision. This is the first time she's caught me alone and now that she has me pinned, she's not going to let me go that easy.

"You haven't said one word to me or even looked at me in over a week. I called you, texted you. And nothing." She's been scorned, hurt, and rejected while she already lay helpless on the ground. If our places were reversed, I'd probably start organizing some horrific thoughts. She continues, "You can't just ignore what happened."

"Sure I can." I never want to look into those violet eyes again, to see the deranged and pained expression on her face.

"Please, Erik…" She starts to pull out a chair.

"Don't." I want to cover my ears to drown her out.

"So you're just going to ignore me forever?"

"Something like that." She's very close already, and still she closes the distance between us.

"Erik, knowing what you can do, that's got to count for something—right?" The high-pitched pleading whisper that wraps around her words vexes my every nerve.

I throw down my pen and look at her. "What do you want, Naya?"

"I just wanted to say I'm sorry. Really sorry." Her eyes drift to the floor. "I should have never set you up for that. It wasn't fair. " She looks at me. "I just didn't know what else to do. So, I thought if you saw her, you'd want to help—"

Beat down and frustrated, I hiss, "Naya, listen to me, it's not that I don't want to help. I hate that you have to watch her suffer like that, and I hate that you're suffering and scared. But, I can't. You have to believe me—I can't."

"I believe in you, and I obviously have more faith in your…ability than you do." Her face is somber, matching her mournful tone.

I sit back in the chair, slap my hands on my thighs, and take a deep breath. "Naya, you have no idea what you're talking about." She rolls her eyes, unconvinced, and I plow deeper into reasons and explanations I don't owe her. "It's not about having faith or believing in me." I realize my voice has elevated and I bring it back down so only she can hear. "You don't know anything about me."

"You're right." She shrugs and I think she's finally conceding to me, until she continues. "I don't understand how you do it or even why you can." She reaches down and lays her hand on my chest. "But whatever it is, it lives in here. You can save her, I know you can."

I shove her hand away from me. "I gotta get to class." Out of words for this conversation, I get up, grab my notebook and

200

backpack, and walk past her.

As I do, she calls out to me. "Erik." I turn. "Please," she mouths. Her pleading expression is heavy, begging me with those violets eyes to save her mother from her final death, and to save her from being alone in this world. I turn away from her and try to ignore the soul-wrenching guilt Naya has laid on me. But, I can't help her. I can't help either of them.

When the bell rings for lunch, I rush to the oak tree, eager to see Addison. I get there a couple minutes before I see her walking toward me. She's so beautiful, but the look on her face is an expression I haven't seen before. I start to say hi when a folded paper floats down from above and falls at my feet.

"Can you please explain this?" Addison says. I hold out my hand to block the sun. Her face is a concocted brew of sadness, hurt, anger, confusion, and hopefulness all blended together to make an expression that I have just realized I hate.

Confusion must be imprinted all over my face. I pick up the paper and stand facing her. Her arms are crossed over her chest waiting. As I unfold it, I know immediately I can explain it, but at this very second, I want to throw up. I want to laugh. I want to tell Addison everything. I want to lie. I want to run. But, I don't do anything. I don't say anything. I only nod as I stare at a picture of me with a dragonfly on my palm, and the baiting words printed at the top: Come See The Boy Who Awakens the Dead.

"I thought since Naya was the one who gave this to me that it was some kind of sick joke. Hoping," she says in a softer voice, "hoping might be a better word."

"Addison," I say her name, but I think I don't say it loud enough for her to hear because she keeps talking over me.

"What? Did you just think you could ditch the eyeliner and voila you're a regular high school kid?" She looks down at the ground and then to me. Tears are running down her face. "You must have been laughing your ass off when I suggested you and your family were gypsies in a traveling show." She lowers her voice. "I feel like such an idiot." She wipes away tears.

Her words are ripping me apart. My stomach is folding in on itself. "Addison, you're the only person I've ever felt close enough to even—I didn't want to scare you away."

"I'm not scared. I'm disappointed."

"It's not like drawing and keeping a secret about what you want to do when you grow up, it's—"

"I don't care what it is," She flicks the paper in my hand. "What hurts the most is you didn't trust me enough to tell me. I thought...I thought—it doesn't matter." She turns and takes a step before I grab her arm. "Let go of me."

I do. She starts walking away from me, her pace quickening. "Addison, wait," I call out.

She doesn't. I ball up the piece of paper and throw it on the ground.

I watch Addison walk past her brother as she walks out of my life. He doesn't try to stop her. He looks to see where she came from and his eyes lock onto mine. I pick up the balled evidence and shove it into my backpack. From across the courtyard, Naya is staring at me. I want to run to her, grab her by the throat, and squeeze every bit of life from her for ruining one of the best things that has ever happened to me. At the same time, I want to thank her, because this will make the next 216 days easier. The lie sounds very good, but it's still a lie.

But, I stand frozen. And like some sick game, Aiden, Naya, and me—the three of us—stand point to point in a wicked triangle. One set of pale green eyes and one set of violet glare at me with such hatred and revulsion. The feelings are so mutual, and a harsh laugh barks from my throat.

~~~

I only have one more class to go. Addison wasn't in any of my afternoon classes; she must have gone home. I've tried to text and call her a thousand times and every time nothing from her end. I just want to apologize, then I can and will move on. A shove to my back sends me slamming into the lockers. My books and folders skid across the floor, homework and notes litter around me. Mumbled conversations cease. Moments ago the busy hall was a jumble of laughs, words, and shuffling feet. Now, complete silence pervades the space. When I look up, all eyes are on me. I duck as Aiden comes at me full force, his arm reaching out with his hand balled in a tight grip around itself. I'm able to get my balance just in time to ward off and prevent his fist from bashing my face. I catch it in my hand and push him back into the gawking crowd.

He raises his hand—his pointer finger is his new weapon of choice—drilling it in my direction. "You think you can come here and do whatever the hell you want. Well, you can't." His head shakes back and forth, reinforcing his words and I can hear the seething hatred for me in his voice. Suddenly, Addison is between us.

He turns on her and I immediately step between them. He can say, and try to do whatever he wants to me, but I'll be damned if he thinks he can get to her. He throws his head back and forces out a dry, sour laugh. "Oh, so you're her almighty protector now?" he asks.

"Does she need protection from her brother?"

He doesn't answer. I see Naya from the corner of my eye. She's like a statue waiting, hovering nearby—like the one in the cemetery, waiting for the perfect moment to blurt out the secret I hide behind. To break down the wall I keep up with one word— "freak." I ignore her. My brain shifts to Addison, she must still care, still want to be with me if she's here, between me and her brother who wants to beat the shit out of me.

"Don't let her good girl, quiet attitude fool ya. She's the bitch who always gets her way."

His words are like ice cubes sliding down my back. I feel

myself readying for the punch of my life, the one in the last round for the title when Addison's hand touches my back, attempting to warm the words that chill my spine. Her touch, as much as I love it, is nowhere close to simmering the anger that boils inside of me. Her voice is soft and light behind me, "No, Erik." I want to ignore her plea for peace, but it's Addison. She comes around to my side and says, "Please don't." But the urge to knock him to the floor is overwhelming. "Erik," she says.

"Ha! She's got you whipped," Aiden hollers while holding his chest and laughing. And even though Roy said the same thing to me, from Aiden the words are insulting. "I never thought my sister would give it up to anyone, but it looks like she gave it up to you. That didn't take long."

And that last set of words is all it takes for me to gear up my fist into action and take aim for his face. I don't miss. He goes down and doesn't move for several minutes. A stream of blood runs off his split lip and onto the floor. Addison bends to check her brother. The betrayal I feel is devastating, worse than any punch I could ever receive. She looks up at me and says nothing. Her expression is blank, unreadable...empty. I mouth, "I'm sorry."

She doesn't say anything and looks away, stroking her brother's hair.

An eye for an eye, a betrayal for a betrayal. I want so desperately to touch her, but instead I back away from her and walk back to my locker, pick up my books, and gather my papers. Ash is next to me when I stand up, and I jump back a little, not expecting her small frame to be looming over me.

"You did good," she says and mockingly punches my arm.

"It wasn't planned. Just kind of happened—"

"Who cares? You know, I wasn't sure for a second there, and I was ready to send Rip in for the assist." She laughs. "But you handled yourself." At hearing his name, Rip walks over to her side. He gives me knuckles; I'm reluctant but hold out my fist.

"Man, you laid him out—"

Alex and Brent break through the crowd and stop at their friend's body. "What the hell?" Alex yells.

"Hey guys. What's up?" Ash says. She just became my spokesperson for the event. She looks down at Aiden and shrugs. "Yeah...well, you're a little too late to be coming to your friend's rescue."

Alex takes a step toward me.

"Enough!" Mr. Tauras yells. He's on us a little too late but the crowd instantly disperses as soon as they hear his voice. And the hall livens up again to the way it was before the action started, only this time, everyone's talking about what they just saw. Motioning to Alex and Brent, he says "Pick him up and get him to the clinic." He looks at me and says, "You, to the principal's office. Now!"

Addison, through tears she's trying to hold back, helps with Aiden and goes with Brent and Alex to the clinic. I finish gathering my stuff. No matter the punishment, it was completely worth it. It might all be worth it.

On my way to the office, I get a mixture of smiles and sneers and a lot of pointed fingers in my direction. Aiden is the quarterback, and even I have to admit, he's good. He's brought many wins home for the school and even a couple championships. But, he's a cocky asshole and people know that, too.

Principal Tacker is a huge football fan. Not good for me. His secretary is shaking her head when I come into the office; I guess the word spread fast. Thoughts of detention, inside suspension, out-of-school suspension, or worse...expulsion, start running through my head. I bet if I clocked anyone else besides the quarterback and sent him to the clinic, I wouldn't be here. Or maybe I would.

"Go on in, he's waiting for you," the secretary says. Her wrinkled skin is the color of the vanilla pudding they serve in the cafeteria and her hair reminds me of my mom's pineapple upside down cake. As I walk past her, I get a whiff of flowers, like the

205

dying ones in the cemetery. I want to cover my nose, but instead I settle for holding my breath. She tilts her pineapple head, gesturing to the office behind her. I hike up my backpack and prepare myself for whatever awaits me behind that door.

He sits on the other side of his desk in a big black chair. His form is statue perfect in front of the large windows silhouetting his intimidating size. I put my hand over my eyes to shield the sun to try to see him better. Total scare tactic; he wants to get a look at what he's dealing with before he lets me really see him.

"Let me close these." He reaches around and closes the blinds. My eyes take a minute to adjust and I look around. I'm in a sea of framed degrees and awards. They cover every inch of the walls. "Mr. Davenport, please," Principal Tacker says, motioning me to take the chair across from him. I sit. I decide not to say anything until he asks me a direct question and stare at the silver hair that wafts perfectly on top of his head. He must spend hours in the mirror each morning perfecting it. I have the urge to pat it down, just to see it bounce back into place. "We haven't officially met, and I'm ashamed to say, I'm sorry for that. But, I'll also say, I'm even more sorry for you, that our first encounter is under these circumstances." He leans back in his leather chair and steeples his fingers.

Reading the degrees, it looks as if he's graduated from everywhere and majored in every field. A degree in psychology from Florida State hangs above one from University of Florida for business. I thought it was sacrilegious to attend both of those schools, but what do I know. Another degree in engineering from Alabama is plastered on top of an award given to him by President Bush. And I wonder why he chose to be a principal here? "Aiden has recently expressed concern to me, regarding his safety when in your company." My mouth falls open and I do my best not to laugh. "Any reason he should feel this way?"

Realizing he's serious, it's time to answer. "No, sir."

"I'm sure you're well aware by now, Aiden is our star

quarterback." I don't answer. I'm not going to play this game; just give me my punishment and let me be on my way. "Of course you do," he says, a carnivorous grin spreading across his face. "I'm sure you also know that we are currently undefeated and we have Aiden to thank for that. And, I hope for your sake, and his of course, that he's able to play come Friday." He starts to twiddle his thumbs under his steepled triangle. "So, what to do with you now? Obviously, fighting is strictly prohibited and the penalties are severe for breaking that rule, rather, that *law* here."

He's expelling me. His degrees blur together and I lean forward to put my elbows on my knees and my head in my hands. This isn't happening. I can't get expelled my senior year of high school. My life is slowly crashing down around me, each wave defeating everything I've tried to do.

Principal Tacker's voice explodes in my head, crushing my self-deprecating thoughts; I lift my head to look at him. "Now, I know it's hard to adjust to a new school, starting in the middle of the year, in your senior year, no less. But, I will not tolerate that kind of primitive behavior in this school." He leans forward on his desk and slides a sheet of paper toward him. Reaching into the pocket of his pressed shirt, he pulls out reading glasses and perches them on his nose. "Since this is your first offense, I expect it to be your last." He pauses and looks directly into my eyes, branding this statement into my head and letting me know he's letting me off lightly. In turn, I should be kneeling down to him with gratitude for this merciful act.

He slides the paper to my side of the desk and I see the checked punishment:

Out-of-School Suspension for (3) days. I let out a whoosh of hot air and in a low voice say, "Thank you," and add, "sir."

"Your suspension starts today," he says. "I'll see you back here on Friday and hey…who knows, maybe I'll see you at the football game." He stands and I take that as my indication that I can go and walk back into the reception area.

"He went easy on you this time. You don't want to screw up again. Trust me on that," pineapple head says as I walk by her desk. "Better keep yourself in check with the rules around here." I don't acknowledge her. All I know is I'll never eat pineapple upside down cake again.

I stop at the mini-mart for my usual chips and a Coke before going to work. When I come out, Aiden's car is parked in the parking lot, but no Aiden. A loud thunderous crack sounds on the side of the building. I follow the noise of another deafening crack. And realize it's the sound of metal hitting metal.

*CRACK!*

Aiden, Alex, and Brent are beating my motorcycle with a metal pipe. "Hey guys. What's up?" I say smiling, knowing they want me to react. And I want to, I want to run over and beat the shit out of all of them, but I use everything I've got in me to keep my cool.

"Not much. What's up yourself?" Aiden shrugs. Half of his grin is slightly fatter than earlier. He swings back the pipe and smashes the headlight.

"Oh. Not much," I say, as nonchalantly as I can even though I'm boiling inside.

"We were just waiting for you," he says as he raises the pipe over his head and slams it down on the side mirror. It crashes to the ground.

"I see you guys know how to keep yourselves busy."

His smile falls into a sneer. "What the hell did you do to my sister?" He winds up again and the other side mirror takes the blow.

"I don't think it's any of your business."

"I'm guessing you think my warnings weren't clear enough or you don't give a shit." He throws down the pipe and takes out a knife, flipping it open. He takes a step toward me, but I don't move. He kneels by the tire of my motorcycle and stabs the front tire, then the back. I'm close enough to hear the air hissing out.

"Yeah, I'd go with option B on that one," I say. I don't like the direction this is going. They came with an agenda, and I'm next on the list after they're done destroying my motorcycle. I know I'm not helping the situation with my smart-ass comments, but I can't back down and show them I want to run like hell in the opposite direction.

"Maybe you *are* as stupid as you look," Aiden says.

"I'm thinking this isn't about your sister so much, especially seeing the way you treat her like shit, and more about me knocking you on your ass today in front of the whole school."

"Yeah, I'll admit, Addison, is a pain in my ass, but you..." he trails off, and pushes up his sleeves. "I think it'll just be easier if I show you." He nods to Alex and Brent, and they're on me in seconds, each one grabbing one of my arms. My Coke drops to the ground and combusts, soda spraying everywhere. There's no point in struggling, they're as big as I am and their grips are tight. Aiden folds the knife and puts it back in his pocket. At least there's a chance he may not kill me.

"It takes three of you? You can't show me on your own?"

"It's just more fun this way," Aiden says, more confident now. We're face to face and I can see the punch I landed on him earlier left his jaw swollen and bruised.

"Sure it is. And easier, pussy," I taunt.

He spits, and a thick hot spray of saliva splatters onto my face. I turn to wipe it on my shirt but Alex and Brent are holding my arms too tight.

"I'm sure I heard you wrong," he says.

"Will you stop acting like you're deaf whenever you're being insulted?"

He pulls back his fist and strikes. The blow lands on my upper cheek near my eye. The bone explodes and fireworks blaze inside of my head and eyes. Another blow to my face, this time my jaw takes the punishment. I taste blood in my mouth. When I look up, he's coming at me again. An uppercut to my gut sends me doubling over. They release my arms and I fall to the ground gasping for breath. I hear the pipe slamming down on my motorcycle, again. It would probably be louder if it weren't for the ringing in my ears. I spit out the blood pooling in my mouth.

"Don't talk, stare, or even look in my sister's direction again. Or, there will be more beatings."

I wish I could laugh at him, but I can't breathe. The air isn't going in or out of my lungs. "Assholes," I say in a low grumble only because I haven't caught my breath, not for lack of conviction.

"Have a nice day, dick," Aiden says.

I ignore him. I ease my way to my feet using his car for a crutch. He kicks my legs out from under me and I go down hard.

The Mustang's engine rumbles to life. Aiden guns the gas and the engine roars above me. He screeches out of the parking lot.

I crawl to my trashed motorcycle and sit there until I catch my breath. The frame is dented to hell, the gauges are smashed, mirrors, tires, all trashed. I bet I don't look much better. I can feel my eye slowing swelling shut. I pick up a piece of the mirror. I'm afraid what's going to be looking back, but slowly turn it over. Oli is going to freak.

When I feel steady enough on my feet, I go back into the mini-mart and get some ice.

"Holy—what happened?" Vern asks.

"Nothing. I just need some ice."

"Yeah, that looks like nothing all right. I'll get ya a bag from the back." He disappears in the back. He returns a minute later. "Here." He hands me a bag of ice and I put it over my upper cheek and wait for the freeze to numb the pain. "Who did that to you?"

"Some jerk that doesn't like his life too much and decided to take it out on me."

Vern laughs, and says, "Yep, that's happened to me before, too."

I laugh with him, and the release feels good. But the motion makes my chest hurt and I wonder if I have a broken rib.

"Man, you're gonna hurt tomorrow."

"I hurt now."

"Then tomorrow, you're gonna wish you were dead."

"Thanks," I say.

He holds up his hands in defense. "I'm just sayin'."

"I gotta get to work. Can I leave my motorcycle in the back, and I'll get it this weekend?"

"Man, they trashed that, too?"

"It looks worse than my face."

"Damn. That's bad. Yeah, no problem. I'll help you get it back there. Hey, I gotta skateboard in the storeroom, you wanna use it?"

"Sure."

When I come out of the mini-mart, Naya is sitting in a car staring at me through the windshield. Her hand hurries to cover her mouth. I look away, ignoring her. As I drop the skateboard on the sidewalk, the driver's door open.

"What happened?" she asks.

"Nothing." I turn away from her and put my foot on the skateboard and push off.

"I'm sorry I told Addison. I didn't mean to—I thought she'd—" she yells broken sentences behind me.

I stop, turn and look directly at her. "No, you're not." I bark out a harsh laugh. "You knew exactly what you were doing." I put my arms out. "Congratulations, it worked, I lost Addison, got the shit beaten out of me, and my motorcycle is totaled. Your little fit of vengeance has taken everything from me. There's nothing left. But, I want to thank you."

"For what?" Her eyes brighten.

"Reminding me why I'm really here and that it's temporary." I push off on the skateboard.

211

# CHAPTER 29

"Damn, son. Who'd you piss off?" Roy asks.

I'm going to be drilled by everyone who sees my face for the next few days, so I'm going to have to minimize the on-lookers.

"You should see the other guy," I say.

"Well, if he looks worse than you, I better start diggin' his grave," he says, letting me keep my dignity. "That's gonna hurt tomorrow."

"So, I've been told." I touch my cheek and can almost feel the hue of purple decorating my face.

"Seriously now, who did that to you?"

"Aiden Bailey."

"The quarterback?"

"That's the one."

"I never did like that boy, a spoiled…never mind." He doesn't have to continue, our thoughts are the same on that asshole.

"You sure you're able to work looking like that?"

"Yeah, maybe I'll look a little better in a while and Oli won't freak out as much."

Roy chuckles and says, "Son, I doubt that on both counts." He's right, of course. I put the skateboard in the golf cart. "Where's your motorcycle?" He doesn't give me a chance to answer, "Oh, hell, he got a hold of that, too."

"Yeah. Can you help me later with it? It's behind the mini-mart. I want to get it back to my house so I can work on fixing it."

"You got it. We'll load it in the bed of the truck. Instead of bringing it to your house, we can take it to Donny's garage. I've known him for a long time. He can fix it for ya, if ya want."

"Yeah, that'd be good. Thanks."

"Help me get these tools on the golf cart and I'll go get the backhoe. Meet me over in section 3, lot 5. You'll see Frederick Johnson's grave, that was Maureen's husband. She'll be buried next to him tomorrow." He walks over to the backhoe and climbs on. "I started digging it this morning, but Bulldog's giving me problems. Let's hope she holds up long enough to finish this grave or we'll be doing it the old fashion way and trust me that ain't no fun."

I pile boards, a shovel, and gloves into the golf cart and drive to section 3 of the cemetery. Some of my frustration and anger thaws into self-pity. When I get to the grave, I get off the golf cart and unload the supplies. The backhoe rumbles in the distance, then it goes quiet. I slump down against the tree at the foot of Frederick's grave and wait for Roy. The sky is darkening; gray clouds float by shutting out the sun, and a hint of cool air blows across my damaged face. The physical pain is nothing compared to the emotional pain of losing Addison, and I hate that she weakens me like that. But it's not like I could be mad at her; it's not her fault I'm a freak.

Another thin wisp of air drifts off the nearby pond, and I watch a dragonfly dance and shift on the invisible breeze. At the base of the tree and only inches from my hand is another—its colors exactly match the one on the inside of my wrist—and it's dead. As I nudge the lifeless insect, I can't help the energy that begins to writhe in every one of muscles. The release of it will bring relief only for the briefest moment, but I want to feel it so desperately. I can't deny it as the warm current quickens into a raging fire racing through my veins, thrashing against my bones, and lashing out and beating against every organ in my body. I'm filled with pure exhilarated

213

madness and all of the emotions that accompany it as I touch the dead dragonfly.

"Holy God."

Startled by his voice, I jerk upright; the dizziness is faint but there. I never heard him come up behind me. It's too late. The dragonfly takes flight and darts off into the air towards the pond.

"I've seen a lot of sh—stuff in my time. But, I ain't never in all my days…"

Panic and horror pound in my chest. Was I in such a trance that I didn't hear the roar of the backhoe? Roy just witnessed the only thing I wish he hadn't, and it feels worse than being pounded by Aiden. And the wound, deeper still, will have its own consequences. I can't think of anything to say. *Defend yourself*, I think, but I can't speak.

Then stupidly, I ask, "How long were you standing there?"

"Long enough."

"Roy, I…ah…it's not…" He shakes his head as if to say don't go there, son. His face is raw with shock, amazement, and bewilderment. And like Naya, he knows exactly what he just saw. I haven't known Roy for very long, but if I've learned anything, he was right when he told me nothing gets past him.

"Roy," I try again, "Please…I—"

He holds up a hand to stop me. I close my mouth without another word. "Son, you don't have to worry 'bout me. I'm not going to tell a soul, that ain't my place." I believe him, he's a man of his word. Gratefully, I nod. "That was…" he points to the ground where the dragonfly was and then lifts his finger pointing to the sky where it flew off towards, "nothing short of a miracle. Maybe one day you can tell me, hell, show me how in the world you did that." He points again aimlessly to the sky.

I leave his request hanging unanswered between us.

He claps his hands together and rubs. "What do ya say we get the rest of this hole dug so we can go home?" He climbs down into the half-dug grave. I pick up my shovel and join him in the ditch. He never again speaks of what he witnessed.

~~~

"Oh my God!" Oli's hand rushes to her mouth. She jumps off the porch swing and hurries down the steps stopping right in front of me.

"It's no big deal," I say.

"No big deal? Did you see your face?" She doesn't let me answer before she asks, "Who did that to you?"

"It doesn't matter. Trust me, it won't happen again." I put my hands on her shoulders. "Oli, really, don't be worried. After I take a shower, I'll look brand new." I kiss her cheek.

Roy gets out of the truck, nods to Oli and says, "Hello, Olivine."

"Hi." The word seeps out as she continues to stare at my face in disbelief. "Erik, where's your bike?"

"It looks worse than my face. Roy and I just dropped it off at his friend's garage."

Oli looks at Roy then. "Thank you."

"Least I can do," he says. "Well, ya'll take care now." He turns to leave.

"Roy," says Oli, "would you like to stay for dinner?"

"That'd be nice. Thank you."

~~~

The steam from the shower fills the bathroom. I rub a circle into the fogged mirror and get a good look at the damage. My right eye is almost completely swollen shut, the right half of my mouth is split and fat, and hues of purple and red stain my cheek and chin. Aiden can definitely throw a punch, especially while his friends hold me still. I watch the steam swirl and shift around me and it looks like a hundred souls are being carried away in the mist; for the briefest moment I wish I was one of them.

I shake off the self-pity, turn away from the monster in the mirror, and step into the shower. The hard spray pounds on my back and neck. Water streams down my face over the bruises and gashes and it stings like a thousand bees attacking at once.

I can't take it any longer. The tears that I've forced back all day, folding them into the layers of pride, humiliation, shame, and pain have found their way out and they're hovering at the very edge of my lids. I finally let them come. I lean against the shower wall and cry. I've come to the conclusion that the normal world sucks and I am failing majorly at living in it.

All day, it's been impossible to keep Addison out of my thoughts. Watching her rush to her brother's aid hurt worse than any punch he could have thrown and I push the thought away. I wonder if she knows what he did to me and if she even cares. I've fucked things up so bad with her. The evil hand of love has wrapped itself around my neck neatly and conveniently choking almost everything else to death. And I know without a doubt that I'll do whatever it takes to make it right. Even if she never wants to see me again, I can't have her hate me. I have to fix it. I. Have. To.

There's a knock on the bathroom door and I shut off the water. "Erik, what are you doing? You've been in there forever." I open the door with a towel around my waist. A cloud of steam floats over CeCe.

"Holy Toledo!" Her eyes are huge and her mouth still hanging on the 'O' in Toledo.

"No worries, I'll be as good as new in no time," I say and force a smile.

"Whatever you say." I walk past her and she follows me towards my room. She lowers her voice. "Can I ask you something?" I turn around. "I was thinking today, I know you're supposed to be resting and stuff, but have you brought back anything—you know, lately?"

I think about the dragonfly today. "Not in a long time." I don't know why I lie to her. She lowers her head and nods at the

216

floor. "What's wrong?"

"I guess I'm just missing how things used to be. And I miss watching you do it."

I hug her. "Me too, CeCe. Me, too."

"I miss Naya, too." I stiffen at her words. "She's the only person that understands and I haven't seen her in a long time. I don't think she likes me anymore."

"I'm sure that's not it, she's probably just busy."

"She's probably not gonna come to my party."

Let's hope not.

# CHAPTER 30

¶ open my eyes and then immediately close them. The sun feels especially bright shining through the window. My dreams helped me escape, but it was only temporary.  My thoughts now shift, and flashes of yesterday slam into my head: Aiden, fight, Addison, Naya, freak.

I leave at my normal time in the morning, but instead of going to school, I go to the cemetery, riding the skateboard the couple of miles to get there.

Roy's pickup pulls into the entrance. "You working today or just hiding out?"

"Both," I admit.

He nods once, purses his lips, and hands me the keys to unlock the padlock on the gate. We drive down to the shed. He climbs down from the driver's seat and I jump out from the bed. "Son, your studies better be good, if you're skipping out on a school day."

"They are," I assure him. "But I got suspended until Friday for yesterday."

"For fighting at the mini-mart?"

"No. For punching Aiden at school."

Roy laughs. "You failed to mention that yesterday. I get it now, though. His ego needed some petting, so he did that?" He points to my face.

"Something like that. He doesn't like to fight alone, so he let his friends hold me while he pounded on me."

Roy shakes his head. "I have a hundred names coming to mind for that boy, but I'm gonna be a gentlemen and keep my mouth shut."

"Roy, about yesterday—"

"Listen," he holds up his hand, the other still grasping his suspender, "it's none of my business, fascinating and strange as hell as it may be. But, none of my business."

I squeeze my mouth shut and nod.

He opens the shed. "Come on, grab those tools. I'll meet you at the fountain by the angel in section two. Let's get that thing working again; it hasn't pumped water in a month. Then, after that, we'll take a look at Bulldog. If I can't figure out what's wrong with the damn thing, then I'll call someone."

I walk around the statue that oversees the broken fountain. A bee floats in the still water. I hesitate, but pick up the dead insect. I refuse to give its life back and fight against the energy swelling in my veins. Instead, I hold it by its plump body and tear off its wings. It makes me think of tearing off flower petals to see if she loves you or not. And then I think of Addison. Defeat builds in me, and I throw down the dead bug. I take out my phone and call her. Nothing.

"You alright, son?"

"Yeah. Fine." I try to smother my emotions, shoving them under my mask of bruises.

"I swear this damn pump is cursed, but let's give it a shot anyway."

We spend most of the morning fixing the fountain. I drag the hose over and fill it with water. Finally, the pump starts and water begins to trickle over the side. Roy wipes his brow and checks his watch. "It's almost eleven, let's take a break, then we'll take a look at Bulldog."

The golf cart poses as our picnic bench, and we take out our bagged lunches. "Whatcha got in there?"

I pull out a PB&J. "The usual."

"Ha, that was my usual growing up, too." He holds out a bag of chips. I take some. "Olivine handled your face pretty good last night?"

"Yeah, as good as could be expected, I think. She was a lot more understanding than my mom would have been." I sigh and take a bite of my sandwich.

The morning is quiet, only a few cars come and go visiting their lost loved ones. We eat the rest of our lunch in silence.

"Let's take a look at Bulldog," says Roy.

After two hours, we come up with nothing. "Damn thing won't stay in gear." Roy climbs down from the backhoe. "I'm gonna go make that call. You had better pray while Bulldog is down no one dies." He waves his arm. "Pack up these tools and meet me at the front gates."

Fifteen minutes later, Roy drives up in his truck and parks off to the side. "Walk to the end of the opened gate and start swinging it." As I do, he pumps oil into the hinges with an oil can that looks just like the one from *The Wizard of Oz*, the one they used for Tin Man. It makes a knocking noise every time you pull the trigger. *Knock. Knock. Knock.* "Open the gate, here comes a car."

I walk open the gate and as I turn around, Addison's jeep is driving through them. "Shit."

"Shit, what?" asks Roy.

"It's Addison. I don't want her to see me like this." I duck behind the cover of Roy's pick-up.

"I'm guessing she's the reason for your new look." Roy says.

"One of them. Aiden is her twin brother."

He returns a twisted grin and single nod. Addison drives

through the gates and parks on the side of the road. She gets out, and I watch her come right towards my hiding place. She's wearing tight jeans tucked into her cowboy boots, a wide belt with a big silver buckle, and a tank top. Reluctantly, I turn away from her.

"Hey." Her voice is strained but edged with kindness, and at the very sound of it, I want to grab her in my arms and pull her to me. But I only turn around keeping my head down so my hat still conceals my face from her and echo her hey. "Aiden's been bragging about what he did to you." She plays with the heart on grandmother's bracelet. "I tried to call you, to see how you were doing, but it kept going to voice mail. So, I thought I'd take a chance and come here."

I take my phone out of my pocket and see that it's dead.

"It was nothing," I say, pulling my hat a little lower over my face. It's so hard to stand here so close to her and not touch her.

"Are you going to look at me?"

"Are you still mad at me?"

"Erik, that's not fair."

I look up without thinking. "Addison, I—"

She takes a sharp intake of breath. "Oh my God." She reaches out to touch my wounds, stopping just before she makes contact. "Erik, I'm so sorry."

I take her outstretched hand before she can take it back. She doesn't protest and lets it rest in mine. "This," I say, pointing to my face, "I could take a thousand times over. But, this," I touch her heart and my chest, "what happened between us...hurting you, hurts a hell of a lot worse."

"I never even gave you a chance to explain, I'm—"

I press my finger to her lips. I don't want to hear her apologies. "Don't go there. I should have told you."

She nods. And then giggles a tiny noise.

"What's so funny?" I ask.

"Not funny. A realization." Her fingers weave between mine.

"Of what?"

"How much I've fallen for you. And if here," she puts her hand on my chest, "hurts worse than your face, you've fallen pretty hard, too."

"You can definitely say that." I comb my fingers through her hair resting my hand on the back of her head and pull her to me. "Shit!"

"What?" she says.

"I want to kiss you so bad, but…" I point to my lip.

She gets on her toes and kisses the side of mouth that's not inflated. I hate Aiden even more right now for preventing me from kissing Addison, but then again, if it weren't for him breaking up my face, she might not be here right now.

"Listen, why don't I come by after work, pick you up and— crap, I don't have anything to pick you up with."

"He was bragging about that, too. I'll come back after you're done—"

"Y'all is bringing a tear to my eye," says Roy. "Son, would you just take off now." He motions to Addison. "Swoop her up in your arms and go, or whatever the hell you kids do nowadays."

I nod and smile at Roy. "I'll see you in the morning."

"Well, I won't be here. Your Oli and I are having coffee."

"What?"

"You heard me." He clicks the oilcan a couple times. Then reaches in his pocket and throws me a set of keys. "Be here by eight. That's when Old Henry's coming to work on Bulldog."

"You got it." As Addison and I walk to her Jeep, I turn and say, "Hey, Roy."

"Yeah?"

"Heads up…she likes tea."

He smiles that rare smile I've only seen a couple times and tips his hat to me. I watch him tuck away the grin that escaped his lips and his face melts back into his work.

222

~~~

"He's a good guy, huh?" Addison says as we pull out of the cemetery.

"Yeah. Really good." I smile. "You know we worked all morning together and he never once said anything about having a date with my grandma."

"I think it's cute."

"Cute, huh?"

"Yeah, cute." Her face is glowing she looks so happy. "Want to go to the lake?"

"Yeah, I have some things I need to…tell you." I almost say show you, but think better of it.

She smiles. "I'd like that."

We pull off the side of the road. "Grab the blanket in the back," she says.

The dragonflies dart around in my gut, hitting the walls of my stomach; I'm getting ready to let her into my world. I'm nervous as hell that she's going to run. Run so far and so fast away from me that I'll never see her again. And, a small part, smaller than it's ever been, wants her to hate me, push me away, hard, so that I can return to my original plan of getting out of here and back on stage where I really belong.

She takes off her boots and sits on the blanket next to me. Here it goes. I plunge into the depths of those green eyes and tell her everything, especially the part that when I bring back the dead it's very, very, real.

"I was nine years old when I first brought back the dead." I huff a laugh as I think back at that day and continue. "I didn't even realize what I had done."

From the corner of my eye I watch Addison's face turn toward me as I begin to tell the tale of how I became a freak, but I don't dare look at her. I don't want to see her spooked or possibly accepting eyes. And I don't know which I'd rather see at this moment.

"We were driving to the next town for my dad's next show when we had a blowout. We pulled to the side of the road and I followed my dad out of the RV to check it out. It was in the middle of summer and the air was stifling, like there was a shortage of oxygen. The day was so bright and the heat animated the highway. I looked down to shield my eyes from the glare on the road. Littering the asphalt were dead dragonflies. I watched the black birds pace along the median waiting for their chance to claim their next meal.

"I picked up one of the dragonflies and put it in my hand. Its huge dead eyes took up most of the space on its bulbous head. When I held it up to the sun, rays of light shone through its wings. Hundreds of tiny uneven squares lit up as if they had their own light as they let the brightness of the day race through them. I brought the dead creature close to me, to inspect it even more closely and a burst of something I've never felt before surged through me. Scorching heat raced through my veins, and something else I've never felt before roared throughout my body. The nerve endings at the tips of my finger started to purr.

"I still held the dragonfly and with complete horrified amazement, I watched as its wings began to pulse, slowly at first, then faster, faster than my own heart. They beat into a rhythm that took it into flight. As if studying me, it hovered over me and just like that, it was gone. I didn't understand what was happening, or what I had done, but I knew I wanted it to happen again. The feeling was amazing and exhilarating, nameless and unexplainable, but nonetheless incredible.

I look at Addison then, and her face is frozen and unreadable.

I continue. "I remember thinking, this isn't real, it can't be. But when I looked up, my dad had this look of astonishment on his face, so I knew he had seen it, too; I didn't imagine it. He didn't say anything, only bent down, handed me another dead dragonfly, and silently nodded for me to do it again. I did.

"He grabbed my hands and examined them, tracing the lines on my palm with his fingers and turning them over and back again. I didn't know what he was looking for. Nothing was there. He picked up another dragonfly and pulled me into the RV. I remember my mom asking, "Did you fix it?" And my dad said, "Fix what?" "The Tire," she said. And then like he just remembered why we went outside in the first place, he told her no, but it was alright, something about it was one of the dual tires.

"He still held my hands as he sat down on the couch and lowered his head into his hands, never letting go of mine. I looked at my mom; I didn't know what to say or do, so I stayed quiet. Then, my dad said, "You need to see something. Don't ask questions because I won't have answers. I don't understand it, but it's very, very real."

I shrug slow and high and offer Addison a small smile. "And that's how I came to realize what I could do."

She never interrupts or asks any questions. She only looks at me, studying me. Intrigued? Scared? Is she going to make a run for it?

And even if I don't know what she's thinking, I can't help but keep talking. I've never shared this with anyone, the release of it all is overwhelming and awesome, and after eight years of keeping it bottled up, it's liberating. I tell her, "When I realized what I could do, what I was capable of...it made me feel scared, hysterical, ecstatic, like a superhero and God-like, all at once. I could actually bring back something that was dead, and I thought I had the entire world at the tip of my fingertips, and I was only nine."

"Do you miss it?" she asks.

"More than life itself. It's part of who I am." I laugh. "I know that sounds crazy, missing the life of a freak. But, I miss my friends, and the thrill of being on stage, the way the crowd looked at me as I performed my trick." I air quote the word trick. "Mostly, I miss bringing back the dead, to feel the jolt of energy and the heat that

225

courses through my veins and bones."

"After you graduate, are you going back to that life?" she asks in a small voice.

"Yes." There's no hesitation in my answer and it feels right.

Addison stands. She's leaving. That's it, but it was only fair to tell her.

"I'm going to go for a short walk, process everything you've just told me. Wait here, I promise I'll be back."

I think I want to throw up as I watch her get up and walk down to the shore. She walks the line of the wet sand letting the small waves lap her feet. She bends down and picks up something, puts it in her hand and looks at it. I watch her as she stands motionless and looks across the water. My heart is beating so fast, too fast. I can't fill my lungs with enough air. The dragonflies inside me are pounding against my rib cage and I feel like I'm covered in ice, unable to take my eyes off her as I wait to hear if she still wants to be with me, the freak, after everything I just told her.

She turns away from the water and walks toward me. Kneeling in front of me, she looks down at her closed palm and slowly opens it. "Show me."

~~~

A small fiddler crab lay on her palm.

I look at her and she meets my eyes. At this moment, I have no reservations about showing her what I can do, and I want nothing more than to open up to her even more than I already have. Without saying anything, I reach deep into the crevices for the thing I miss most. And my body immediately responds. The heat comes, slowly at first, and then faster, whirling in my veins as it finds its way into my fingertips. I touch the crab and in seconds, its claw snaps shut.

Addison takes a sharp intake of breath. We watch as its eyes and legs begin to move and then the smaller claw opens and closes. She looks at me as if she doesn't know what to do next.

Slight dizziness settles over me as I lower her hand toward

226

the sand. The crab scurries off her palm and walking sideways along the sand looks for a hole to hide in.

She looks at me, her mouth opens, just a little, and her eyes are huge. "That was…amazing."

"I'm sorry I didn't tell you. When I met you, I never wanted to be normal so bad in all my life."

Her striking green eyes are muted from the tears that are pooling in them. They threaten, at any second, to cascade over her lashes and fall onto her cheek. "I'm glad you're not," she says and kisses me lightly on the lips. "Can I ask you something?"

"Anything."

"How does Naya know? Why did she try to use your past against you?"

I have nothing to hide from her anymore. And as the dragonflies finally lay still in my gut, I tell her how Naya has seen me perform and the real reason she invited me to dinner.

Addison doesn't say anything for a long time. Then she says, "Can you blame her?"

"No. But I can't help her, either."

# Chapter 31

$F$og surrounds me. No. Not fog. Souls.

They separate from the bodies they once inhabited, leaving thousands of corpses writhing at my feet. Tendrils of vapor swirl and swoop all around me. I run, but it's no use, they're everywhere.

In some places where the fog thins, I watch in terror as the wet bones thrash under the mist. I slip and fall into the broken bodies and scramble on my hands and knees to get up, but they—no, *she*—won't stop reaching out and grabbing for me, pulling me back down. Her face, Madam Selena, Naya's mother, screams and begs me to bring her back to life. Breaking free from her, I'm able to climb to my feet. I look to the heavens and a million dragonflies fill the sky. Iridescent blue and green bodies are being carried through the night by paper-thin wings. I feel their multifaceted eyes bearing into my back as I run from her, believing only for a second that I can escape.

I run and I run, but she's everywhere: every slivering body under me and around me has her face, every floating soul with its gaping mouth is her, all of the pleading wails, and even the soaring dragonflies all have her face. I race past tombstones and statues. I'm in a cemetery. When I look over my shoulder, nothing has moved, all the things I'm running from are in exactly the same place. Addison is there, on the other side, across from all of the bodies and souls of Selena. She's reaching out to me as Aiden pulls her back. I reach out but she's too far, the gap is too wide. I see my name form on her lips followed by the word *"goodbye."*

Gasping for air, I tear the sheets away from my thrashing heart. I sit up and try to fill my lungs with the air they desperately want and need. Short inhales of breath are all I can manage. I focus on breathing normally. I lie back down on the damp sheets and feel my body begin to relax. What the hell was that all about?

*Guilt.*

~~~

I pull hard on the wooden door. The church is thankfully empty, no services on a Thursday morning at seven. I slide into one of the pews. I'm not sure why I've come here: to ask God to erase the nightmare, beg him to forgive me for not being strong enough to save Selena, and ask him to take her from Naya as painlessly as possible? I close my eyes, fold my arms on the bench in front of me, and rest my head in the crook of them.

The door to the church opens. Footsteps walk beside me up the center aisle.

Breathe, I tell myself; just breathe. The scent of burning wax from the candles floats around me. It reminds me of the burning vanilla and lavender candles Mom burns, and I sense comfort in that thought. I relish in the feeling and my body finally begins to retreat to that calm place.

I stand and look at the front of the church. Naya is kneeling in front of the statue there. I turn to leave, to sneak out. I'm almost to the door when she grabs my arm and spins me around. Her violet eyes are almost black in the dim light. I feel as if my outer shell melts away and the reason for my being here is laid out for her to see. I don't trust myself to speak.

"Do you enjoy seeing me on my knees? Begging to a God I don't even believe in?" Her apologies have mutated into anger as she waves her arms around the church. "This is what you've reduced me

229

to." She pushes her hair away from her face. "But I don't know another way. I can't let her die."

I yank my arm away. "Naya, I'm not the one killing your mom—"

"No! You're the one not saving her, either."

"You make it very difficult to feel sorry for you."

Her laugh is humorless and grotesque. "What? You think I want your pity?"

"No, you want something I can't give you."

"Yes you can!" She squeezes her eyes shut and opens them slowly.

I turn and walk toward the door and push it open; light floods the inside. I don't look back to see Naya. I try to erase the guilt I feel. I wish it were as easy as erasing death.

# CHAPTER 32

"It's my birthday! It's my birthday!" CeCe sings as she dances around the kitchen.

"It's Friday! It's Friday!" I sing back.

She stops and puts her hands on her hips. "Hey, that comes every week, my birthday only comes once a year."

I laugh. "Alright, you got a point there."

A horn blares. Addison is sitting in the driveway waiting for me.

"I gotta go. I'll see you tonight and we'll celebrate." I squeeze her small body and pick her up.

"I can't breathe."

"Hey," I say, and she looks at me. "I know Mom and Dad wish they could be here."

"I know." She shrugs. "It's okay."

I run out to Addison's Jeep and get in the passenger side. "Hi," she says.

"Hi."

"I missed you."

"Me, too. Come here." I pull her to me. Her lips are soft as usual, and as the gloss slides across my still swollen mouth, I wince.

"I'm sorry," she whispers against my face. And I pull her tighter to me.

231

*Knock! Knock! Knock!* The banging on the window startles us both and we look up, alarmed. CeCe is staring at us through the window.

I unzip the window. "How long have you been standing there?" I ask her. Before it's completely unzipped, CeCe's top-half is through the window.

"Hi, Addison."

"Hi, CeCe."

"Did you know today is my birthday?"

"No."

"Well it is—"

"CeCe," I say, "slow down."

"Happy birthday," says Addison.

"Thank you. I'm nine and we're having a party tonight, just a small family party, but can you please come? Please."

Addison looks at me, I'm guessing for approval, and I shrug, leaving it up to her. She smiles at me and then spreading her smile even wider just for CeCe, she looks at the birthday girl, and says "Count me in."

"Yay!" CeCe says. She jimmies herself out of the Jeep, her feet hitting the ground. She skips to the front door, turns around and waves with the biggest smile on her face.

"Okay, where were we before that small burst of excitement came through the window?" I ask Addison, leaning in for another kiss.

She pushes me away, and says, "Later, we got to get to school." And with that, she backs down the drive.

We pull into the parking lot; it's packed with people dressed in red, white, and blue for the big game tonight. As we start toward the main building, Candace runs up alongside Addison. Words and laughs start spewing out of her mouth.

"Okay, so tonight after at the game, we'll meet in our usual spot at the lake." Candace has been very clingy to Addison since

Tiffany's death.

Addison cuts Candace off and says, "I'm not going to the game—"

"What?" says Candace, panic in her voice, like her world has just been shattered.

"I have a party to go to," Addison says, brushing her hair away from her face.

"What party?" asks Candace, now sounding offended that she wasn't invited.

"CeCe's, Erik's little sister. It's her birthday."

"Oh…kay. Well, that sounds fun," Candace says, boredom dripping off every word.

"Yup, it sure does," Addison agrees, leaving out the sarcasm.

"Alright, well whatever. Guess I'll see ya later."

"You don't have to go tonight. I'll tell CeCe you had something come up—"

"I'm going to CeCe's birthday party and that's final." Her words are stern and undisputable. And I'm glad. I wrap my arm around her and we walk together to class.

"Hey." Ignoring the familiar voice, I keep walking. "I'm talking to you!" Aiden's voice explodes from down the hall.

Still ignoring him, I send Addison off to class; she doesn't need to be part of this again. None of us do, but I guess according to Aiden, the quarterback who's used to calling the shots, we do. For me, ducking out is not an option. I turn on him and watch him come toward me; Alex and Brent are at his side.

Again, all discussion and movement in the hall ceases, and all eyes are on the four of us. Aiden closes in on my personal space. "You are going to die," he whispers so only I can hear.

"Yeah, one day, you're right. But I can promise you, today is not that day," I say in just as low a voice as his, never taking my eyes off his. Alex and Brent start to close in, just in time for Principal Tacker to make his rounds.

233

"Good morning, gentleman," he says. Aiden and his defense back away from me. The onlookers move along and we're the only ones standing in the hall with the principal. "How's everyone doing this morning?"

"Fine, sir. Everything's fine here," Aiden stammers. He runs his hand over his short hair, blowing off the moment of intense steam that was so prevalent in his threat of killing me less than a minute ago.

Principal Tacker leans into Aiden and puts his arm around his shoulder. "Son, I'm just assuming, and you don't have to tell me one way or another, that that," Principal Tacker points to my face, "is your work." Aiden doesn't say anything. Mr. Tacker continues. "Now, I love football almost as much as my own family. And, I love watching you bring it home every week. But, I will bench your ass if you keep up this obnoxious and unsportsmanlike behavior. Do you understand exactly what I'm telling you?"

Aiden looks away from the silver haired man, and says, "Yeah."

"No," says Principal Tacker unsatisfied with Aiden's response. "When I'm talking to you, you will look at me. And you will answer me with respect. I'll ask again, do you understand exactly what I'm telling you?"

Aiden meets his eyes and says, "Yes, sir, I understand." He actually looks more pissed off at his number one fan right now than he does at me. I stifle the burst of laughter I feel building up inside of me.

Principal Tacker sets his eyes on Alex and Brent. "That goes for the two of you as well. Do you understand?"

"Yes, sir," they say together.

Now it's my turn. His strong gaze lands on me and before he can ask, I say, "I understand, sir."

The bell rings. "You guys better get to class." He waits for us to disperse from the area before going on his way.

I notice a rush of relief fall over Addison's face when I walk into class.

"Nice of you to join us," Mr. Tauras says.

I pass Addison on the way to my desk and lightly squeeze her shoulder conveying everything is fine. Her hand brushes mine and I know she understands what I'm trying to tell her.

~~~

As soon as the bell rings, Addison is at my side asking what happened after she left. I tell her the gist of it. "Good ole Tacker saves the day," she says, mocking the *Superman* song. "I can't believe he almost took Aiden out of a game, whoa!"

The warning bell rings. "I gotta make a run for it if I'm gonna get to class on time." I kiss her on the cheek and bolt down the hall backwards. She gives me a small wave in return. Still watching her, she turns and I see her rub her temple.

~~~

At lunch, I ask Addison about her migraines. She says she's fine and takes my hand trying to reassure me.

"Is there room enough for us or are we interrupting?" We look up to see Ash and Rip standing above us. I give Ash the "you better behave" look, but she completely ignores it.

"Sure," Addison says.

Ash throws her bag to the ground. "Thanks." She sits down next to Addison. "It's been a long time."

"Yeah, it has," Addison says.

"Wait! You guys know each other?" I ask, stunned. Neither of them has ever mentioned anything.

They both hesitate and then look at each other. Addison says, "Yeah, we used to…um, we were…friends—"

"We used to be close in middle school and now we're not." Leave it to Ash to tell it like it is.

"Yeah, we went in different directions," Addison adds.

"So, what have you been up to?" Ash asks Addison.

235

Addison's posture relaxes as she eases into an easy conversation with Ash.

After a few minutes of catching up, Ash prods Rip in the ribs with her water bottle and turns back to Addison. "Trying to keep this guy out of trouble, and believe me, he needs all the help he can get."

"Hey, thanks a lot," Rip says, and jabs her back with his finger.

"You're welcome." Ash takes a candy bar out of her bag, breaks it in two, and hands half of it to Rip.

Addison says, "I guess you could say that I try to do the same with this guy." She laughs and leans back against me.

"I have to admit, you have a bigger job than me in that department." Ash puts a piece of chocolate in her mouth. "By the look of his face, you're not doing too good a job…"

"Yeah, well, unfortunately I took that day off." Addison's nose scrunches and she looks regretful.

Ash and Addison seem very different, but really, they're exactly alike. They know who they are. Rip and I listen to them catch up on each other's lives, laughing with them as they retell stories and moments together.

I feel perfect. I've managed to make real friends—that aren't freaks—and even hold on to a girl who knows everything there is about me and accepts it; accepts me. I look away from Addison's beautiful face and see Naya. She's staring so hard at me, I feel like she's hexing me with those witchy eyes, but I can't help but feel sorry for her.

~~~

"Addison! You came!" CeCe yells from the front door.

"I wouldn't miss the biggest party of the year."

I glance around the corner to see her, and she looks amazing. She's wearing a short pink dress and her hair is up with long pieces cascading down either side of her face. And I swear her green eyes are almost glowing. She's beautiful and sexy and picturesque.

She hands CeCe a glittery bag with ribbons spiraling down the front.

CeCe wraps her arms around Addison's waist. "Thank you! Thank you! Thank you!"

Addison looks up and our eyes meet. I'm torn between two very content places: watching her and holding her.

"Addison, look at what Erik got me for my birthday." She holds up a white bear. "And this." She points to the gold necklace with the dragonfly hanging from it.

"It's beautiful."

"I have to show you what else he did." CeCe grabs Addison's hand and pulls her through the house, passing me, and out to the backyard.

I follow them outside and CeCe is running toward the swing. She jumps on it, kicks off, and starts pumping her legs for momentum. Addison is next to her watching CeCe float past her, back and forth. "It's just like the one in the front yard. But, I have privacy when I'm swinging back here."

Addison looks at me and smiles. She is absolute perfection.

# CHAPTER 33

"Thank goodness for your sake, that Bulldog's fixed, cause we got a grave to dig." Roy hands me a piece of paper.

Selena Roux, Section 3, lot 8, tier 17 North.

I sit on the golf cart, the piece of paper flutters in the breeze. I want to open my hand and let the wind take it to a very far place, a place that I never have to go.

"What's wrong?"

I stand up. "Ah...nothing. I'll get what we need." I walk into the shed and come out with gloves and a set of boards."

"You know her?" Roy points to the paper I left on the seat of the golf cart.

"No. Yeah—I mean not really, no."

"Sounds like ya do."

I ignore him and put the stuff in the cart. It's then that I realize I haven't seen Naya in school the last few days. I didn't even notice; I was too happy.

After a few hours, after the grave is dug and the boards are in place, Roy says, "It's been a long day, come back in the morning. I gotta a couple of odd jobs we didn't get to today."

"Okay."

My phone buzzes in my pocket. A text from Addison: *In the*

*hospital. Please come!* Fear shakes me to my core, and every nerve ending feels like it's been dipped in ice water. I yell to Roy, "I gotta go, I'll see you in the morning."

"Erik!" he yells. "Everything alright?"

"I'll let you know tomorrow," I yell back over my shoulder.

Minutes later, I rush into the emergency room and ask the volunteer at the front desk where they've taken Addison. When I find her, I'm terrified to pull back the curtain, afraid of what I might see. Gathering all my courage, I tug the drape aside. She's in a hospital gown and her hair is sprawled out over the pillow, a light brown fan framing her pale face. I go to her and pick up her hand. She opens her eyes.

"You're here," she says in a weak voice.

"Yeah. What happened?"

She croaks a laugh. "I don't even need to be here. I just have a migraine, and I have medicine at home. But, my mom insisted. I think she has a crush on the doctor."

I laugh. "Do you need anything?"

"Do you mind pouring me some water?" I get up, cross the small space to the table in the corner with the pitcher of water and a few paper cups on it.

"Here." She takes the water. "Are you sure you're okay?" I sit on the edge of the bed.

"I just want to go h—"

Addison doesn't have a chance to finish before the curtain is thrown back and Aiden is rushing toward her. "What the hell happened?"

It only takes a few steps and he's at her bedside.

"Nothing, jeez. Mom is having a fit that I had a migraine and made me come to this dreadful place again."

"That's it?" he asks irritated.

Before I can say anything, Addison says, "Erik." Her voice is so slight, but it's like she's screaming for me.

She doesn't get to finish before her mom comes in. "Oh, Aiden, you came." Her high heels echo as they smack the linoleum floor.

Mrs. Bailey is at Addison's side, and her father steps into the small space and instead of looking at his daughter, he's staring at Aiden and I who are inches from each other. "Why don't you two step outside?"

"Yeah," Aiden says and leaves.

I lean over her and tell I'll be back. Then nod at her father and follow Aiden's lead. Before I'm even down the hall, I hear Addison's voice, "Jesus, Mom, I'm fine."

Aiden's Mustang blows past me as the sliding doors open, and the relief of not having to deal with him runs through me. A reeking whiff of stale cigarette from the standup ashtray about a foot away blows by me and before I turn back towards the sliding doors, someone behind me says, "She wants to see you." Addison's father stands just inside the doors. This time his eyes look worn and distant instead of piercing and judging.

Wordlessly, he walks next to me on our way back to Addison's room. Dr. Bailey pulls back the curtain and Addison is dressed and sitting on the edge of the bed with her mother.

"Addison, you look..." I'm lost for words. Some of her color has returned and she looks...better.

"The migraine shot they gave me finally kicked in." Her smile is weak, but I'm happy to see it.

"We'll go get the car," her dad says.

"I'm glad you're feeling better." I kiss her forehead. "I have to work in the morning, but I'll call you after."

I start to walk away, but she doesn't let go of my hand. "Hey," she says, "let my parents wait a few minutes." She brushes my hair to the side. "What's wrong? And don't say nothing. I can see it etched in those blue eyes of yours."

I want to tell her to go home and rest, but I remember how

240

she reacted when her mother told her that. "Come on, let's walk." I hold her close to me on the way out of the hospital. "I had to dig Naya's mom's grave today."

"Oh no."

"Oh yeah." I purse my lips and look at an ambulance that's leaving the hospital. "It wasn't easy."

"Have you talked to Naya?"

"No. But the last time I did, she basically told me her mother's death is on my head." I put my fist to my mouth.

She leans into me and hugs me close. "It's not your fault, it isn't fair what she was expecting from you."

"I know. But it's still so—"

"Addison, come on baby, let's get you home," her mother calls.

I hug her and hold back my tears. I don't want to let go, she gives me so much strength, but I know I have to. "I'll call you later."

~~~

I'm exhausted but I can't fall asleep. I lay in my bed waiting for sleep to take over but it never does. I feel so strong now, and I wonder if I could have saved Naya's mom. This is the last thought before I close my eyes and try to sleep.

~~~

I pull into the cemetery. Roy is already at the shed gathering the tools we'll need for the day.

"Everything all right?" he asks.

"Yeah, fine."

"Good." He hands me hedge clippers and gloves, and I put them in the golf cart. "We're gonna make this an easy morning: trim the hedge between sections two and three, fill in the grave after the funeral at ten, then we're goin' home."

Fill in the grave. Those words are not lost on me. Selena Roux's grave. I look at my watch. It's nine.

I've trimmed more than half of the waist high shaggy hedge

241

before I realize how close I am to Naya's mother's grave. Only a hundred feet away the green canopy hovers over the hole I dug for her yesterday. Roy must have set the chairs out this morning. Five of them are lined in front of it. But only a single person stands in front of the coffin, across from the priest. Naya. Her long black dress pools around her feet and she's holding a single rose. Her hair is up and rests on top of her head. All of it seems so normal yet surreal until she turns and looks directly at me. Her violet eyes are hidden behind the veil that covers her entire face.

She looks away from me as the casket begins its descent into the grave, and I have to look away. But before I do, I see Naya throw the rose into the hole and then fall to her knees. I look away from the hole that I dug for a woman who at one time had crossed paths with me ever so briefly.

I walk just a few feet behind me and sit under a huge oak. I sit against George McDonald's headstone, 1932-2011, and hold my head up, a lazy breeze swaying by cooling my wet cheeks, and I take a deep drink of water.

I call Addison. I need to see her. I need to hold her. I need her to hold me.

~~~

The ripples of the lake float toward us. Their long journey of wading pushes them onto the shore, only to have the shore force them right back out. The endless motion of ebb and flow seems exhausting and daunting, and oddly tranquil.

She smirks.

"What?"

Her smirk liquefies into an expression of affection and she says, "I'm so happy." I reach in to kiss her and when our lips touch, it's as if nothing else exists. She pulls back and says, "I want to draw you."

"Okay." The idea intrigues me. She's only shown me a few of her drawings and they are amazing.

242

"But I want to draw you as you're bringing something back to life." I look at her. I'm not sure what my expression must look like. "If you're uncomfortable, I understand." She takes my hand in hers. "I've just never seen that expression in my whole life on anyone's face, ever. When you touched the crab, it was like watching pure fascination, bewilderment, joy, animated ecstasy, and a million other things melting together to mold into one infinite enchanted expression."

"Well, when you put it like that."

She jumps up. "I'll be back." She runs through the path toward the road and disappears. I lean back on the blanket and rest on my out stretched arms.

She's back before I can even form one coherent thought. "Here." I hold out my hand and she lays a dragonfly on my palm. "I found him near the road." I smile. How well this beautiful girl knows me. She pulls out a sketchpad and pencil from her bag. "Don't do anything yet, let me draw your body in detail and then some base lines and basic shapes."

It takes her about a half hour. Then she says, "Okay, can you do it now?" Her pencil is poised above the paper over my face. I do what comes naturally. She never speaks during the process. Through the static and heat, I faintly hear her pencil scratching the surface of the paper; quick, short bursting movements, even after the dragonfly flies away.

"As soon as you touch the dragonfly, it's like you're somewhere else, far away. And vulnerable."

I never knew I was showing so much emotion each time I brought back a life. But I need to see what she sees; how *she* sees me. "Are you going to show me your masterpiece?"

She holds up her sketchpad but keeps the drawing held to her chest. "Yes. But, you have to promise if you hate it, you won't tell me."

"Promise," I say and laugh.

She flips it around. I'm flabbergasted and take in a sharp breath. "You hate it." She lowers it to her lap.

"No!" I say too loudly. "No, I…is that how you see me?"

"Yes. Just like that." Her voice is very soft.

I reach for her hand. "I look…beautiful to you?"

"Yes." The portrait is incredible. The dragonfly is alive on my palm, and my face— she's drawn someone I've never seen before, and as many times as I've looked into the mirror I don't know this person. But through her eyes, he's mysterious and happy, magical and content, handsome and generous.

I lean into her and before I even know what I'm doing or saying, I whisper onto her lips, "I love you."

# CHAPTER 34

195 days.

In less than five months, I'll be breathing in the sweet fumes, squinting at the blinking lights, and hearing the exhilarated screams of the carnival. Anticipation dominates all other thoughts until I see Addison walk toward me. As I close my locker, I wonder what will happen to *us* after graduation and suddenly the 195 days don't seem like enough.

She slips her hand into mine. I draw her body to me and kiss her long and deep. "Wow. What was that for?" she asks when we finally break the connection.

"Good morning." She gives me a smile I hope I never forget. I tug her hand and as we turn the corner in the hall, Naya's face is inches from mine. Her bearing is rigid and uncompromising with a pale and makeup-less face that's both pretty and frightening. Dark sleepless patches are smeared under those unusual violet eyes; their beauty obscured by thousands of tiny red veins, a glossy sheen from a not too distant bout of crying, and lined with puffy lids. A sloppy loose dress hangs off one shoulder, the neglected fairy kneeling in torment on her arm.

"Naya." Her name sounds more like croak coming from my throat than the smooth unbroken way the letters flawlessly flow.

"I *hate* you," she hisses through cracked lips.

I tighten my grip on Addison's hand and start to walk around her. Everyone in the hall has stopped and once again, I'm on display with another unwanted confrontation.

She turns and screams into my back, "Don't you walk away from me, FREEEEEEAK!" Stunned into complete stillness, I turn around with cautious ease as bile rises in my throat. Piercing violet slits seize my blue and very wide eyes. Her chest is heaving, like an erupting volcano. With only a few deliberate strides she's standing in front of me. "Let's tell everyone what you can do." Her voice is low and unnerving.

"Naya," I warn, sounding more on the verge of hysteria than measured. Clearing my throat, I continue, "We don't start spreading shit that isn't true."

"YES IT IS!" she screams. No one witnessing this freakish episode moves or whispers a word. "Why can't you just tell the truth?"

"Naya, you're grieving, you're—"

"Don't make me your excuse. When are you going to stop lying to all of these people?" She waves her arms around at everyone who is frozen watching us. "Go ahead; tell all of us the truth." Her voice is so restrained and controlled that her face almost looks calm, but it's a seething calm. A calm that threatens to explode at any second. A calm so precise and horrifically patient as it waits for me to disclose the deepest part of who I am.

I don't say anything.

"Fine, I'll tell them." The calm on her face melts into hideous satisfaction. "Before coming here..." There's no way to stop her. "Erik Davenport was the freak-boy who brings back the dead in a traveling carnival."

Complete stillness and silence surround me. Then, choking laughter bursts out around me. I'm paralyzed. Everyone's amused as they watch our debut of *The Freak's Standoff*. Behind Naya, the crowd comes into focus and they're covering their mouths and pointing at Naya. Their chuckles and accusations creep their way to my ears and I shuffle through them to make out coherent sentences: *"She's lost her freakin' mind." "What the fuck is she on?" "I told you she was crazy."*

Blood stains her face a furious red. "I'm not the freak." From her outstretched arm, her finger is no more than an inch from my chest. "He is!" Even her high-pitched shriek is hard to hear over our audience. She turns and runs through the ridiculing gawkers and down the hall, away from everyone.

Naya has officially ruined herself.

~~~

The day cannot end fast enough. Addison left earlier with her mom to go to a follow-up appointment for her migraines. So, even without all eyes on me as I walk through the halls—thanks to Naya—the day would have still sucked. When the final bell rings, I practically run to the parking lot.

"Where you running off to so fast?" Aiden's voice grinds its way through my nerves. "You know I'm really upset that I missed that whole little episode this morning. Man, that would have been something to see; a showdown with the freaks." I keep walking until he says, "The boy who can bring back the dead." Turning my attention to him, I watch his gritted sneer shift into doubt. "Yeah, that I don't believe. But, what I do believe is the part that you were a carnie before coming here. A freakin' carnie." He laughs so hard he has to bend over to catch his breath. "Don't tell me, let me guess…it was your job to take the tickets from the kiddies so they could ride the merry-go-round or, no wait, wait," he puts one hand over his mouth and the other outstretched pointing at me, "I know, I bet it was your job to keep the fat bearded lady happy. Come on," he bounces his eyebrows, "you know what I mean."

"You're an asshole," I say.

"I'll take being an asshole over a freakin' carnie any day."

247

I gather every ounce of control, take the deepest breath that my lungs can hold, and walk away.

"Hey, Carnie, you know there's a carnival coming to town this weekend. Maybe you can get a job, or put on a little show for us. That is, after you dig a few graves."

As I increase the distance between us, a smile creeps onto my lips as a spark ignites inside of me.

There's a carnival coming to town.

# CHAPTER 35

The first memory I have of going to the carnival was when I turned five. I know I must have been hundreds of times before that since I grew up in them. But, I'll never forget that time, holding my father's hand as he led me through the winking lights, past the clowns walking around with bundles of balloons in their hand, the dat-datdatta-da music playing over and over, the smell of candy apples and corndogs, and a hundred other endless memories. He took me on ride after ride and we played game after game. I remember my mom telling him that I was going to get sick from all of the sugar and twirling. I never did.

Giddiness spreads through me like a kid on Christmas morning, his feet pound the stairs as he rushes down them preparing to be flabbergasted with piles of presents under the tree. My face hurts from trying to contain the smile that won't leave. The taste for the life I miss is so close and overwhelming. And the thought of being able to experience it with Addison is nothing less than incredible.

Oli looks up when I walk by her chair in the center of the room. She sets her book in her lap and says, "My, my, we look awfully happy. Are you taking Addison out? "

"Yeah, how'd you guess?"

"A) The uncontrollable smile on your face, and B) you're all dressed up." She points to my clothes. "Your ripped jeans and faded t-shirt gave you completely away." We laugh together.

"I'm taking her to the carnival."

"Ah…" She nods and I watch as the smile dims just a bit in her eyes, but the smile her mouth forms never wavers. She understands my happiness and it doesn't thrill her that I'll be leaving her in 193 days to return to a life she doesn't wish for me. "It seems you two are pretty serious."

I shrug. But I know the beaming smile on my face doesn't match the lame gesture I offer, and I give in. "Yeah, I think so. I don't have anything to compare it to."

"Love isn't something you compare. It's something you feel here." She points to her heart. "And here." She points to her stomach. "And here, and here, and here," she continues to point to her arms, legs and toes.

"I get it." I laugh.

She holds up her hand and points to her head. "But, not here. The rational knows not love, but only the process to make you fall into it."

"Who said that?" She tilts her head, nods and holds out her hands in a sitting bow. "Well, Old Wise One Oli, let me get this straight…so basically we become giddy and stupid by way of a strategic, well thought out plan—we have no memory of planning— and hope it works out for the best?!"

"Exactly."

"Then, so far it's working out pretty damn good." My mom would have cut me down for the minor swear word, but not Oli. She gets up and hugs me and tells me how happy she is for me. When I pull back, I ask her about Roy. She sits back down in her chair and I wonder if she's going to answer me when CeCe comes around the corner. "They're doing great," my little sister says.

"Oh really?" I ask.

"Yep," she says. Scooter is perched on her shoulder like he was born to be a parrot and juts out his nose, his whiskers twitching.

"And how do you know this?" I ask.

"Cause I just do."

Oli snickers behind her book and I get the feeling that CeCe is right on. I raise my eyebrows at Oli and she just laughs.

"Alright guys, I gotta go, Addison's waiting for me."

"Where are you guys going?" CeCe asks.

"To the carnival."

"PLEASE! PLEASE! PLEASE! CAN I GO?" CeCe jumps up and down. And I know she misses it as much as I do.

"Not tonight. I'll take you tomorrow."

"Promise?"

"I promise." She hugs me and I hug her back.

"By the way, how's your motorcycle?" Oli asks.

"Awesome! Roy really hooked me up." I love the smile that's on her face at the mention of him. She looks happy.

~~~

Addison is waiting outside when I pull up to her house. She runs over her lawn and kisses me. "Yay! You got it back!" She jumps onto the back of my motorcycle. "Let's go. I'm so excited!" She's wearing jeans and her cowboy boots. God, I love those things.

I put my hand under her chin and use her mouth as a puppet and say, "Hi, Erik, how are you? I missed you so much and I couldn't wait to see you again."

She starts giggling. "I'm sorry."

"I'm teasing." I hand her the helmet. "In fact, I owe you."

"Why?"

"Because I don't have to stand in the presence of your parents who hate me."

She slaps my arm and says, "They don't hate you."

"Yeah right." I pat her leg. "Hold on."

When the lights of the carnival come into view, Addison

drums on my shoulders and I hear a muffled squeal. Rocks and pebbles spray up from the tires as I turn onto the dirt road. Tall pines are scattered in the lot already lined with rows of cars. I find a spot and park.

I take her hand and pull her through the crowd. Suddenly, I'm absorbed in a world that's home. The smells, ambiance, and screaming laughter; I'm ecstatic. For the last couple of months I've only daydreamed of being lost amidst all of it and now I get to share every second and every inch of this place with Addison. "What do you want to do first?" I ask her.

"Eat. I'm starving."

Addison pulls my hand and I follow her around one of the kiddie rides. We come face to face with Aiden and Candace. Both of them are laughing until they see Addison and me. "Look, the freak made it to the show," says Aiden.

"Wouldn't miss it for the world," I say grinning.

"Let's go," Addison says. She starts to tug on my hand, and I let her. I don't want a confrontation tonight.

We walk away from them and order two corndogs and a Coke from the closest place we can find. "What do you want to go on first?" I ask. The thumping music is already moving through me and the feeling is exhilarating. "We should probably start out easy and go from there."

"Perfect. So the merry-go-round?"

I laugh. "I was thinking more like that one," I point to a ride that's pulling, shifting, and pushing in all directions. "Or, the Ferris wheel? What do you think?"

"The merry-go-round."

"Come on." I take her hand and head toward the Ferris wheel.

"I've never been on one of these before." Her voice is simultaneously loud and small, nervous and excited.

"You'll love it."

"Don't let go of me."

"Never," I say and wrap my arm around her.

When we reach the top, the world surrounds us and the view is breathtaking.

"I've never seen anything like this. I mean I've been in planes before, but there's something thrilling about being this high off the ground in the open air," she says. The car jerks and rocks and she grabs hold of my shirt.

"It's okay. I promise." The giant wheel spins onward as we start our descent. We're almost on the ground when fat raindrops begin to fall. The moment the carnie guy unhooks the latch, rain pours from the sky, as if the car's handle was also the release to open up the clouds. We make a run for a nearby tent, jumping over and through puddles on the slick ground.

Addison's hand slips from mine and I turn around to grab it again. And I watch her fall to the ground. I run the few yards back to help her up, but she's not trying to get to her feet. She's perfectly still.

# CHAPTER 36

¶ pick up her collapsed body and cradle her in my arms. The closest tent is still thirty feet away. As soon as we're in, I lay her on the ground. The rain pounds the tent and I have to yell her name. "Addison! Addison!"

Nothing.

I want to go get help, but I don't want to leave her. Propping myself against the supporting ropes of the tent, I pull her unmoving body onto my lap. The rain has matted her hair to her face and I smooth it away. She looks peaceful and that scares the hell out of me. I hold her very still, afraid to move her. Her fingers twitch against my arms and her eyes flutter open.

Thank God. I collapse over her as the breath I was holding explodes from my chest. She tries to sit up. "Relax, don't move yet," I tell her. Then, her eyes roll up and her body goes slack against me.

"Addison!"

"Erik," she croaks without opening her eyes.

"I'm here." I try, but I can't hold back the tears streaming down my face.

"Don't leave me," she says in a low, hoarse voice.

"I won't." I feel her start to fade, her body going slack.

Through the opening in the tent I see Aiden. Candace isn't

with him. "Help!" I scream to get his attention. Finally, he turns and sees me and runs into the tent.

"What the hell happened?"

"She collapsed. Get help!"

He doesn't take out his cell or even move. Shock freezes him in place. The rain drowns out whatever words he's mumbling. Unlike the Aiden I know and have come to hate, he's coming unhinged. I know right then, he won't be of any help. I feel the hysteria taking over, the realization of this horrifying situation becoming very real by the second.

Slowly Addison opens her eyes and reaches up to touch my face. "Why are you crying?" she asks, and wipes the tears away. The wind picks up, and the walls of the tent billow and creak behind me. A light misty rain sprays into the tent, and I pull her tighter to me to keep her as warm and dry as I can. Her eyes close again and I watch her face wince in pain. So badly, I want to take it away but I don't know what to do.

I feel her body go rigid and then relax. "What's wrong? What hurts?"

"My head."

"Is it a migraine?" She doesn't answer. "I won't leave you. I'm right here," I whisper. My tears won't stop coming.

There's movement outside the tent and I look up. Naya. She's in the rain coming toward me. I can't even begin to know why she's here.

"What happened?" she asks as she kneels in front of me.

"Addison collapsed."

"Erik," she whispers my name over the rain and I don't like the way it sounds. "She's going to die."

Her words take only seconds to penetrate the horrifying moment. "No! Shut up, Naya." She puts her hand on my arm. "No. No. No. No," I chant the words, aching for them to be true, and shake my head in denial.

255

Naya doesn't argue. "Are you going to bring her back?"

I don't say anything and look back down to the girl I love in my arms. Her eyes barely open again, and I watch her fight to stay with me. My heart is being torn from my chest and the ache is unbearable. Her eyes close again. "Addison, stay with me. I love you. I love you. I love you," I whisper. "You're going to be fine." And in the middle of all of the unknowing, I know this to be true.

In my own selfish way, I could stay in this moment forever, just holding her in my arms. Her head lies against my chest, and her wet hair fans out over my arm. She looks so beautiful. I sweep the few strands of hair away from her face. Her lip-gloss is almost gone and her make-up is smeared under her eyes, shadowing the green pools that captivated me the first time I ever looked into them.

She tries to keep her eyes open, and I can tell it's difficult for her. A smile barely touches her lips and I bend to kiss it. More tears fall from my eyes. One lands on her cheek; I start to wipe it away and she moves her head, and my hand hovers above her face. She says, "Leave it there." She looks so content in my arms and I can't take my eyes off her.

Her hand tightens over my arm. "Are you in pain?" I ask.

She shakes her head a little and says, "No." But I can tell she's lying. Anything but pain, I don't want her to suffer. If any person deserves not to suffer, it's her. She's waiting to die; I can see it in her eyes. She expects it.

"I love you," she whispers as her last breath blows onto my lips.

I kiss her but she doesn't kiss me back. "I love you."

Aiden is pacing back and forth back and forth back and forth. I want to shout at him to stop, but before I find my voice I feel the pulsing in my veins, the heat writhing through my body and when I realize what's happening, everything becomes clear; my gift to bring back life becomes so very, very clear. And, I smile. I can't help but smile.

"Erik, you have to, now," Naya whispers.

She's right. I think about the lifespan of a dragonfly and how I, like them, only lived the last couple of months in the last stage of my life. I found someone I loved, and in return who loved me back for everything that I am.

"You can do this," Naya says.

I breathe in so deep my lungs want to explode. The heat is radiating off my skin. I don't remember it ever feeling this angry. Then I think back to when my grandfather died; it was this same blistering heat shuddering through me.

Naya touches my arm and quickly jerks her hand away. "You're burning up."

"I know," I can hardly get the words out, "this is what happens when I…" I look into her violet eyes and I can't finish. They're filled with sadness, regret, and shame.

"I'm so sorry. I didn't realize how much I was asking for." She's crying now.

I nod. And for a brief second I laugh. Not a real laugh, more like a sick hollowed-out noise.

"What?" she asks.

"You always believed in me."

"Yeah, I did." Naya puts her hand on my arm again, and this time leaves it there. Every nerve under her touch is electrified and humming, and even in this horrific situation, I love the sensation. I look at Addison's peaceful face, and like liquid heat, the energy to save her jolts through my veins, darting and shifting like a dragonfly, looking for an escape.

"Erik, you could die, couldn't you?" Naya whispers over the rainfall.

"Yes. But I *have* to do it." The devastating demand is excruciating and there's no other choice. I have to do this. I have to try.

"You have your whole life in front of you."

257

Her words mean nothing to me. I kiss the dragonfly tattoo on the inside of my wrist.

A thin smile slides across Naya's lips. "That's why the dragonfly—it was the first thing you ever brought back from the dead." She doesn't need an answer. Her cries and her weak smile wither away as I close my eyes.

A thousand memories slam into my head: CeCe on her swing, my parents laughing, Oli and my grandfather at the lake, and dragonflies—dead and alive. I don't expect to live, or to take another breath after I give her every ounce of energy in me so that she can live. There won't be any left. I can't say I don't care, I will miss this life, I will miss giving life back, and I will miss the dragonflies.

As I take my last breath, I wonder what she'll feel. I never thought about that before, what the creature I'm bring back to life feels. Then, I wonder what I'll feel. It never hurt before; the funny thing is…I'm not scared—not for me—I'm scared for Addison.

I need to slow the torrent of energy or my body will fail before she even has a chance. What if it doesn't work? The weakness comes and I can barely hold onto the girl I love. She's so beautiful, and I try to hold onto the memory of her, but like all memories, she too starts to fade. I hear broken threads of her laughter, and catch glimpses of her face, a blip of her smile, the small hollow area between her nose and lips, and her green limitless eyes.

"Don't," Naya's last plea is whispered against my ear. I open my eyes to look at her. All along, I knew she didn't understand the consequences, but now, by the look in those violet eyes, I know she does, but there's also the hope she always had. And then she fades.

The shadows ooze from the corners of my mind, creeping up behind me. I fade too, just like a memory, leaving only the empty shell of a boy who once fell in love with a girl.

# CHAPTER 37

$\mathcal{W}$ithout opening my eyes, I realize the drumming of a million raindrops has ceased, leaving nothing except a detached white noise to fill the void. I try to open my eyes, but the task seems so daunting. Silly, I think, for such a simple act. No matter, my lids stay folded over my eyes, refusing to lift. So, here I lay, helplessly listening to echoes of cries and indiscernible words floating through me like I'm not even here. A ghost.

Breath, as soft as the petals on the flowers I once gave a girl, seeps out through my lips, tickling them. Every molecule of air escapes from my lungs, deflating me. But the panic for oxygen doesn't come, and I don't understand why. It's as if a warm blanket has been thrown over my entire being and the sensation is strange and comforting. Peaceful.

A single dragonfly manifests from somewhere in my dreams. As if beckoning me to follow it, it hovers and waits, glaring at me with its bulbous eyes. Then, so fast, it whips away and like a shadow, I hurry after it. It whirls and soars like a tiny helicopter with translucent wings. We fly over trees and mountains, and then high up into the clouds. Darting over wisps of vapor and through veils of white, it finally rests on a thin tendril. The moment is bizarre and oddly familiar. I almost expect the creature to speak to me, but it doesn't. The blue and green iridescent body is so still. We stay like this, staring at each other, the clouds swirling and shifting around us.

Without any warning, the dragonfly dives.

Down.

Down.

Down.

And for lack of knowing what else to do, I follow it.

# CHAPTER 38

Distant sounds of chaos and chatter echo around in my head. I grasp for anything that makes sense, but my effort is useless. An urgent feeling of happiness rushes through me and possibly, it's difficult to tell, I smile. Then reckless fear takes its place. Fragments of horror explode through the glimpses of joy, tearing them apart. And I try to gasp for a breath and fail. I don't want to know she's dead, that I couldn't save her. My empty arms tell me I failed.

Far away, from another part of the universe, a voice I recognize calls my name. "Erik!" It's filtered through a million other disoriented noises. Now I know I'm dead.

Then, that same voice calls my name again. I feel distant from everything that's happening. But, I'm sure I'm right here, in the middle of this madness.

Another voice—Aiden's. "Addison, he's gone." He's trying to pull her away from me.

"NO!" Addison's breath is hot against my face.

No! No! No! I'm here! Right here damn it! The words reverberate in my head. I'm screaming at him to leave her alone. I want Addison's arms to stay wrapped around me, but I don't know how to tell her or to show her. A soft wetness smears across my face. Addison's cheek is against mine and she's crying. Her tears are silky and sad and I want to wipe them away from her beautiful face, but my arms won't move.

"Please wake up! Please, please wake up." Muffled through blackness as thick as tar, Addison's voice reaches me.

New voices sift through the chaotic sounds.

"Help! Help him!" Addison's voice.

Air is suddenly being pushed into my lungs. An insistent whooshing sound, followed by a hiss is on the other side of my consciousness. Again. Again. Again. Then pressure lunges down onto my chest over and over.

Addison! Addison! Her name sounds loud in my skull but I don't think it leaves my mouth. I want to hold her in my arms as I remember our last kiss, stolen by my lips, unable to help myself, and her final breath. Tears, hidden and trapped by my eyelids threaten to break the dam as they build and build until the flood can no longer be contained.

Finally, a breath that I thought was lost forever fills my lungs. Streams of air continue to course through me. The surge of oxygen, fueling and heating every membrane in my body—it's a feeling I know well, but this is slightly different, better, stronger, invigorating. As it flows through every vein, I feel each cell awaken.

When I have full control of my breath, I fill my lungs until they might burst. I'm being rejuvenated as the oxygen feeds the adrenaline and I ache to open my eyes to see what's happening around me, *to me*. But my lids still won't cooperate and I remain blind; fear is no doubt the culprit.

I breathe in the scents of vanilla and woods, and a thousand memories slam into me: the Ferris wheel, a gold bracelet with a dangling heart, running with Addison through the rain, her collapsing, the tent, holding her as she died. I think of her long golden hair splayed out around her face, and those green pools looking up at me, and her lips touching mine.

The struggle to open my eyes is fierce. Finally, my brutal

efforts pay off. Slivers of unfocused faces surround me, but all I want to see is just one. And she is nowhere. Frantic, I try to sit up and someone pushes me back down. My head is heavy and lolls to the side. Naya. She's tucked into a ball against the wall of the tent. Her arms are wrapped around her knees and black tears run down her face. She looks at me and I want to ask her about Addison, but I haven't yet found my voice. Her eyes widen when she looks at me, and she cups her hand over her mouth silencing her sobs. On hands and knees, she crawls towards me through the throng of people.

I feel her wilt in front of me, and her weight on my shoulders. She pulls me in for a hug; her embrace is warm and the closeness feels amazing, but not right. Everything around me falls away again and I'm disappearing into nothingness. *Addison*, I think. Addison.

The blackness closes in on me until unconsciousness completely chokes off the light.

# CHAPTER 39

A dragonfly lay on my nightstand. It's propped on its wing, the other lifts high and the sun bursts through it spreading iridescent light over the dark surface. Its colors exactly match the one I followed into the clouds.

Clouds.

Diving.

Down.

Down.

Down.

Dying.

Dead.

Addison!

Flashes of memories rush into my head and I try to rake through mounds of them. The sensible part of my brain is failing miserably. But the fantastical part—HOLY HELL! Was I able to save her? And I *possibly* may not be dead? I mean who dies and then wakes up in their bedroom to find out it's really Heaven?

Easing myself into a sitting position, I wrestle off the dizziness, pick up the dragonfly, and lay it in the palm of my hand and…I wait…I wait longer…nothing. Not even a spark of simmering energy radiates.

A shadow emerges over the hand holding the dead dragonfly. When I look towards my window, brightness silhouettes a figure.

"It was lying next to you when I woke up," she says.

No words come for a long time. I know I have a million things to say and to ask, but I only take her hand and pull her to me. Addison lies down next to me and together we cry. Our bodies shudder against each other as we cast away every unwanted memory and embrace every perfect one.

"Thank you," she whispers.

I lift her chin and those amazing pale green eyes look into mine. "I love you." I kiss her.

Not too long ago, she lay dead in my arms, and then I in hers. Irony can be cruel at times and whimsical at others; but that's the beauty of it, its unpredictability.

When we stop kissing either for reason (a) her mouth got tired, or reason (b) she finally reached the brink of disgust from my mouth tasting like sewage waste, I ask her what exactly happened.

She takes in a deep breath. "It went something like this: I died, you brought me back," she pauses, smiles and then continues, "when I woke up in your arms, you were..." I nod; neither of us wants her to say it. "Of course I lost it, and my brother," she huffs, "completely useless. I didn't know what to do. But, Ash and Rip somehow found us. Ash gave you CPR—"

"You're kidding?"

Addison shakes her head. "I forgot her mom was a nurse until Rip said something."

"Huh," I say stunned. "Okay, sorry, go on."

"Naya was there. She stayed away from everyone until you came to the first time, and then she wouldn't leave your side. She might be crazy, but she really is a good friend for you." I couldn't agree more. "Anyway, everyone wanted to bring you and me to the hospital or call the paramedics and Naya and I basically had to fight them off." She laughs a little then.

"How'd I get here?"

"Aiden," she says.

"Now I know you're joking."

"I swear I'm not." She chuckles. "I have never seen him like that before." Lowering her head to look at her hands, she continues. "He knows what he saw, what you did, and for that I know he'll always be grateful."

I nod. "What day is it?"

"Sunday morning. You only missed a day." Relief floods me. She kisses me lightly on the lips and says, "There's a little girl who really missed you."

The sun is so bright and welcoming as we step outside. It's a new day, and I get another chance to live. CeCe is by the flower bushes following a butterfly. I watch my little sister, and I'm hit with how much I've missed her, even though it's only been a day. I tug Addison's hand and we walk into the yard.

CeCe studies the butterfly that now rests on its side. Please don't be dead, I think. Not in front of this little girl dressed in her pink tutu, who has had so much happened to her to in only a few short months. The tutu surrounds her as she squats on the ground. She picks up the dead insect and puts it in her hand. I stay silent, captivated by her. She touches the lifeless wings that are the color of gold. We watch in amazement as they slowly begin to pulse, and then faster, and in an instant the butterfly takes flight.

She looks up at me, winks perfectly, and the most amazing smile spreads across her face. Tears of pure adoration and amazement slide down my face. I wink and smile back at this beautiful little girl, who has the gift to bring back life.

# Acknowledgments

Kevin, thank you for never giving up on me. Your confidence in me is more than I could have ever asked for. Thank you for taking care of our family while I was writing. I'm fortunate you're mine.

To my oldest daughter, Emma, thank you for being so proud of me, and for all of your support. I love you all the way to the moon. My dear creative Katelynne, my desk has become an ongoing art show thanks to you. And I wouldn't have it any other way. Thank you for all my homemade cards and crafts you make with so much pride and love. I love you very much! And for my sweet Lew Lew, you have more patience than a three year old should. You've heard "Let me just finish this sentence" more times than I can count; thank you for putting up with Mommy. I love you all more than life itself.

For my parents: Mom, thank you for always believing in me, I love you. Dad, for all of your support and enthusiasm through this endeavor, and your continued belief and in me, I love you. Jan, who always asked about my writing and has continued to encourage me along the way. Thank you for so much, I love you! And, to my brother Kyle, who always asked, "Hey, sis, how's the book coming?" Love you!

Miranda Hardy who has been there for me every day since the day we met, and who never tires of listening to me (at least she says she doesn't.) She's a pure genius in the brainstorming department. I couldn't ask for a better writing partner or business partner. There is so much that I am thankful for in our relationship: our genuine friendship being the first.

For Wendy Sternberg, my best friend who has always believed in me. And, no matter how busy she is, she always insists on a writing update. Thank you for being there.

Nancy Curran, Lisa Keating, Dena Esteva, and Madalyn Olejniczak, thank you for the great feedback. You'll never know how much it meant to me that you read this book.

Lauren Oliver, thank you for teaching me the only algebra I need to know! Your books have been an inspiration to me. Thank you for always being so nice.

Thank you Harrison Demchick, with Ambitious Enterprises, for suffering through the first draft of this book, and putting me on the right track. Through my consultations with you on this novel, the changes have been drastic, and quite painful at times, but all well worth it. This novel wouldn't be what it is today without you. You were always right on.

Tee Tate, thank you for your invaluable advice.

I can't thank Todd Barselow enough. You polished every page to a magnificent sparkle. Your love for the written word is transparent in your work, and your expertise is downright brilliant. Thank you for always being kind and respectful.

Najla Qamber, my cover designer. Thank you for putting up with a million changes and complete cover transformations. You're an amazing artist and your work is beautiful. *HUGS*

To my readers, thank you for spending your precious time reading my book. I hope you enjoy it as much as I enjoyed writing it.

# About the Author

Ainsley Shay avoids insanity by living mostly in the fiction world. She believes surrounding herself with positive people, and strives for balance in everything. She owns more jeans with rips and holes than without; and has recently found the magic of patches. For her, reading or writing the perfect sentence is better than the smoothest piece of dark chocolate melting in her mouth. She is a deltiologist for pure enjoyment, not for the study of. She longs to move north one day, even though she hates the cold. (Go figure!) So, for now, she continues to live in warm south Florida with her incredible husband, three beautiful daughters, and two lazy cats. (We won't mention the dog.)